HOMEWARD-BOUND HAUL

THE SECOND ARKLE WRIGHT NOVEL

RAYMOND S FLEX

1 SOME GODFORSAKEN PLANET - SOME GODFORSAKEN TIME

A S THE TRAFFIC LIGHT switched from go-green to warning-amber, the driver slowed the hover cab down —*way down*.

Hell, there must've been time for just about every last single instrument within the vehicle to power off; get checked over by some snub-nosed, meticulous mechanic—get everything oiled-over, all greased-up; even recalibrate the thrusters—before the traffic light switched all the way over to red.

But the goddamn driver stuffed the brakes on all the same.

All squashed-into the back seat of this tiny, wannabe vehicle with Foy and Milky—members of my noble, and *sizeable* crew— I was rightly beginning to lose my patience.

I've never been what you'd term a 'small' man, and I sure as hell wasn't having anything approaching a good time with my knees stuffed way hard into the back of the driver's seat in front of me. In retrospect, my usual garb of a beaten leather jacket over a pair of jeans—and, of course, the standard-issue, battered ankle-high boots—didn't seem such a great choice of wardrobe given the circumstances.

I would be onto Clive Wodd—my Ship's Engineer, and the mastermind behind this job—when we were all through . . .

Foy and Milky were much better dressed; the two of them wearing no-nonsense, non-descript grey-blue overalls, looking more like a pair of mechanics than useful members of my ship's crew.

I breathed in the stink of polish or disinfectant, whatever the hell the driver had been spraying about in his transport without remorse. I could taste the remainder of some fish soup I'd chomped down on back at the market—at least it'd had the nerve to *call* itself 'fish soup'—rumbling its way up the back of my throat.

The driver—this guy maybe the other side of a hundred—lightly tapped his leather-gloved hands against the finger indentations in the steering wheel's plastic coating.

Calm as you *like*.

"What was that name again?" he said, tapping something or other into a vidscreen.

He wanted my name so he could bill this epic—in the bad sense—taxi-cab journey to my account. I was of a pretty brutal mind to give him one of my rival smuggler's names for his crimes.

"Wright," I said. "*Captain* Arkle Wright."

The driver squinted at his vidscreen, tapping in the details.

There was a satisfied *ping* from the machine . . . at least it *sounded* satisfied to me.

Out of nowhere, this loading vehicle blazed by us; its after-burners carrying it caterwauling over the still-deserted intersection, somehow managing to keep those ten or so vital centimetres above the surface of the road. I just about managed to catch the name on the side:

The Delights of Fonch!

I caught a shudder for my trouble of reading the name, and turned away as the vehicle made it across the intersection—with time to spare—and then disappeared off along the road; devoid of traffic for the time being.

The driver shook his head, whistled, then glanced up in his rear-view mirror to catch my eye. "All that just because he couldn't wait five minutes, huh? A fellow might rightly break his neck doing something like that—what'd his family think then, huh?"

From my experience, the only thing worse than waiting at all is to believe that anything positive will happen as a *result* of said waiting . . .

But I buttoned my lip.

Sneered a, "Yuh", back at him by way of reply.

As we *waited*, I stared out through the window, to the traffic surrounding us on all sides, seeing only those distinctive, bored faces of those who've become prisoners of ground transportation. And all because they had to 'settle down' on some planet or other; all because they had to have this 'living space'; all because they *gave in* to that biological urge which tells a man, once upon a time, that he needs to 'take responsibility'.

Yeah, the day that happens to me do me a favour and stick a laser blast between my eyes.

Poor bastards.

Hell, I couldn't even tell you the *name* of the planet I was on that particular day, and since I have strict policies in place aboard my ship—*The Navaplastas*—as regards storing travel data, I wouldn't even be able to find out if I wanted.

I glanced to take in Foy and Milky.

Against my better judgement, I supposed I'd started to put together the beginnings of my very own merry little family. But who in their right mind could say no to those two?

To Foy, a twenty-something gal with honey hair, peachy eyes, and pinched-red cheeks.

Or to the teenage Milky—just about your standard-issue, tragic, orphan case—long hair tied up in a plait and hanging down to his waist. Back where I'm from—back on Arkle-4—a kid'd get himself beat on for daring to have hair longer than about five centimetres.

More importantly, though, as regards my crew, Foy was just about the meanest gunner I, or anybody else, has ever seen. Milky, meanwhile, was adept at fiddling with droids, bots, whatever else, and making them do his bidding—or, more importantly—*my* bidding.

I turned my attention back front-and-centre.

To the driver.

He was whistling.

Actually whistling.

As if he was having the time of his life.

Damn, if there's anything worse than having to hire a taxi driver while stuck down on some unlucky fig's planet, I don't know what is. First things first, you're at the mercy of whatever

4

the hell the driver wants to do—*whichever way he wants to go; however* fast *he wants to go.* You're no longer a free-roaming, liberty-indulging pedestrian . . . Nah, you're now a fully paid-up prisoner of some other punk's property. And that's something I should know better than most. Being a space smuggler's *all* about property. Who's got what. Who's being taken *where.*

. . . And, make no mistake, the old mantra of *My Ship, My Rules* will apply right to the end of existence. At least to the end of *my* existence.

The traffic light changed.

Finally.

The driver hummed the taxi up off its spot.

I felt my neck snap back in reaction to the movement.

I never will be able to understand just how people can live their whole lives planetside, with all the inconveniences that come with it. I guess I've just been spoiled what with having Big Black and nothing at all to tie me down . . . just one fella and his adventures . . . and his *crew* too, I suppose . . .

As the driver channelled into traffic, I couldn't help but notice some muscle across my stomach tighten. Like one of those prescient moments. Like I knew just what was going to happen. Like I could *see* what was going to happen. Or maybe it was just my mind playing tricks . . . trying to make out it was smarter than it truly was.

All I knew next was we were no longer neatly suspended just above the road, but instead being hurled off in some direction I couldn't make much sense of.

And then everything went black.

2 THE NAVAPLASTAS

WHEN I CAME TO, it was like this whole army of worms with pointed noses had somehow burrowed beneath my skin. And now they were trying to burrow their way out. If that sounds funny, then you can't have ever suffered from one of the more exotic, outer-space venereal diseases.

Everything came to me pretty bleary. The bright white light didn't help any at all. It just made me have to screw up my eyes in a squint.

My brain felt like it'd taken a good licking, which is to say that my brain felt an awful lot like all the other times it's taken a good licking. I could smell disinfectant all around me, and it felt like someone had wodged a pair of cotton balls up my nostrils.

As I reached out to touch my nose, I realised that I was lying on my side. That accounted for all the odd angles; all the twisted dimensions happening in front of me. I also found out that the reason it felt like I had cotton balls stuffed up my nostrils was because I *did* have cotton balls stuffed up there. I soon got shot of those, blowing them free into the *nada* surrounding me.

A few good lungs of air later and I felt like I was getting my senses back.

The world came just a touch clearer.

Details became finer—*pricklier*.

I soon realised I was in a medbay . . . and then, a moment or so later, I realised the bright white light shining down on me looked awfully familiar. A second more, and I twigged that I was in the medbay of the *Navaplastas*. I got a warm, fuzzy feeling which, I suppose, is akin to the sensation a baby might go through when its mother shows up after what seems to the baby like a lengthy absence. Just who was the mother and who was the baby . . . well, it speaks for itself . . .

"Easy, there, Captain."

I squinted some more, now able to see beyond the bright white light.

I could tell from the voice, the fact I was in the medbay of the *Nava*, that it was Brian who had spoken to me. One of Foy's two cousins on board.

Brian of the bushy afro with that single corkscrew curl twizzling down onto his forehead. In an effort to be of use to my burgeoning crew, Brian had taken on the role of Ship's Doctor, or whatever the hell that role might be called out in space . . . I was only ever an army man in occupation; never in spirit . . .

I held up my forearm to guard against the light.

That helped me out some.

I finally made him out.

He was wearing that white coat of his as if he *actually had* some kind of medical credentials. From somewhere—*God* knows where—he'd dug out a stethoscope which hung about his neck limply, like some long-dead snake.

I found my voice.

Finally.

"You think you could shut off the light, or what?"

"Aye, aye, Cap'ain."

That just sent a pounding pain to my temple. "We've spoken about *that*. Don't talk that way, okay? None of this 'aye, aye' crap." I paused, regained my senses. "It's *Captain* or *Sir*. Got it?"

"Yes, sir," Brian replied, sounding a fraction chided.

Then again, a boy's gotta know his place.

Especially when he's on my ship.

Thankfully, though, Brian had already made good progress on *finding* his place.

The other one—Brian's twin brother; Terry, of the matted, straw-yellow hair—hadn't yet found his vocation, but, at least today, seemed to be giving the role of Ship's Nurse a good working over. And he looked just as thrilled as might be imagined.

"Nurse," Brian said, deadpan.

"Shut the hell up," Terry shot back.

Terry, I could see, was wearing a pair of dungarees; a striped polo shirt on underneath. The way he stood with his thumbs hooked into the belly pocket made him look more than a little like some kind of dunce. The way he allowed his mouth to just latch open, as if it might be adept as a flytrap, really didn't help out much.

"Gonna need some more cotton balls," Brian said.

"Get them yourself," Terry replied. "I've got work to do on one of the starboard laser cannons."

Terry was always trying to get himself as close to the *Nava's* guns as he possibly could; no matter that he'd shown, time and time again, in the heat of combat, he simply couldn't hack it when it came to pulling the trigger—like he'd just freeze right up; not be able to do anything at all. Maybe it had something to do with his penchant of dressing up in dungarees; in what job—anywhere in the universe— are you taken seriously when you dress in dungarees?

I decided that, like always, I was going to have to step in, like the de facto dad I'd sort of become to these middle-to-late teenagers; I never did bother asking them for their ages, and they never seemed all that eager to tell.

"Shut the hell up, *both of you* . . . there's not gonna *be* any more cotton balls, got it?" I squinted some more. "And switch off that *damn* light."

Finally, Brian—or Terry; I wasn't really paying attention— flipped off the light.

And all was good again.

The ambiance of the *Nava* was just how I liked it, which is to say that it was something like a perpetual twilight; perfect conditions for any kind of smuggling antics you might be inclined to get up to. I reached about, grabbing hold of the edge of the examination table. I hauled myself upright, into a sitting position.

"Uh, Captain . . ."

I wheeled on Brian. "What? You gonna tell your captain to *relax* or something?"

"No, sir," Brian replied, averting my eyes.

I switched to looking at Terry, realising that he too was giving me a good staring.

"What is it?" I said. "Didn't I get all the cotton balls, or what?"

"No, sir," Terry replied.

"Then *what?*"

Terry shifted a glance at Brian, and then Brian appeared at my side, this time bearing a mirror.

When I took the mirror from him, I couldn't help wondering at it for a few moments. The mirrors that had existed on the *Nava* never spent very long in any tangible state of existence; they were extremely liable to get broken in times of great distress. This particular mirror had survived either through fluke or by design. Not so much as a scratch on the fucker.

It was almost a side issue when I got around to considering my reflection.

I looked beyond the hamster-pouch cheeks; the mottled, red complexion; and, of course, the pushbutton nose which'd been broken a few more times than it'd been fixed.

And I noticed the giant hole up in my temple.

That I could see a bit of my brain within; just peeping out to say hello.

I turned to Brian and Terry, in something like shock.

"Now, which one of you's gonna tell me what the hell happened?"

———

In the end, for whatever reason, neither one of them authorised themselves to tell me the whole story—it seemed that they either didn't know or someone had told them to hold out on me. My best guest was without doubt Foy . . . for all intents and purposes my Co-pilot, if such a thing ever existed on the *Nava*.

Although I could remember the taxi ride . . . that *infuriating* taxi ride . . . I was having a lot of trouble reconciling just what'd gone on after that set of lights.

I could sort of recall a large explosion . . . the blackness . . . but then there'd been nothing at all. Nothing till I'd woken up in the medbay of the *Nava* with the Gruesome Twosome bearing down on me, playing Doctor and Nursie.

On the bridge, though, I found only Clive Wodd; my Ship's Engineer.

As with the rest of my crew, how exactly he had ended up on the *Nava* was a mystery.

Though my nose wasn't anything worth writing home about, at least it wasn't as afflicted as Clive's was. Clive's nose was bent this way and that, all over the place, as if in his childhood his parents had held a bi-annual gathering where they'd got the neighbours round to tap dance all over his face. And, from his skinny physique, the fact that his parents had obviously neglected his alimentation needs, that bi-annual gathering invention of mine didn't seem such a long shot.

Good man, though, Clive.

He'd got the *Nava* back purring after more dings and flat-out crashes than any engineer *I'd* ever heard of. And any friend of the *Nava* is—by extension—a friend of mine.

Clive was wearing a simple, if slightly raggardy-looking emerald-green shirt over the top of a pair of black tracksuit trousers.

I've always wondered if I should do something about the dress code around the *Navaplastas*, but, then again, being a smuggler—as I proudly am—I feel that it'd end up cramping my style . . . shattering the carefully constructed *ambiance* of the ship.

Skipping the fact that Clive was staring at the hole in my forehead, I blurted out, "Where's Milky and Foy?"

Clive shifted a glance at the twins—Brian and Terry—who'd apparently followed me through to the bridge. Maybe they were waiting for me to simply keel over and die before them . . . I guess with me gone, and with no written will available, they'd plan on putting something disgusting like a *timeshare* scheme in place with the *Nava*; sharing her out among them like a cheap whore.

I kept my concentration fixed on Clive. "What's going on? Why won't anybody tell me *anything*?"

Finally, Clive turned his attention back to me. "They're . . . uh, *missing*."

" 'Missing' ?" I replied. "What the hell're you talking about?"

Clive shook his head, and looked a touch perplexed—maybe understandably so seeing that he'd apparently explained the situation to the best of his ability.

I held up my hands, deciding that I should go for a different approach here. That I should take things just a little slower. "Okey doke," I said, "let's take this back to Square One . . . just *what's* happening here?"

Again, Terry and Brian exchanged glances.

Said nothing.

Then both looked to Clive.

He shifted an apprehensive glance back at the *Nava's* vital systems—no doubt hoping that something might've come up; something that needed fixing.

Nothing, apparently, had.

"We were back at the terminal—*planetside*," Clive said. "Waiting for you three to return to the *Nava*. Next thing we knew, Milky set off his distress beacon. We set off as soon as we could for the location. When we got there, there was this whole wreck . . . the totalled hover taxi in the middle of an intersection."

Clive shifted a glance back to the twins, as if needing them to corroborate his story.

He turned his attention back to me—his *captain*—soon enough.

"The only one remaining in that hover taxi was you . . . and the driver, of course; he seemed pretty much unharmed, just groaning and stuff, but conscious." Here Clive shook his head. "Tried to get some words out of him, but he was jabbering nonsense—wanting us to get him to a hospital." Clive jerked his thumb over his shoulder, as if we were back planetside. "I could hear sirens approaching—didn't seem much point in waiting around. Didn't want you to go missing like Milky and Foy. I made a judgement call, decided that we should bring you back . . ."

"And here we are," I finished for him.

Clive nodded.

"What about Foy and Milky?"

Clive shook his head, eyed the twins. "We had a quick scan of the networks, working out if they'd brought Milky and Foy in . . . if somebody picked them up for medical care. Or some kind of an interview with the authorities." He fixed his stare on mine. "Results came back negative . . . whoever dug them out of the wreckage, it wasn't anybody official; nobody who's playing by the rules, in any case."

I thought this over, wondered at what it might mean.

And then the most obvious point struck me.

"Where are we . . . *right now?*"

Without so much as needing to glance at the *Nava's* instruments, Clive informed me that we were about a day's journey from where we'd been; the time it'd taken me to come round from the crash.

I immediately instructed him to turn us around.

As Clive headed for the controls, preparing to put the *Nava* to work, he hesitated. He turned back to me. "I . . . know what this looks like, Captain . . . like we *deserted* them . . . like I made the decision to leave them behind." He stared into my eyes. "But it was just this feeling—down in my gut; like something wasn't right."

I held myself still, feeling my own gut shifting slightly; I wondered if the twins had thought to drip feed me any sort of sustenance . . . if they had, then it hadn't been especially *sustaining*.

"Not to worry," I replied, to Clive, trying to brush it off as nothing at all. "You did what you thought was best—might've saved all our bacon, who's to say?"

But, as I sat down in my captain's chair, my brain began to work away. It began to go all of those most-paranoid of places which I'm convinced only exist within the realms of a smuggler's skull. All of those places which implore the career smuggler never—*not under any circumstances*—to trust anyone.

"Captain?"

I glanced up, saw that Clive was at the controls.

He nodded behind me.

I turned, saw that Brian was there, afro and all.

"Shall we take care of that hole in your head?"

3 BACK PLANETSIDE

EFFICIENT SOUL HE WAS, Clive got us back to the terminal.

We got clearance fine, and we weren't brought down in a shower of laser fire . . . that said, a smooth landing should never be mistaken for a warm welcome. In fact, some of the smoothest landings I've ever had have been followed by perilous, and —*quite frankly*—unhealthy situations. I wasn't taking chances with the rest of my crew neither, instructing them all to stay behind in the safety of the *Nava's* belly.

I wasted no time at the terminal, not bothering to even take note of the planet's name, even at second pass. Unlike other smugglers, who seem to have a natural aversion to planetside authorities, I went to the cops right away.

Asked them flat out to do a scan for the members of my crew.

One of the unexpected benefits of having a crew as a smuggler means that there's a kind of unspoken ambiguity in the air. As far as the cops are concerned, they're suspicious that you're up to no good because, let's be honest, smugglers aren't the most *hygienic* of creatures. But the fact that you've got a crew *at all* seems to paint you as being at least semi-legitimate.

And, to give myself the requisite credit, I've always considered myself as being somewhere approaching semi-legitimate.

Most of the time . . .

The station was fairly modern—vidscreens all over the shop —and a dozen or so busy-looking cops zooming in on particular details. It smelled of coffee and sweat, though not the elbow-grease, hard-working kind. It was *office* sweat. The sweat you cook up tapping a screen all day.

Then again, being a space smuggler as I am, and spending a good portion of my life with a similar kind of setup, I suppose I shouldn't have been having such grandiose pretensions.

When I put my enquiry to the cops, they were unable to help me out.

I told one of them—this guy with cosmic-blue hair—about the crash, about the hover taxi at the intersection. His expression, the way he scratched his skull before searching the database, told me that he got quite a few of such incidents on a daily basis. And that there was nothing remarkable about them.

The blue-haired cop ran me through the footage from that day; or the 'highlights reel' as he referred to it.

I soon pointed out my particular crash, and he duly set about slowing down the images, bringing into focus the components as they fell into place.

I watched on as the taxi driver sat at the red light, observed as that hover truck passed us by at flat-out speed; the one with *The Delights of Fonch!* scrawled onto its side in a childish cursive font.

If only those kids knew the truth about Fonch . . .

The video remained focussed on the halted traffic. When the light changed, I felt a strange churning in my gut, like my body was craving a moiser, or something like it—I always tend to do my best work when I've got just a touch of alcohol running through my blood.

In the end, I guess the sensation had more to do with anticipation; anticipation for finding out just how the crash had transpired.

How I'd got the hole in my head.

The taxi pulled off its spot. Hummed onward. The rest of the traffic gently picking up speed behind. It was then that I saw the truck—the same one which'd blazed through the lights in the first place; the one with *The Delights of Fonch!* written on the side. As it ploughed right—*smack*—into the side of the taxi, I felt my whole body seize up; like someone had reached out and slapped me on the cheek.

It was a weird feeling to watch myself in that taxi—crushed just as easily as a tin can in a fist—tumbling its way across the intersection.

The truck with *The Delights of Fonch!* written on the side didn't so much as slow down.

It just kept on going.

"*Holy . . . shhh-sugar,*" the cop exclaimed, as he manipulated the image. He called out to one of his colleagues, "Hey, Thorpey, come take a look at this one—hit and run."

I heard footsteps behind me, but I kept my attention fixed on the monitor, watching as the reel spun onward. I held my breath, never taking my eyes off the taxi as it lay there—on its roof. I could just make out the others—me, Foy and Milky—all packed into the back seat.

The video ran on another few seconds, and then promptly cut right out.

When the screen flickered to black, I jolted so hard in surprise that I jumped clean up out of my chair. I turned on the cop who'd been running the video—who'd called out to his colleague. "Where's the rest of the tape?"

The blue-haired cop, now deep in conversation with his colleague, his back turned, held up a flat, no-nonsense palm. That's something I've never been able to stand with cops; how they have this superiority complex just because someone handed them over a uniform and a blaster pistol.

Finally, the conversation apparently done with, the cop turned back to me; his colleague marching on out of the room, apparently to go fetch a superior, or whatever.

The blue-haired cop didn't wear anything like that slightly jovial expression he had before; that expression which told me, pretty plainly, that he was looking for some diversion in what was otherwise a Mainly Boring Day. "Sir," the cop said, "I'm gonna have to ask you to leave."

" 'Leave' ?" I snapped back, feeling like my eyeballs almost rolled right out of their sockets. "I wanna know where the *hell* the rest of the tape got to. Where the *hell* my crew have got to."

The cop stared long and hard at me, perhaps only then realising I was a smudge taller than he was. His eyes casually drifted down to my waist where he no doubt spotted my laser blaster hanging off my thigh. If there's one thing about cops—especially in urban places like there—they want to play down confrontation wherever they can manage it.

The cop glanced at the monitor; to the screen showing nothing but black. He looked to one of his buddies, over on the other side of the room. One of them shifted me a glance, looked back to the first cop, then shook his head. He resumed whatever task he was bothering his vidscreen with.

Blushing now slightly, the cop looked back at me. "Listen," he said, "nobody reported anything out of the ordinary. It was a bad *fender-bender*, that's all."

I felt likely to sock him in the jaw if he continued this way.

Or maybe I could just show him the hole in my head.

"The only one we've got a record of pulling out of that crash is the driver. Everybody else had skedaddled by the time recovery services turned up on the scene." He shook his head. "Why, from our records, you weren't even *in* the crash."

I bit my tongue, doing my best to ignore the pounding pulse I could feel in my temple. How I could feel that my brain was rapidly being attacked with a blinding migraine. I suppose any *normal* person would've been taking it easy after catching a hole to the head . . . not me though, apparently.

"Yeah?" I said, taking care to keep my tone cool, calm and collected, or, at least, as best as I could manage. I indicated my forehead, and the plastic or whatever the hell Brian had filled my skull in with. "What's that look like to you?"

The cop scowled at my forehead as if—more than anything —he wanted to deny the evidence.

But, as every cop knows, they live and *die* by the evidence they uncover.

"Wind the video back," I said, standing my ground, allowing my hand to fall away from my forehead and then to hover—ever so slightly—closer to my blaster pistol. At the same time, on some gut-level, I knew just how dumb I was being to get threatening in a *police* station.

Did I *want* to end up with another hole in the head?

For the longest time, I was certain the cop wouldn't do what I asked, but, in the end, with a quick, efficient nod from one of his colleagues, he stomped back on over to the vidscreen which'd shown the crash unfolding. With a couple of wild gestures, he ordered the tape back to the beginning.

And we watched the video through one more time.

It cut out in the same place.

The cop glanced back at me, the resentment on his face having vanished for the time being, replaced by a sense of intrigue—that childish quality which, I'm sure, attracts its fair share of kids into police work in the first place. "Cuts out—same place," he said.

I shook my head. "Has someone tampered with the tape?"

The cop shrugged. "Looks that way, don't it?"

I stood back from the monitor, as the cop, without me prompting him this time, reeled through the video another time. I lowered the tone of my voice. "You think anybody about the station might've been responsible?"

The cop remained focussed on the screen for a long time, freeze framed the video and then glanced about himself casually. "Nah, I wouldn't think it."

"Then how?"

Again, the cop shrugged. "Hacked from the outside, I'd guess."

"That happen often?"

"More than you'd think." The cop leaned in closer to the screen, squinting. "It may surprise you to learn this, but there're certain criminal elements about this planet—and they've got far superior resources when compared with our bumpkin police force here."

I could almost smell the sarcasm dripping off his words.

The self-effacing tone brought a slight smile to my lips.

Perhaps I'd got this cop wrong after all.

"Take a look at this, Captain."

Finally, a little respect; calling a man by his proper title.

It was almost as if he was *trying* to get into my good books now . . .

I bent down to take in the screen, feeling my knees creaking out loud in protest as I did so. On screen, I made out the flickering, frozen image. As before, everything was in black and white; the focus being on maintaining a high contrast. The cop'd brought up the moment right before the crash. Even though the image was good quality, the interior of the taxi was still set in shadow; it was impossible to make out the passengers or driver within.

The occupant of the truck neither.

The cop focussed the image down onto a stamped serial number on the truck's fender, explaining as he manipulated the vidscreen controls, enhancing the resolution further and further, "Vehicle came back negative when we ran a scan." The cop shrugged. "Standard for vehicles being used for illegal purposes—or even just some old lady who forgot to file the registration." He shook his head. "Damn, I could tell you stories—some days it feels like less than half the vehicles on this Godforsaken planet are unregistered."

I gave him a solid "Hmm," to acknowledge his pain, and he went on.

"I'd venture to suggest, though," the cop continued, "that this wasn't any benevolent old lady out doing her shopping." He leaned closer into the screen. "Nah, this's someone out to do harm."

Finally, he leaned back from the image, relaxing in his chair. He knitted his fingers together.

It was a long, reflective moment, as if the two of us were taking the time to consider the implications of the crash; of what the two of us had just witnessed play out on the vidscreen, and what it might mean.

Right then, from across the station floor, I heard a wild *screech*—something like a chicken getting unexpectedly stuck with a pole.

I turned to see a towering, bean-pole scrawny female cop emerge through a doorway. It took me several moments to realise that what was coming out of her mouth were *words*; and that those *words* were directed right at me.

And that they weren't pleasant words by any reckoning.

Before I'd so much as got my thoughts straight, she was right up in my face, jabbing a sharply manicured finger into my chest telling me to "Get out! Get out! Get out!"

More out of panic than anything else, I nodded my thanks

to the blue-haired cop who'd taken me through the footage of the crash, and then hustled my way for the door.

It was only when I was out on the street, with a door being slammed shut behind me, and—from the sounds of it—a bolt being slid into place on the other side, that I caught my senses. That I wondered what I was going to do next.

Well, I might not've seen anything helpful in the crash footage, but I did have one thing.

I'd happened to see the truck's registration.

That truck which'd smashed right into the taxi.

The truck with *The Delights of Fonch!* written on the side.

. . . Never did have all that much of a sweet tooth . . .

4 ANY PLACE, ANY TIME: PLANETSIDE

.

W HENEVER I'd come across anything vaguely technical—which, for me, was anything involving numbers—I'd be sure to call Milky to task as soon as I could possibly manage. Now, though, since Milky was MIA, I had to resort to my—admittedly *useful*—backup option:

Clive Wodd.

I got on the line with him using the inner-ear comms which Milky had put together for each member of the crew. When I called him up, he sounded as if he was somewhat vexed, as if I'd disturbed him while he'd been doing something important . . . most likely, though, I knew the truth would be that Terry was getting on his nerves; not allowing him to do his work in peace . . . the work Clive did as the Ship's Engineer.

I gave him the vehicle registration, and he muttered something about not knowing all that much about handling those kind of databases; not knowing all that much about how these systems *worked*. While Milky loved nothing more than to get tinkering with screens, just as much as he enjoyed tweaking with electronics—making stuff *blip* and *bleep*—Clive hated just about everything to do with computing systems, programming, and the like.

What Clive loved most and, quite frankly, what he excelled at most, was poking and prodding at engines, at all the actual *real-life* systems which kept the *Navaplastas* in the air.

But that didn't mean Clive couldn't handle computer systems just as well as Milky could; or perhaps—I've always had my suspicions—*even better* . . .

Sure enough, Clive got back to me within the minute. He sent me over a full listing of the truck's address. I thought once or twice about hailing a taxi cab, and then, plugging the information into my GPS systems and finding that it was a good two-hour walk away from my current location, I decided to bite the bullet.

I flung out a chunky Bingo wing.

Mercifully, this time I got myself a bot-piloted hover taxi—this meant a one-hundred-per-cent discount on all small talk. Bots are notorious for sticking to the central details; to the *where to* and the *this much*. And—considering the type of business it seemed I was about to mess myself up with—it was the best option.

The bot dropped me off some place well out of the city.

I paid the credits, got my canned "Thank you" and then got on out.

As I'd been riding along in the cab, the twilight had been snapping at the fender. Now, the planet had taken the plunge into full-night. I had to admit that I was somewhat surprised to find that the street lights even lit up at all this far out of town . . . apparently in the middle of nowhere.

This was the sole house on the whole street; all the others seemed to have been flattened for some long-ago planned—and long-ago *forgotten*—renovation works.

The house itself looked to be a decent-sized, five-bedroom property. The garden had grown wild; the grass growing up to somewhere just beneath my armpits.

The path to the front door wasn't clear.

As I took in the façade of the place, I couldn't help but notice the truck—the one which'd been responsible for the crash in the first place. It was parked up—*unsubtly*—around the side of the house. I glanced over the windows, seeing if there was anybody peeping out, and, since I could see no one, I decided to have a butcher's.

Just as I'd seen it the day of the crash—just as I'd seen it on the vidscreen back at the police station—the truck had that precocious *The Delights of Fonch!* slogan basted on its side. What I noticed now, though, that I hadn't noticed either on the day of the crash, or from the tapes I'd witnessed back at the station, was that it seemed run down.

In fact, when I reached out and ran my fingertips along the side of the vehicle, they came away covered in black dust and grime. On closer inspection of the truck's tarpaulin, I noted many tears; parts where the tarp itself had peeled right away to reveal the much more sedate, dirty-white bodywork beneath. As I completed my tour of the truck, coming around to the front, I noticed that the windshield was cracked in no less than seven different places.

Man, oh, man did this send a creep up my spine.

Just *what the hell* was some guy doing ploughing about town in a truck belonging to a now-defunct company? And what was more, just *what the hell* were they doing driving said truck into traffic?

Realising that I wasn't going to get the answers to my questions by just sniffing about the bombed-out truck, I turned my attention back to the house itself.

Before I approached the place, something nagged me to check in with Clive. I suppose that's been one of the big benefits of outfitting the *Nava* with a crew . . . it gives me someone to watch my back right when I'm about to do something especially *dumb* . . .

All-checked in with Clive, and warned to 'take care', I set my attention onto the front door, a sneer firmly fixed right across my lips.

If there's anything I've learned about dealing with objectionable individuals—objectionable individuals *just like me*—it's that you've gotta go in with a no-nonsense, here-to-bust-balls attitude . . . anything else just *bleeds* weakness.

With that in mind, I slipped my blaster pistol free of its holster, and squeezed it down at my thigh. I reminded myself that this person—either directly or indirectly—was responsible for Milky and Foy's disappearance.

I rang the doorbell, settled back on my heels, and waited.

From within the house, I heard nothing but silence for the longest time. One of those silences which tells me, instinctively, to prepare for laser bolts coming sizzling past my skull.

But, then, out of nowhere, there was a nimble *snap* of a locking mechanism disengaging followed by the door opening in on itself.

Standing there, in the hallway, was a little old lady.

She wore a dressing gown, slippers and glasses that could have quite easily doubled as microscopes.

———

I was a touch stunned for the ensuing twenty minutes.

In fact, I don't think I fully regained consciousness until— with a warm, milky and sweetened cup of tea in my hand—I got a message through from Clive, wanting to know if I was okay. If I was in need of any sort of 'assistance'. After assuring him that I was 'fine, just *fine*', I turned my attention back to where I found myself.

It was the proverbial grandmother's sitting room. Patterned, faded wallpaper. Some world-weary, wilting flowers over by the window. The gentle smell of lilac perfume mixed in with an overwhelming stench of damp. And, under my arse, just about the most comfortable armchair that I'd ever sat in. Considering that I'm including my captain's chair, back on the *Nava*, that's *really* saying something.

I turned my attention to the old lady, sitting opposite me, in her own armchair.

She had a shawl draped about her shoulders, her own cup of tea already finished and set down on the coffee table between us. The cup sat on top of a stack of paper books which—I could tell from the many dozens of milky rings on the top volume—served only as coasters.

The old lady was mumbling about something beneath her voice. I knew what old folks got like at this age, starving for company, glad to have just about *anybody* around.

Even a space smugger like me.

I wondered if she was even speaking to me at all. If she didn't think that I was some long-lost grandchild who'd returned here to converse with her for a while before heading back to the Land of the Living.

I sipped at my tea, winced a touch at the oversweet taste, and then set it down on the coffee table, neglecting to use one of those books as a coaster. Since the old lady said nothing about it, I presumed I was in the right.

"Uh, ma'am," I began.

The old lady glanced up at me, and I noticed how her hair was almost like stressed cotton wool that'd been set in place with some modelling glue.

"I was just wondering." I leaned forwards, sat on the edge of the armchair cushion, then jerked my thumb in the direction of the outside, as if this movement might help me convey my message. "Couldn't help noticing that truck of yours you've got parked up out there."

The old woman cocked her head to one side.

Smiled pleasantly.

As if I was complimenting her on some freshly baked brownies.

I waited out a couple of beats—an old lawyer trick—to see if she would fill in any of the blanks; if she would *volunteer* any further information.

Realising that she was waiting for me, I continued.

"You see, a day or so ago, I was in a crash . . . back in town." I eyed her closely, wondering just how much of this she was truly grasping—how much she was truly taking in. "Anyway, I went to go see the police about it, to see if we could thrash out just who was responsible"—here I grinned widely—"and your truck *out there* showed up on the vidscreen."

I paused, waiting for a response.

But I got none.

I slouched back in the armchair, crossed, then *recrossed*, my legs and went for a different tactic. "You don't happen to have a *grandson*—a *granddaughter*—who likes to borrow the truck, who, uh, takes the truck out for a spin every now and again?"

Here I expected the old lady to screw up her features—for frown lines to score her forehead. But her full attention remained fixed on me, her smile and eyes just as bright as before, as if she would listen to me for the rest of eternity.

But I didn't *have* eternity.

Foy and Milky didn't *have* eternity.

"Ma'am?" I said, prompting her.

"Hmm, oh," the old lady replied, blinking a couple of times —perhaps clearing the daze of Memories Long Passed from her eyes. She glanced back at me, and I wondered if she was going to ask me who I was . . . if she was going to ask me *why* I was in her home. Instead, though, she said, "The pension scheme here is really daylight robbery." She shook her head, but maintained her fixed, bright-eyed demeanour. "I could tell you things which'd make your toes curl. A woman's got to find a way to make ends meet *some* way, you know? And, with all due respect to this planet—my *home*—there really aren't all that many part-time employment opportunities for an old biddy like me."

"Ma'am?" I replied, not quite following.

She smiled wider still—seemed to cock her head at an even more acute angle. "The leaders of organised crime throw me a bone every now and then—just a little morsel for me to do." Her eyes shone brilliantly now. "A dash of *adventure*."

My brain stopped working for several seconds.

Then I caught up with reality.

"Let me get this straight, ma'am," I said. "You're saying that you were the one driving the truck—the one who did the hit-and-run on the taxi?"

"Oh, yes," she said, smiling even wider still.

She paused for a beat.

Then added, "Can I get you some more tea?"

———

Feeling just a touch shaken, and not a little confused, I left the old lady's house behind.

She had revealed that her name was Amber, and that—just as she'd said—she ran several small deals for the local mobsters. Whenever they required someone to fly under the radar—say when they needed someone to crash into a *taxi*; no questions asked—they would get in touch with her. When I'd pressed her for the location and contact details of these mobsters, she'd been only too happy to give them to me.

What I'd expected was, at best, a whispered phone number, or perhaps even a scrawled, near-illegible address written on a napkin.

What I *hadn't* expected was a glossy white business card with gilt lettering pressed onto the front; someone by the name of Richard 'Ricky D' Hernandez with the admittedly vague title of 'Independent Business Owner' beneath. I trekked back into town all the same, giving that Fonch truck one final glare for old times' sake.

Being out in the sticks, I didn't have the same privileged of being able to pick and choose my hover taxi; this time I got stuck with a human driver. All the way into town, from the moment I gave him the address, the driver went on—*and on*—about how 'Ricky D' had solved a hernia that his great aunt had, and, in general, about how he was an all-round swell guy. In fact, when I eventually arrived outside the indicated building, I couldn't help but feel somewhat positive myself. If people had such good things to say about this guy then how could he be truly responsible for the kidnapping of Foy and Milky?

And—if he did prove to be responsible—then surely he would be kind enough to listen to reason?

. . . Yeah, sometimes I forget the way the world works . . .

As the hover taxi began to pull away from the street, I glanced back at the business card, realising that there was no floor or office number listed. I caught the driver just before he left me behind in a high-pitched *whine* of electrical engine.

When I explained my predicament, the driver cracked a wide smile. Then he leaned out of his window just to give me some sort of a friendly *pat* on the shoulder. "Oh, buddy," he said, "you really *are* new around here, aintcha?"

Not seeing any reason to keep my cards close to my chest, I replied, "Yeah."

The driver, apparently finding my question something approaching side-splitting comedy, reached up to wipe away a tear. When he'd got some modicum of control over himself, he said, "Ricky D; he owns the whole damn building, pal," then drove off.

I took in the building for the first time.

Just like the business card, the building was bridal-veil white. Its windows had a silver coating which allowed the occupants to look out, but nobody outside to look *in*. Each of the windows was framed with a glittering golden coat of paint. The whole building was lit up against the night sky by a series of bright white spotlights.

I couldn't help but feel, as I stepped into the lobby, breathing in the overpowering odour of mint, that this might be some kind of a religious institution . . . or perhaps it was just an *institution* . . .

By the time I'd reached the reception desk, I was convinced that the blond-haired, blue-eyed secretary sat behind it would shoot me down without delay; that when I asked after 'Ricky D' she would declare that he was 'unfortunately occupied', 'out of the office' or that I should 'make an appointment'. It was enough of a wonder that the place was open at all at this time of night.

Then again, for all the trimmings, this *was* a gangster I was dealing with.

Night, I suppose, was peak profit time.

I was hit pretty hard with surprise when—upon presenting the business card, enquiring if I could have a word with 'Ricky'—the secretary told me to go right on up.

To the thirty-third floor.

Now, from my experience of gangsters, I've found a few constants.

Number one: there's security *everywhere*:

Muscle wrestling to get free of tight-fitting suits.

Blasters itching to break out of holsters.

Number two: a sense of threat hangs over *everything*:

Stainless steel, medically anonymous interior decorating.

No natural light.

. . . And, well, apart from the perfectly explainable fact of it being *night*, I could hardly accuse Ricky D of any of these.

When I emerged up on the thirty-third floor, there was only a secretary tapping away at a vidscreen. She barely glanced up when I announced myself, when I informed her that, down in the lobby, they'd told me to go right through and see the big man himself. She just smiled sweetly and confirmed what the secretary downstairs had said, adding only, "Mr Hernandez prides himself on his accessibility—that at any time of day anyone can get in touch with him for a face-to-face."

Feeling stunned by this whole experience, I pinched myself as I passed through the sliding doors to Ricky D's office.

—————

By that point, since my expectations had been well and truly shattered at just about *every* opportunity along the way, I can honestly say that I would've been prepared for anything.

But, most of all, I was prepared for it to be a trap.

For all of this to be some elaborate setup, designed to capture the unwary; those who were dumb enough to come at Ricky D out in the open.

My throat wound too tight to speak as I stood in the doorway. I stared in at the bespectacled man curled over his desk, hard at work. He couldn't have been much out of his twenties. He had slick, well-gelled hair and a finely groomed pair of eyebrows.

I don't know what drew my attention to the eyebrows other than some sort of eyebrow-grooming *envy* . . . it's been bandied about that my eyebrows more than just resemble a pair of extremely well-looked after caterpillars.

"Just one minute," he said, remaining coiled over his desk, tapping away at the screen before him.

I took in his office, seeing the trio of moons which hung over the planet shining in through the skylight. Ricky did have at least *one* gangster-like vice. His office was the penthouse. Then again, I guess if I'd had my own building, I'd make sure that I got the sweetest of sweet spots.

There were also bookshelves lining the walls, rising all the way up to the ceiling. And these weren't just decoration—bare walls hadn't simply been programmed with the rendering of stuffed bookshelves—they were *real* paper books that'd been well thumbed through.

Just standing in the office, I felt like my IQ had risen two points.

With a large intake of breath which seemed, of itself, to draw his body out of its curled-up position, Ricky straightened up and then rose from his chair.

As he rounded his desk, I noted that his chair was one of those old-style, brown-leather recliners. A kind of circular shape. The sort which Earth presidents might've been proud to own. The desk wasn't too shabby either. It looked—and probably was—authentic Earth-grown oak. Polished within an inch of its life, too.

Ricky trod towards me, grinning all over, stretching his hand out. Despite his perfect, pearly-white smile; despite the sharp suit—everything which screamed *used-car salesman*—I couldn't help but *like* him instantly.

As I gave him over my hand, complete with horned, gnarled fingernails, he shook it as if I was some kind of envoy. He even pressed his other hand over the top of mine—the *two-handed handshake* . . . he was clearly glad to see me.

Or else *awfully* good at pretending.

Ricky broke off the handshake, took a couple of steps back. He held out his finger, pointing directly at my chest. "Arkle," he said. "Arkle Wright?" And then, on impulse, he slapped himself on the forehead. "*Captain* Wright," he corrected himself. "I *am* sorry."

And he actually sounded as if he meant it . . .

Still dumbstruck, Ricky eased me over to the chair which sat before his desk. A chair just as plush—if not *better* maintained—than the one he used. He made extra-sure I was comfortable before taking a seat himself. He propped his elbows on the desk and knitted his fingers together.

His concentration firmly fixed on me.

"I imagine," Ricky said, "that you're here about your crew." He blinked a couple of times, but I'm certain he didn't look at any notes or consult any sort of neural implant. "Foy Undine and Petur Hay-gun."

I held myself still.

Braced myself by squeezing the armrests.

I had known Foy's first name, of course, but never her surname . . . Foy *Undine* . . . interesting.

As for the other name, I could only imagine that Ricky was referring to Milky; that this was Milky's *real* name. Once more, I had never thought to press Milky for his name; it had seemed too personal, in a way. Or, maybe—*just maybe*—I'd been too fixed on trying to make as many credits as I possibly could to the detriment of human relationships.

I had to admit that my suspicions had now been well and truly raised.

Although I did my best not to show off any emotion—to display any sort of surprise about what Ricky had just told me—I couldn't help but narrow my eyes.

"How'd you say Milky's name again?"

Without so much as batting an eyelid—instantly knowing just who 'Milky' was—Ricky said, "Peter Hay-gun . . . it's spelled P-E-T-U-R, then, the surname, H-G-U-N."

I focussed on Ricky all the more, trying to fathom just how he'd got hold of all of this information; all of this *data* on my crew.

Then again, I came to realise that there could be only one way.

That he had taken the two of them—Foy and Milky —prisoner.

"I would like to apologise straight away," Ricky said, that smile still fixed to his lips. "I realise how *uncouth* this whole situation no doubt strikes you." He rolled his shoulders a touch; one of those irritable tension-loosening exercises that Office People so often go through . . . people who live lives dominated by vidscreens.

I waited a few moments, trying out my silence trick again; to see if Ricky would add in more details of his own accord.

But he was waiting for me.

I had to admit that he had me thoroughly stumped.

"I . . . I don't really *understand* the 'situation'."

Ricky kept up that smile; no sign of faltering.

Not even for a second.

"It's quite simple, Captain, I have some associates a few systems across who were very much interested in acquiring the services of your crewmembers on a temporary basis. They got in touch, and put a plan in place to *acquire* them."

Here I noted a slight chill entering Ricky's tone.

Or maybe it was just me.

"You mean," I replied, "you *kidnapped* them?"

Ricky shrugged and spread his arms wide, indicating that I could use whatever nomenclature suited me but it changed things not one jot.

Silence pressed down on the sizeable office.

Suddenly I felt as if the space wasn't as ample as I'd once thought.

Again, Ricky was playing me at my own game, leaving the silence out there for me to fill. Once more, I decided there wasn't another option. "Why didn't you just come to me?" I said. "Why didn't you just *ask* them directly if they wanted to do something on the side?"

Ricky pouted then perhaps smiled more widely than he had at any other time in the course of the discussion. "There was no time, Captain. If there *had* been time then, believe you me, I wouldn't have had reason to get involved." Ricky shook his head, smiled some more. "Really, I'm as much in the dark over all this as you are." He gestured to me, and then back to himself. "And we're really not too different, you and I, are we? I mean, we're both freelancers; both of us *fierce* independent businessmen trying to make a living in an unforgiving universe, hmm?"

I couldn't help but think Ricky was doing far better than simply making a 'living'.

"As for the means," Ricky continued, "I *am* terribly sorry for the robust method employed to 'kidnap' "—here he made bunny ears with his fingers—"your crewmembers, but, really, if you'll forgive me, I could see no other way." He glanced down to his hands, swallowed hard, showing off what I could only take to be genuine regret. "I had everything all lined up . . . medical care to hand, but"—here he glanced back up at me, wagged his finger —"your crew were *extremely* efficient at extracting you . . . and I can see"—he gestured at my forehead—"they've done a really quite complete job in patching you up."

I took a moment to consider the relative merits of having

been cared for by Brian, as placed alongside the potential care which Ricky might've offered me. I couldn't help but think that the skin where I'd had my hole punctured might've been somewhat better 'finished' if a true medical professional had had his way with the wound.

But no point crying over spilled moiser . . .

"Now, Captain," Ricky said, rising up from his seat, coming around to where I was sitting; placing his arm about my shoulders, "I really must wish you a safe journey—there're, no doubt, many other people who're waiting for a meeting . . ." He paused, removing his hold for a moment, making it seem that, although he had pressing matters to attend to, he didn't wish to seem rude in showing me the exit. "Unless there's anything else I might be able to help with?"

I held myself still for a moment, trying to gather my thoughts.

It'd been a long time since I'd found myself at the business end of a charm offensive.

"Uh," I just about got out, stumbling from my chair, and being escorted to the door of Ricky's office. "When will I get my crew *back*?"

Ricky halted.

Made a show of staring me in the eyes.

"Well, I imagine that's at the whim of my client."

"And who's your client?"

Ricky gave a wry smile.

He wagged his finger at me again.

"Did they tell you, Captain, what the 'D' in 'Ricky D' stands for?"

"No."

"*Diamond.*"

I tried to reconcile this information for a few moments, working out if there was some sort of a subtext I was missing. In the end, it seemed that my beleaguered expression was more than enough to prompt Ricky to elaborate.

"That's my reputation," Ricky said. "*Diamond* . . . my promises are not only *valuable* . . . they are *unbreakable* . . ."

"Ah," I managed, "that kinda makes sense now."

"I'm so glad, Captain," Ricky replied, easing me the last few steps out of the door. "Take care, won't you? And do come by to visit next time you're in the neighbourhood."

With that, I felt myself thrust out.

It took me several seconds to get my thoughts back together.

And when I did, I couldn't quite convince myself that they made any sense.

5 BACK ON BOARD THE NAVA

"**C**APTAIN? Captain?"

I returned from my bleary, addled thoughts.

I wondered if I was maybe suffering from some kind of delayed concussion . . . in my extensive experience of holes to the head, concussions—or at the very least *headaches*—usually turn out to be the very start of the symptoms.

I glanced up.

Saw Clive's nostrils peering down at me.

That pair of never-ending, furry tunnels.

Slowly, I pieced my surroundings back together.

Realised where I was.

The *Nava* . . . on the bridge . . . in the *captain's* chair, no less . . . in all of its well-sprung, impossibly comfortable glory.

I glanced up to the navigational screen, saw that we were floating somewhere in space, apparently in the middle of nowhere. I rubbed at the hole in my head—the one which Brian had so neatly filled in—and I turned my attention to Clive. "What's up?"

Clive gave me the shred of a smile. "Need to know where to, Captain . . . where we should take the ship."

Although his request sounded reasonable enough, I couldn't quite bring myself to put all the pieces together in a completely logical fashion. Almost as if there was something blocking me— something stopping me from grasping the *thrust* of the idea.

"Huh?" I said, expressing my confusion succinctly.

"The next job?" Clive tried again, then rubbed his finger and thumb together. "Money? Credits? *Lifeblood?*"

Somehow Clive always knows how to get through this thick skull of mine.

I straightened up in the captain's chair, focussed on him.

If I did have concussion then at least it wasn't affecting my vision.

There was only one Clive Wodd, and that was how I'd always remembered him.

Singular.

"Did I . . . uh . . . tell you about . . ."

Clive rolled his eyes. "Yes, Captain—you told us that some hood called Ricky D contrived of the crash, as a means to snatch away Foy and Milky."

I blinked a couple of times.

Realising that I couldn't have put it as well myself.

"Uh, yeah," I got out, stumbling free of my chair, and then, surely heading for a tumble if it wasn't for the good old sturdy wall of the ship, I added, "that's it."

It was right then, thinking things through, trying to work out if there were any tiny bits of skull floating loose in my brain that I realised I could hear the joyful *pitter-patter* of footsteps coming along the corridor. Someone approaching the bridge.

I knew that it would be one of the twins—as Clive had reiterated, Foy and Milky were still both AWOL—but I hadn't quite realised how fixed I had it in my mind that it'd be Brian to come bounding onto the bridge till I saw it was, in fact, Terry.

In a great big tangle of straw-coloured hair.

And as I suppose many parents act when their less-favoured, or less-talented offspring shows up, I put on what I believed to be a 'receptive' face, showing him that I was waiting for him to impress me in some way. That he would *always* have the chance to illustrate just what he could do.

Terry glanced about the bridge, dumbstruck for several moments.

"Out with it, boy," I said, determined not to have any nonsense.

Terry attempted a smile.

It didn't much convince me or Clive.

Soon it slipped back into the more familiar teenage grimace I'd grown to recognise as Terry—and his brother Brian's —*neutral* expression.

"I've been checking over some of the databases; impressions the *Nava* took while we were parked down at the terminal."

Not quite sure about trusting my legs with the full weight of my body, I continued to support myself with the wall.

Terry glanced from me to Clive then back again. "Landing records," he said, as if this explained everything.

I stared Terry down, wondering if he might have the nerve to take the piss out of me.

Most likely, though, it was just the concussion talking.

Making me take reality in the wrong way.

Apparently sensing that his captain's patience wasn't to be tested, Terry continued with his explanation.

"After Clive had run the check on the truck's registration, I decided to take a look at the larger database; to see if I could access the landing records." He chanced a smile here. This time it stuck. "I did a search for crew information; for Milky and Foy."

"You telling me you knew Milky and Foy's real names—surnames and all that?"

Terry shook his head. "Nah, I just searched using their You-Lick."

I blinked hard, now sure that Terry was trying out some extremely ill-judged wise routine with me. But being the benevolent captain I am, I decided to give him another opportunity. "Come again?"

"U-L-I-C . . . the ULIC . . . Unique Landing Identification Code."

Terry shifted a nervous glance in Clive's direction, looking for support.

Clive gave me a no-nonsense nod.

That's the thing with Clive, you always know where you are. There's very little sense of humour in the man; almost as if he exists on some other plane where irony, metaphorical language in general, just doesn't play a part.

"Yeah," Terry went on, turning his attention back to me, "I

searched the codes and it came up with the name of the ship they departed on."

Feeling my head getting caught in a spin, I reached up and massaged my temples. I decided that now the time was right for me to leave the ever-supportive wall behind. Time for me to try and stand up on my own two feet.

It was shaky—*otherworldly* uncomfortable—but I managed to stay upright.

Just.

"Hang on," I said, daring to hold my palm up—a gesture which damn near upset my whole sense of balance. "This sounds like something Milky was working on." I glanced back to Clive, who was still concentrating on Terry.

Clive gave me a subtle nod to confirm this.

When I turned my attention back to Terry, he was blushing slightly. He was actively averting my gaze now, as if ashamed. He shouldn't have had any such worries seeing that, whatever it was he was saying—whatever sort of *technology* he'd used to get his hands on this information—it was well and truly beyond me. As with all technology, my attitude has always been to take whatever benefit I can from it with the tiniest amount of energy and effort expended in understanding it as possible. It's a way to live . . .

"Well," Terry replied, sounding ridiculously bashful, "*yeah,* it was this program Milky was working on." He flashed his eyes at me and Clive, almost in an aggressive way. "But do you want to know what ship they left on, or what?"

Yeah, it certainly smelled strongly of teen spirit all of a sudden . . .

"What's the ship?" I said.

Terry held back a moment, crushed his lips together, and then told us.

————

As I lounged back in the captain's chair, Clive, slouched over a screen, did all the tricks that were required. He plugged the information Terry had garnered into the ship's computers. He told me—in an offhand way—that the ship was called *Ghost Wave* . . .

Just to hear that name sent a shudder down my spine.

I couldn't quite identify the reason why.

But it sounded *so* familiar.

When Clive came back with a registry for the area, he turned to me. "Okay, Captain, they were plotting a course out of the system."

"You see any further than that?"

Clive turned back to the screen.

He shook his head.

"Most likely they've already left the system behind."

Both me and Clive looked back at Terry, who was still standing in the doorway to the bridge, looking thoroughly lost; with no immediate duties to attend to.

Terry shrugged. "I can dig around Milky's programs, see if he was working on a real-time tracking map . . ." Here Terry trailed off. "But I get the impression—even if Milky *was* working on something like that—it'd take an awful lot more processing power than the *Nava's* systems possess . . ."

It was almost as if somebody had fired a blaster shot right between the toes of my boots.

I rocketed up out of my captain's chair, my finger already set to waggling before I'd even got close to Terry. "You think long and hard about what you're going to say *before* you say it."

Terry visibly gulped. "Sorry, Captain."

I held myself back.

One eye closed.

Finger still waggling.

Every piece of grey matter my brain possessed attempting to conjure up a suitable punishment for such a clear insult of my beloved; of my One and Only . . . of the *Navaplastas*.

Catching Clive's eye, and getting the impression that homicide might not be the best way to start off our search for Foy and Milky, I acted the bigger man and stood down, trudging my way back to the captain's chair. I could still feel myself boiling with rage, even as I allowed the cushiony, incredibly comfortable springs to caress my poor, weathered spine.

Without looking at Terry, I said, "Go on—you were *saying*."

Clearly still somewhat shaken from the near ass-kicking I'd given him, Terry took a moment to gather his thoughts, and then said, "I was just thinking . . . well, if we've got the ship's course, then why don't we, you know, plot its most probable route and follow—see where it goes?"

Although I would've liked nothing more than to be able to shoot down Terry's idea in some way—or, better yet, to use his idiocy as a reason to drop him off at the nearest port—I didn't have any bright sparks of my own.

And I decided that there was nothing to be done.

The kid had *by far* the best idea for the time being.

Besides, if we ever did manage to track down Foy, I knew she would near enough kill me for having lost one of her cousins.

People get so attached to one another . . .

I raised a limp wrist in the air, made a vague twirling motion with my fingers. "All righty, then, set course to *follow* that ship." I paused for a moment, feeling something stirring in my stomach . . . not hunger; something *else*. "Let's get on *Ghost Wave's* tail."

6 IN PURSUIT OF GHOST WAVE

TERRY REMAINED ON THE BRIDGE, apparently having nothing better to do. And what with me being the loving captain I've always been, I said nothing about it. If the kid wanted to see something of the smuggler lifestyle, then who was I to begrudge him? That said, he would've looked a whole lot more like a legitimate smuggler if he just ditched those dungarees of his . . . the open-mouthed expression could stay . . .

I suppose Terry was keen to see his plan put into place; he wanted to see if he was going to have any sort of tangible effect on the attempted rescue of Milky and Foy. Although I didn't want to get the kid's hopes up—only for them to be shattered, like so many times before—I couldn't help but feel a tad excited to be thrown into hot pursuit.

Well, just about as *hot* as pursuit gets out in space.

Clive cranked the *Nava's* engines up as far as they would go and I whispered, underneath my breath, a few choice words of apology for this brisk treatment; not wanting the *Nava* to take this to heart, as some kind of sign that I no longer loved her . . .

It took about half a day to get some distance along the estimated flight path of *Ghost Wave*, and already it was looking like Terry's idea—although noble; and coming from a good place— would ultimately be a failure . . .

It takes a failure to know one; and I—*sure as anything* —am one.

Seeing on the navigational screens that there was nothing but empty space opening up on all sides, nothing that was going to require any steady captaincy—any *sharp-tack thinking*—I decided to allow myself to nod off in my chair; slipping away into a land of giddy dreams brought on by my aforementioned head injury.

———

I woke with a start—as always seemed to be the case whenever I allowed my crew to take over things for a while; whenever I allowed them a more or less free rein over the *Nava*.

"Wha . . . wha . . ." I just about got out, before Clive was stooped over me, a look of absolute terror on his face.

"Captain, Captain!"

I realised, slowly, but surely, that he was gripping my shoulder, and shaking me lightly.

I wondered how long he had been trying to stir me from my sleep.

I blinked away my daze, looked about the bridge, noting that Terry was nowhere in sight. I supposed that the poor kid had got his heart broke to realise we were headed into nothing but emptiness . . . that there was no sign of *Ghost Wave*.

It was right then that Clive dashed that assumption.

"We're missile-locked, Captain!"

One thing can be said for Clive. Although he might not be the most interesting man to look at—not by a long shot—and although he's one of those types who simply *vanishes* in a crowded room, he knows just how to command attention when he wants to.

Well, at least he knows how to command *my* attention.

I stumbled up out of my chair, threw myself at the navigational screens.

I half expected—in a kind of doped-up, sleepy way—to see a rendering of *Ghost Wave* on the screen, headed right for us. What I in fact saw, though, wasn't that at all.

Nope.

Much worse.

There must've been a dozen of them—I've never been all that great at counting; especially when velocity is required.

All of them were closing on the *Nava*.

Every last one of them—I could clearly see—with their missiles, indeed, locked on us.

"Holy *shit!*" I blurted out, turning away from the navigational screen since it was such a disturbing sight. Because there was nothing else I could usefully do at that point, I wheeled on Clive, and asked, "Just what the hell has gone on here?"

His attention still—understandably—distracted by the navigational screen, he answered me while staring at all those neon dots and swirls. "It happened about a minute ago—they just cropped up out of nowhere, well . . ." Here Clive trailed off and pointed at the navigational screen again.

I followed his finger, took in where he was pointing.

Realised there was a planet.

I turned back to Clive. "Just where the hell did that estimated course take us? Where are we right now?"

Clive held himself very still, eyes fixed upon the navigational screen. "Arkle System, sir. That's Arkle-4, right down there."

He might as well have clocked me a good one, right in the gut.

It felt as if all the air had been immediately squeezed out of my lungs.

A swiftly squashed pair of balloons.

"Arkle . . ." I just about got uttered from my dry throat. "Arkle-4."

"That's right, sir," Clive replied, finally turning back to me, squinting. "Sir?" he said. "Are you all right? You've gone pale."

I just about managed to force a smile onto my lips, and then to reach out and place my hand on Clive's shoulder; a *reassuring* hand, I hoped.

"Send a message to the mother ship," I said. "Surrender."

———

The ships closed in quickly, creating what I took to be an

unbreakable cordon about the *Navaplastas* . . . at least I didn't have much interest in testing out whether or not it could be broken. As me and Clive stood up on the bridge, awaiting our fate, I heard the unmistakable sound of running along the corridors. Although I ordinarily would've strongly castigated anybody crazy enough to pay the *Nava* that much disrespect, I couldn't help but grin and bear it in a situation like this.

Sure enough, the twins appeared in the doorway to the bridge; Brian dressed, as he always was these days, in his white jacket; and Terry still in that pair of nondescript dungarees.

They wanted to know what was going on, of course, but I couldn't quite bring myself to blab anything by way of reply.

My mind was off on another planet.

At least metaphorically if not literally . . .

It had been so long since I'd been back to the Arkle System. I had gone out of my way to avoid it for so many years; for *such* a long time. In fact, I can honestly say—hand on heart—that I would've been quite happy never to have seen the blasted place ever again. Never one more time to feel the warming glow of Mertinon—the star of the Arkle System—on my cheeks.

Then again, neither one of those things might come to pass.

If we got lucky these ships might blow us up.

But it didn't seem like we were going to get lucky.

Soon enough, the proximity alarms were sounding.

Then the docking notification; waiting for the captain to grant permission.

I granted it.

There was a long, almost gut-wrenching wait as the *Nava* jerked a touch from the impact of the ship pulling up alongside.

I could just tell that it'd made a nasty dent in the bodywork; probably take a whole job's worth of credits to sort out . . .

Cackling laughter rebounded its way along the corridor, arriving on the bridge, the walls of which served only to bounce the laughter all about us; as if we were surrounded by maniac space hyenas. Acting on impulse, I took a couple of steps forward, keeping my crew behind me; at my heels. I knew that, if the worst came to the worst then my enlarged bulk might give them a fighting chance of survival in the event of a fire fight.

Soon enough, we got to see their faces.

Three of them.

A captain.

A guard at each shoulder.

I glanced to the guards, seeing, instinctively, that they were each packing a blaster pistol strapped to their thigh. Also, I couldn't help noting, they had a blaster rifle slung over their backs. There could've been *no* use for a blaster rifle on a ship; it was all simple intimidation tactics, wanting to show off the firepower they possessed.

Well, they'd succeeded.

Each of them wore a uniform—a sleek black colour . . . way different from the faecal-brown colour I remembered the officials wearing on Arkle-4 the last time I was there.

They also had on knee-high, black leather boots; all polished up.

The jackets they wore were also black leather.

I vaguely wondered if Arkle-4 had struck some kind of trade deal with somebody, someplace, and they'd got a surplus of leather dumped on them.

That sounded just like something the *politicians* there would do . . .

My eyes slowly swept along to pick out the captain.

He had a leathery face and wore a cap which was drawn down, leaving his eyes in shadow. Tufts of grey hair stuck out from the sides of his head. His name patch read: Captain Norbortwitz.

Just because he could, he hocked back a great deal of phlegm and gobbed it out; right onto the floor of the bridge.

A little of it splattered the toe of my boots.

Then, apparently pleased with this greeting, he grinned at me wide. Inside his mouth were all the colours of the rainbow they don't tell you about as a kid.

"Captain Wright," Captain Norbortwitz declared. "Welcome home."

Again, it felt as if someone had straight up punched me in the gut.

I held his watery-blue eyes.

"Do I know you?" I replied, deadpan.

Captain Norbortwitz smiled wider still, showing off a little of his tongue; enough so that I could see he had a large chunk missing from it. He gave a shrug. "Should do, I'd say," he replied. "Not that I'd like to presume."

That word—that *tone* he was striking . . . it all sounded so alien in his mouth.

Coming from between his lips.

I couldn't help but catch the impression that this was someone who'd been promoted above his station. But, then again, I supposed that there most likely wasn't an official in the world who *hadn't* been promoted above their position.

From my—*admittedly biased*—experience of officials I've found that those who seem magnetically attracted to strutting about in uniforms are almost *always* the very same types who can't be trusted with scissors . . . not without parental supervision, in any case.

"Toss the guns," Captain Norbortwitz said.

As I reached down for my blaster, stuck in my thigh holster, I noticed Norbortwitz's guards getting awfully twitchy; they were no doubt sensitive about anything happening to their captain; understandably so . . . they most likely wouldn't get their paycheque if they allowed their boss to get snuffed by some two-bit smuggler.

I dropped my blaster.

Heard a trio of *clunks* behind me.

That threw me for a moment or so.

Although I could recall having issued Clive with a blaster, I couldn't think of a time when I'd ever handed one to either Brian or Terry. Then again, I suppose that I hadn't exactly kept the twins on a tight leash; they'd surely got up to all sorts that I had little or no idea about.

"Good stuff," Norbortwitz said, turning on his heel, heading back along the corridor. "You all follow me, now. There's some good boys."

As I led my crew off along on Norbortwitz's heels, I snatched a final glance over my shoulder at the bridge of the *Nava*, unable to quite shift the feeling that this could quite easily be the last time I ever got to see it . . . then again I suppose some part of me, whenever I set out on some new adventure—or the latest *idiocy*, depending on how you term it—prompts a little emotion.

The thought that I won't return to the *Nava* is never far away.

This time, though, it really did feel like the end.

7 ARKLE-4

WHAT I EXPECTED NEXT was for Norbortwitz to take me and my crew prisoner; for all of us to get shoved in some jail cell. So I was somewhat pleasantly surprised to find that we were only dumped into a shuttle and fired down to Arkle-4 terminal . . . creatively named The *New* Terminal; although that name was starting to sound somewhat ironic given that it was built a good few decades ago, and wore *every one* of those decades in its endless cracks and broken glass.

I could tell, from the looks of my crew that they were not overwhelmed by Arkle-4 itself but the situation they found themselves in. They, too, were surely surprised we'd been turned free so easily; albeit after having been relieved of our beloved *Nava*.

The morning light wasn't kind to Arkle-4. The tangerine glow from Mertinon seemed to bring out all the sludge greens; to throw a spotlight on the ugly, dirty-purple rising smokes. To make all the puddles scattered about the street look like they were molten iron.

And not *fine* molten iron.

More like the kind that'd been through a war, or two.

As we emerged from the terminal, I couldn't help but notice the many homeless people lining the pavements. All of them slumped up against the cracked concrete wall, coming down from some sort of drug-induced high or other.

I got all sombre as I surveyed them, thinking that, if I'd remained on Arkle-4, I might quite easily have ended up among their number.

When I passed by a particularly grim-looking specimen; a homeless guy who seemed to be entirely naked aside from the flattened cardboard box encasing his body, I had the overwhelming urge to toss him some coin.

So I did just that.

On impulse, I turned to look over my crew—Clive and the twins—and saw their combined expression of total surprise.

"What?" I said, flat-out. "Can't a guy give a little back to humanity?"

Having just lost my ship—the only thing in the universe I *loved*—I was ready to brawl with anybody at all. So I suppose, on some level, I was daring one of them to make a peep . . . to attempt some gentle *jab* by way of response . . .

But none of them said anything.

Only the homeless guy.

"Humanity's all well and good," the homeless guy said, "but you ain't ever gettin' off this planet, sonny."

I felt my gut twist; pure, unadulterated rage.

"What'd you say?"

The homeless guy either refused to take the fury in my voice seriously or he was still coming down off something and so was pleasantly numb to the world.

At least it'd make the ass-kicking I was about to hand him a little easier to bear.

As I drew back my foot, ready to give this DIY philosopher a philosophy of my own, he responded to me.

"I *said*, You *ain't* ever gettin' off this planet."

It took a great deal of strength and—come to think of it—Clive's stronger-than-average hold to keep me from swinging the toe of my boot into the homeless guy's chest.

In the end, realising that I wasn't going to get any sort of a physical vent from this encounter, I settled for replying, "*Says who?*"

In retrospect, just about any self-respecting kid on any given playground in the entire universe would've laughed at my comeback. But, again, perhaps because this homeless guy wasn't exactly playing with a full deck, I didn't get my rightful comeuppance.

The homeless guy just stated the case flat-out. "Says *Big Jo.*"

It felt like someone had just stuffed ice down the neck of my shirt.

" 'Big Jo' ?"

"Yuh-huh," the homeless guy replied, counting through the coins I'd thrown him; seeming to be perplexed for one reason or another.

My mind began to flicker back to my childhood—to *another time.*

Thankfully, though, Clive tugged me away from the home-less guy before I burst out in a fit of rage which'd see me breaking free of his grip . . . or else breaking down in tears.

I couldn't rightly say which would've been worse.

We headed back along the terminal road, toward what I knew, a little too well, as being the main street of Bomberlee City, the capital of Arkle-4, and, among other things, one of the very best places in the entire universe to get deep fryers repaired.

As we trudged down Fryer Street, I couldn't help but feel a new bounce to my heart.

It wasn't quite sadness; and it most certainly wasn't *joy* . . . the best I could pin down the feeling was as some kind of expression of *nostalgia*.

Fucking nostalgia.

"Captain?" Terry said, from behind me.

"What?" I replied, continuing to trudge on along the street, feeling something moist, and greasy, and *papery*, splatter against the side of my boot.

"This place is called Arkle-4 . . . and, well, *your* name's Arkle."

"Uh-huh, astutely observed."

There was a long pause, and I wondered if Terry had decided he was going to clamp his gums shut for the good of his continuing vitality.

"Is this your home planet?"

"Got it in one, kid."

I breathed in deeply, trying to keep my patience. Attempting to ignore the constant rush of blood to my brain, overpowering any of my sensible thoughts . . . or any of the thoughts that had the *potential* to be sensible.

Then came another question . . .

"Who's Big Jo?"

It was the moment I'd been waiting for—the chance to *explode* that I'd been craving.

I would've been well within my rights to flip on him . . . to at least get into some *shouting* . . . something which'd clear all of the pain I was feeling right then from my veins; get me back to feeling something like the red-blooded, hardened space traveller I've always imagined myself to be. But, when I looked over Terry's semi-innocent, teenage face, I just couldn't bring myself to throw all my ire on him. It wouldn't be fair. *He* wasn't the source of my angst . . . *he* wasn't the reason I felt at a loose end . . . *he* wasn't, quite, the reason the *Nava* had got impounded; or whatever had happened here.

I did something out of the ordinary.

I put myself in my *crew's* shoes.

Wondered how *they* must be feeling right then.

Wasn't *I* supposed to be the local authority—the local *expert* —at that moment in time?

. . . Of course I was.

And, until I answered Terry's question, I was holding out on them.

Holding out knowledge on them.

I stifled a sigh, looked over my crew, and their curious little faces.

"Big Jo," I said, out into thin air at first, as if I was testing to see how it'd sound to my ears. "He was this small-time gangster back when I was a kid . . . used to run everything about here; *drugs*, mainly."

When I glanced up, I caught a strange look from Clive. Maybe he wanted me to lay off the heavy themes for the kids. But it'd been one of the kids who'd asked, and now I'd worked myself up to spill the details, I wasn't likely to dilute any of it.

"Always was talk of him getting legitimate, if you can call it that. There was always this talk of him getting himself into politics—wanting to get a better foothold in Arkle-4."

I couldn't help but cast my mind back to Ricky D . . . and thought about how it looked as if Big Jo had gone one better. That he'd now ended up running the whole *damn* planet.

This time Brian spoke up. "So he's, like, the president of Arkle-4 now?"

I shrugged and gave him some gormless expression. "What'd I know? I just got here . . . just like you all did."

"You mean," Terry said, picking up in that way twins seem to do often, "you don't know what's going on here—on your *home* planet?"

"Nope," I replied.

This seemed to shut Terry, and his brother, up for the time being.

I couldn't say I wasn't contented with the development.

"Captain?"

This time it was Clive speaking.

I turned to him, ready to be receptive, for whatever it was worth.

"Where to now?"

I looked over my crew—what *remained* of my crew. I

couldn't just tell them what was on my mind; that we were well and truly *fucked*, that there was no light on the horizon; that we'd gone and got ourselves trapped in the rectum of the universe known by its human name: Arkle-4.

Nah, I couldn't tell them that.

So I just decided to lie.

"This way," I said.

———

I had very little idea where I was going to take them—if I was going to take them anyplace at all—and so I suppose it was only natural that some kind of horse sense, whatever the space smuggler equivalent works out as, led me back to my old neighbourhood.

To Green District.

I took in the tower blocks, and how they all seemed to be like jagged giant's teeth sticking up out of the foul, green-brown mud which passed for earth on Arkle.

The buildings looked like they should've been knocked down the very same day they were put up. Those grey-purple washed walls, the uncountable blackened-out windows which punctured the sides. Then the doors at the bottom of the buildings, leading to the lobby, like some kind of yawning throat; starving for just a bite of *real* meat.

I held back for the longest time, unsure about how I should proceed.

In the end, it was Terry, again, who made himself heard.

He appeared at my side, unsolicited and unwelcome.

"Is this where you used to live?"

Trust the kid to show that he had a talent for *intuition* right then—right when he'd gone and got me at my most exposed.

But, somehow, I couldn't feel angry.

Not anymore.

It seemed almost as if I felt nothing at all.

As if someone had ripped my heart out of my chest and replaced it with a fistful of sawdust.

When we'd all been standing there for maybe ten minutes—perhaps a little longer—Terry spoke up once more. "So, you gonna take a look, or what?"

"Yeah, kid," I replied, my tone far more sedate than I felt—far *crisper*. "I'm gonna go take a look."

———

I guess I expected the others to follow me into the building —*hell*, I don't think I would've been able to blame them if they had done . . . just what was a crew meant to do when there was no ship to see to? However, they all mulled about outside, on the patch of ground which passed for greenery on Arkle-4 and I was left to go in alone.

. . . I could still remember seeing kids chucking a ball about between themselves on that patch of ground, finding some joy amongst all the dirge.

I could still remember *being* one of those kids.

I couldn't help feeling a shred of anger—directed at my parents—long since kept dormant within me, but now being brought—*bubbling*—up to the surface.

I eyed the doors, taking in the busted fingerprint scanner attached to the wall.

Its glass had been smashed long ago . . . whether or not it'd ever worked—back when I'd been a kid—I couldn't quite stretch myself to remember.

As I trudged in through the doors to the building—the doors I'd passed through countless times, returning from school—nostalgia got me again.

My brain seemed to almost *shudder* within my skull.

As if it was afraid of what I might find.

I reached up, touched the welt which'd popped up around the plastering job Brian had performed on me. I couldn't help but feel a touch ashamed to think that Brian had come from similar circumstances to my own. But he'd never—*never once*—given up on attempting to better himself; turning his mind to medicine, of all things.

I'd never had delusions of grandeur.

Never thought I'd turn out to be a doctor.

But, then again, neither had I ever thought I'd turn out to be a space smuggler.

Was a space smuggler *really* so low on the celestial totem pole?

. . . One thing was for certain, it would be way less hassle telling people at parties I was a doctor rather than a smuggler . . .

The air inside the building stank of linoleum tiling gone bad. It was almost as if the whole place was decaying from the inside out, and that, one day, it'd just all sort of fold in on itself; like an apple collapsing into its rotten core.

But it wouldn't crush me with it.

I'd got out.

And, from the looks of things, just in time . . .

Our place—what'd *been* our place—was up on the third floor.

There was no lift to get there—it'd never been working in all the time I'd resided in the building.

Stairs all the way.

Some things never change.

I eyed up the plaques on the doors, taking in the codes as I paced:

3 – 14

3 – 16

I paused.

Drew in a breath; absorbing all the damp from the place into my bloodstream—it seemed—at the same time.

Knowing I could put it off no longer, I reached the fateful door.

The place I'd once called my home.

The place that'd existed before I'd *escaped*.

Before the *Nava* had even been a twinkle in her creator's eye:

3 – 18

The door was just as I remembered, which was reinforced steel, with a mean set of matching locking mechanisms. Nothing digital. Nothing automated. Everything was worked with a good, old-fashioned key.

I remembered about how, at school, we'd even had a retina scanner; the test we had to pass simply to get in through the doors. And Green District Comprehensive certainly wasn't a wealthy establishment by any stretch of the imagination.

I eyed the doorbell, wondering if I could simply reach out and depress the button.

If it'd be that easy.

I caught myself getting side-tracked, wondering about when the last time I'd seen an actual *live* doorbell had been.

Maybe not since I'd left here.

Forever.

I sunk my teeth into my lower lip.

Felt the faint throb of blood to my brain.

I reached out.

Pressed the button.

Perhaps the longest seconds of my life occurred while I waited on the doorstep of what had once been my family home; what'd *passed* for my family home. I didn't think anybody would come to the door; the whole damn building was surely on the point of falling down, after all . . . and yet, I couldn't be shifted from the spot.

Something was keeping me there.

Call it a supernatural force—*aliens* . . . whatever . . . something made me stick.

When the door did finally open, it happened so quickly. Although I'd never thought much about it until I was standing right there, actually *waiting* for someone to come to the door, I'd seen this situation play out so many times in dreams; once during all those naps I'd stolen on the bridge of the *Nava*; or else with my head cushioned by a pile of travelling bags; by a stock of stuff I was meant to be moving from here to there.

Moving stuff about the universe.

And then everything returned to that one moment.

The Right Here, Right Now.

I sensed the figure standing in the doorway, but I couldn't make out any of their features. There was no light lit in the apartment. I wondered if the whole building had been sliced free of the grid, among other things.

From the stench of sweat, I supposed this was a man, and slowly, even despite the dank darkness closing in on all sides, I made out something of the features.

The beard sprouting free of the chin; wiry, out-of-control, long ago rendered untameable.

And then, the gut which bulged and hung low over the waistband.

I centred on the eyes.

Peered into those dark, gently glinting spheres.

I opened my mouth to speak, but was beaten to the punch.

"Arkle? That you?"

It felt like somebody had head butted me in the chest.

But I somehow found my voice.

". . . Yuh?" I got out, feeling the sound vibrate my whole ribcage.

The figure breathed in deep.

I saw his whole body rise with it.

And then he reached back, scratched his neck.

I heard the *scrub-scrub* sound of loose skin becoming caught under his fingernails.

"You gonna stand there, or you gonna get a drink with your brother?"

8 ARKLE-4 - FORMER RESIDENCE

I WASN'T TOTALLY SURE I even wanted to walk through that door; even knowing that it was my brother, even knowing that it was Mertinon. Even though I'd passed through that doorway so many times before. In some ways it felt like I was gonna die, or something; like this was my own personal vision of heaven, or hell, or purgatory . . .

Maybe I hadn't come round from that head injury after all.

Mertinon produced a match from somewhere. It sparked into life and he lit up an oil lamp, or something equally medieval.

"You cut off?" I said.

"Could put it that way," he replied.

The flimsy light danced its bronze glow about the room.

Slowly tugging the room free from the tar pit of memory.

I stood over a mildewy armchair.

I recalled it from my youth; from all those times when I'd

slouch back and stare at the vidscreen through half-opened eyes till it was time to go to school again. I learned more from that vidscreen than from either one of my parents.

Good thing too since they both ended up as dealers.

I hadn't even sat down before my brother, Mertinon, said, "Mum's dead. So's Dad."

I paused midway down onto the cushion.

When I eventually made contact, the surface was a touch damp, and the cushion itself felt strangely squishy; as if it'd been stuffed with garbage or some such.

I breathed in the murky air of the apartment, processing this news.

Of course I'd presumed my parents long dead and buried, but it somehow made it more *real* to hear the news spoken to me . . . from out of my own brother's mouth, no less.

He snorted hard; one of those habits, I guess, he'd picked up from being solitary for so long—not having to impress anybody any longer . . . except maybe the Health Inspector.

In the end, I didn't allow myself to lay my full bulk on the armchair. Though I've hardly ever been the most hygienic of specimens, even I've got my limits. And that chair, well, I was pretty sure it had some interesting life forms growing away on it. An ambitious, uncompromising scientist probably could've made a good fist of studies from the mould.

I sat there for a moment, just to think things over.

It was overwhelming in so many ways for me to have returned.

More than I could ever have imagined.

"Why'd you come back?"

I glanced up at Mertinon, eyed him. "You gonna sit down, or what? Feel like you're gonna pounce on me all of a sudden—when I let my guard down."

"Well, maybe I should," he replied.

"And why's that?"

Mertinon stared back into my eyes. There was a sharpness there, for just a few moments, and then it was gone. He gave a shrug as if to pass off his reaction as nothing at all.

But *I'd* seen it.

"How 'bout we start with the idea you left me here to look after Ma and Pa—how 'bout you get to telling me just *where* the hell you've been all these years." He snorted harder again. "What you been *doin'* . . ."

It was then that I noticed just how much of the old, bumpkin Arkle-4 accent I'd managed to lose over years. In some way, it made me glad to think that these days I was speaking more or less standard Basic. In another way, it made me feel a touch sad.

I guess it hurts when you see just how far you've left your roots behind.

I gave a sigh. "It's a long story," I said.

Mertinon smiled slightly at this. "It's okay. I got time." He shook his head. "I got *nothing* but time to spare." He held up his hand, then added, "First things first, though, before I go grab you a moiser from the fridge, before we sit down for some jaw-time . . . I want to know just what people out there—*up there*—think about you being called after your home planet."

I couldn't help giving a slight snigger. "Probably just the same as they feel about anyone called after a star."

———

Once the first moiser hit my bloodstream, I started to feel every last bone and muscle in my body grow looser. I chewed Mertinon through my entire story—all the way from my time in the FSA—and then on into my current life as a space smuggler. Every couple of minutes, I glanced over at him, where he sat, beside a window looking out over the piles of muddy land which surrounded the building.

The first few times I saw him peering out through the netted curtains, out to the dying daylight, I thought he'd lost interest; that he'd turned his mind to thinking about other things. And, far be it from me to keep someone hanging on listening to me jaw away when they weren't really paying attention, I stopped speaking.

But, each time, he glanced up, gave me a simple nod.

And I continued.

It surprised me how quickly I got through with the story— after only four moisers—and, finding myself at a loose end, I forgot about my seating situation and allowed myself to slump back. I caught a gross *squelching* sound as some kind of punishment.

Gathering that I'd got through with my story, Mertinon glanced up. He lifted his head off his fist, where he had kept it propped up; resting during the course of my stories. "That it?" he said, with the kind of nonchalance only someone sharing my bloodline could manage.

"Yep," I replied, short and sharp.

"A smuggler," he said. "A *space* smuggler."

"That's right."

"And that's what brings you back here—back to Arkle?"

"Sure."

Mertinon turned all pensive for a long while, clearly attempting to get to grips with something or other. He glanced back at me. "Good news is that Ernest Harry's no longer prowling about here." He gave a wry smile. "Not even enough business to be had around these blocks for Ernest Harry—not since half the neighbourhood moved out."

I felt a flash of anger to hear this . . . to hear *that* name again . . . finally, though, I let it go. It was something in the past; something which couldn't be changed. To be fair to him, Ernest Harry—as my parents' employer—had most likely put more food in my mouth than the Fritten Space Authorities—the FSA— during my service.

I rolled the empty bottle of moiser within my hands, knowing that I was sitting on the limit now; that I had two choices: Stop drinking; deal with the onrush of melancholy. Or —preferable—keep on drinking and preserve the warming feeling for a little while longer.

Realising that I wasn't truly in any sort of situation which'd be improved by being hung-over, I shot for the first option. When Mertinon hoiked himself up from his own seat, to go and refresh his drink, I turned him down.

As I listened to the *creak* of the fridge door opening wide, and then the gentle *clinkity-clink* as Mertinon sorted through the bottles of moiser—no doubt searching for a *lucky* one—I realised that I had to get out. That I just *had* to get out of the place.

It wasn't simple enough to explain away the feeling as a single emotion.

I just *needed* to get out.

When Mertinon returned to the sitting room, I was already halfway to the door.

It felt like I'd got caught in the act.

"Guess you're not searching for signups for your crew."

My heart sank to hear those words tumble free of my long-lost brother's lips.

It was difficult to piece together just how much I owed him; for everything he'd done—for *being here*—while I'd been swash-buckling about the universe.

Maybe I needed some time to think it over.

To think of a way to repay him.

Then I remembered.

I shook my head. "Ship's been impounded," I replied. "Not got anything to offer you to crew on, I'm afraid."

Twisting his mouth into an odd shape, his hands uncon-sciously working to free the cap from his latest moiser, Mertinon cocked his head to one side. "What were you thinkin', Arkle, coming back here? What *good* was ever to come of it?"

I wanted to explain to him that I'd delegated the task of trailing a ship to some of my crewmembers; that if I'd ever had the faintest *inkling* we would end up on Arkle-4, I would've soon put a stop to it. Throughout the years, when I'd had jobs which'd necessitate me coming within a day's journey of the Arkle System, I'd reroute . . . sometimes giving me twice as hard of a slog to get the job done; but it meant I wouldn't have to return here.

"Well," I said, my hand on the apartment door latch, "I *did* . . . and now it seems like I'm stuck here." With a final nod to Mertinon, after all these years—all this *time*—I trod out of the place, leaving him standing there, a fresh moiser in his hand.

———

Every step I took away from the buildings of Green District— with every single *metre* I placed between myself and my past—it felt like a weight was steadily being relieved from my shoulders.

It seemed as if my heart kicked on a touch harder; as if my body itself became *more vital*; *younger* just from leaving the oppressive, damn place behind.

The Arkle-4 air, though it'd always had a sulphur note to it —at least in my memory—seemed to coil up my nostrils several degrees fresher. I breathed it in, allowing it to cleanse my body. To bring me back to life.

"Captain?"

I turned, found myself nose-to-nose with Clive Wodd . . . not such a difficult feat when you're dealing with Clive.

Clive's expression was neutral; stone-faced, almost. There were times when I was glad for Clive's unfeeling, logical outlook . . . how he could make it seem as if there was nothing in the entire world which might throw him off; which might make him stumble.

"Find what you were looking for?" he said.

I stared back into his eyes, managed a smile from some-where, and then looked off to the horizon. I pressed my lips together, shook my head. "Nah," I replied. "Afraid not."

I took another moment for introspection before I got over myself and shifted my attention back to the task at hand; namely the recovery of Foy and Milky, and, with any luck, along the way, the recovery of the *Navaplastas*.

I glanced about.

Turned back to Clive.

"Where's the twins?"

The right corner of Clive's mouth tweaked back in the approximation of a smile. He jerked his thumb over his shoulder. "They were getting restless, so I cut them loose. Thought they might want to go roam."

I looked about, wondering if I'd catch sight of them anyplace.

But I couldn't see either of them.

I felt an unpleasant, shifting feeling in the pit of my gut.

I turned back to Clive.

"When was the last time you saw them?"

Clive shrugged. "I . . . don't know, Captain." He rolled his eyes up in their sockets, as he often did whenever he was doing some intensive thinking. "Maybe an hour ago; maybe two . . . depends how long you were in there."

Feeling something like electricity dancing through my veins now, and my heart leaping up to my throat, I snapped to action. Something just felt wrong about this.

Something.

"Wodd," I said, barking his surname almost.

"Sir?"

"I think they've been snatched."

9 ARKLE-4 - FULL PANIC, NO PLAN

C LIVE WAS CONSTANTLY trying to catch my attention, snapping about my heels like some kind of insistent Jack Russell terrier.

I paid him no mind, though.

Despite being away from Arkle-4 for a long while, I hadn't forgotten its ways; its little *quirks* . . . how when you couldn't say exactly where somebody was then it usually meant believing the very worst of the situation. That they were missing . . . or something else.

Night was closing in fast now. Whereas the moisers I'd swigged back with my brother had seemed to send me floating up to the ceiling before, they only seemed to weigh my feet down now. It took a great effort on the part of my legs to keep moving forwards.

We made it back into the heart of Bomberlee, and I did my best to placate Clive with some assuring words about it being really 'nothing'. Of course he made a whole bunch of noises about being sorry—about how he felt responsible for what'd happened to the twins.

All I wanted was for him to shut up.

There was no point in dwelling on past mistakes.

Not if we wanted the twins alive.

It was strange to be back in Bomberlee; everything was so familiar, and yet there was a *twist* to everything and anything. Each time that I stood still, tried to get a hold on my surroundings, I would see all the old storefronts; those elaborately carved cornices and such, but then, when I'd check over the storefront itself, I'd see some unfamiliar name there.

Nothing remained of my childhood.

Of my *past*.

This was like a Bomberlee from a parallel universe.

Why I kept on rushing through the streets, bumping up against the wretched-looking commuters, bundled up tight in their winter coats, with their hats pulled down to keep their features in shadows, I really had no idea.

Not until I arrived.

To the place my mind had known I'd get to all along.

Hanx's Hoarders' Haul

One of the few places that I recalled from my childhood.

And—oh, my—*how* I recalled it.

I recalled it just like some kind of a recurring nightmare.

That same intimate, skin-prickling sensation ran through me.

I turned my attention to the pair of carved, stone gargoyles which stood to either side of the entrance. And then I looked up, to the emerald-green tarp which hung down, apparently on the pretence of keeping the windows free from the most adverse of weather.

And here, on Arkle-4, there was certainly adverse weather . . .

The windows, as they'd been in my childhood, were all blacked-out.

I felt Clive breathing down the collar of my jacket.

I glanced back at him.

There was something about *Hanx's Hoarders' Haul* which caught the attention, though I wasn't sure what. One thing was for certain, Clive was just as occupied gawking at it as I was. Clive was the one to break the silence. "What's this place?" he said. "You think the twins are in here?"

"Nah," I replied, shaking my head. "But I'm fairly certain Hanx will be able to tell us just *where* the twins have got to . . . if not where Foy and Milky are being held up."

"Sounds good," Clive said. "So let's go in."

I wasn't quite as enthusiastic.

I knew that I had to take care.

It wasn't like I wanted to broadcast the fact that I was back in town.

The way I'd wanted things to pan out—the second I'd discovered just where *Ghost Wave* had led us—was for me to go to ground; to take an *incognito* turn . . . then again, I suppose that there's something deeply uneasy—perhaps 'evil' is the right word—which runs thick and pure through Arkle-4. Certain forces that I'll never understand.

I looked back to Clive, nodded, and we ventured in.

A cracked bell sounded over our heads as we crossed the threshold.

I noted the sensor beam which was set across the doorway, and which was, apparently, connected to the out-of-sight apparatus of the bell.

I wondered vaguely if it was anything more than a simple sensor beam; if there might be some other, more clandestine, use it could be put to.

Just as I remembered it, the floor was carpeted—with something I would've described to be a Persian design; all gold and rich, royal reds. Even after all these years, after all the foot traffic which'd surely passed through the store, it felt slightly springy.

Comforting almost.

Though not quite.

Bits and pieces of memorabilia—or *crap* as I'd've described it, given half a chance—stuffed up the shelves of the place. I took in the many plastic animals all congregated together and staring out blindly as me and Clive passed by. The series of miniature, plastic statues—of *Earth* touristic attractions—drew my attention next.

The Eiffel Tower.

The British Houses of Parliament.

Taj Mahal.

And then, of course, the Pacific Space Elevator.

The piece of equipment which'd sent mankind spewing out across the universe like some badly stifled sneeze.

The air smelled strongly of incense; like the stink of burning tyres and dark chocolate.

Nobody was at the counter of the place, though that was hardly unusual. My attention drifted upwards, to the camera which hung off the wall; watching me and Clive's every movement. No doubt someone safely out of sight was scrutinising our appearance, trying to divine just what it was we wanted . . . though, probably most important of all, from their perspective, they were trying to work out if we were armed.

Neither of us was, of course, what with that Captain Norbortwitz relieving us of our weapons back up on the *Nava*.

Even to speak the name of my beloved within my own mind gave me a clenching feeling deep down in my gut. My heart throbbed. I wondered if this was how star-crossed lovers get to feeling when they're suffering from separation anxiety.

A beaded curtain, behind the counter, maintained the back room in some sort of secrecy, as well as keeping the flies out . . . and, on Arkle-4, if there's something we've got in spades, it's *goddamn* flies.

When I got to standing at the counter, I decided I'd come a long way—managed to tread over some fairly heavy *personal past* shit—that it'd be an idiot move not to go just a little further. With a quick glance back to Clive, and a swift thought to myself that I was glad not to have *his* nose with that bizarre stinking going off, I laid my palm flat on the counter and called out.

"Hello?!"

It was like shouting at a mattress.

Just as there was the Persian rug draped over the floor, there was also carpet which hung down from the walls. It'd make this the perfect place to torture someone—especially if the person being tortured was the kind partial to screaming.

Thankfully, I wasn't able to spend much more time speculating about those fantasies of mine . . . is it any wonder I'm as hangdog-faced as I am?

There was the *scrub* of soles on carpet.

And then, with a *clickety-clack* of the bead curtain, a young lady; maybe in her mid-to-late twenties, by my poor reckoning, emerged.

She was dressed in a floaty, deep-purple tunic. It was embroidered with gold and silver thread. There were a few gems stitched into the design, too. I noticed that she wore a pair of strappy, leather sandals on her feet. Nobody wears strappy leather sandals . . . not on Arkle-4 . . . at least not without having a more than adequate amount of muscle to beat the brains out of the ones doing the cackling.

I took in her face.

Sparkling green eyes.

Purple eye shadow, to match her tunic.

Neatly cropped black hair.

Voluptuous lips.

She was quite stockily built, *chubby*—apparently never really having grown into either a famous, movie star, hourglass shape or slimmed down into a sleeker, elegant, up-and-down figure.

Not that I gave this much of a damn.

If there's one thing working all these years space smuggling has taught me, it's that romantic entanglements are just *bad* for business.

And when you're an independent businessman you've really gotta know where to cut back on the expenses.

As I finished up my inspection, I couldn't help but notice that, like me, she had a misshapen part of her forehead. It strongly resembled my own hole in the head. I lingered staring at it for several moments.

"Can I help you?" she said, striking an innocent tone I found remarkable.

Feeling Clive staring at me, and wishing he'd stop it, I did my best to affect a kind of friendly, middle-aged uncle smile. Maybe I managed to pull it off, too.

At the very least, she didn't run away . . .

"Looking for a pair of kids—*twins*—wondered if you might've seen them rushing past your shop; along the street outside."

The girl pouted, glanced to Clive, then back to me. She shook her head, sending all those gems sewn into her tunic bouncing about; that cropped hair dancing, also.

I could tell she knew how to handle clientele.

"No," she replied, finally putting it into words.

She shot us with another smile.

"Nothing like that."

I took in a good deal of air, glanced about the interior of the shop, wondering what my next move should be.

I turned back to her.

"You see, they were exploring . . . they must've *wandered* off . . . I can't believe that they wouldn't have ended up here."

"I'm sorry, sir," the girl said, still holding onto that smile against all odds. "I haven't seen anybody around here."

"Captain?"

I glanced back to Clive.

"Maybe we should go—sounds like she hasn't seen them."

I held myself still, then turned on the girl again. "What's Hanx up to these days?"

" 'Hanx' ?" she replied, scrunching up her eyebrows.

"Yeah, you know, the name on the storefront."

This seemed to capture her attention. "Oh, he's helping out in terminal security now."

" 'Terminal security' ?"

She nodded, breaking into yet another smile.

"Doesn't drop by here much anymore, huh?"

She shook her head.

I drew in a deep breath, deciding that I had to give her one more chance; that I needed to give common sense one more chance. But then, seeing that there was no common sense to be had, I burst off my spot, rounded the counter, making a beeline for the beaded curtain which covered the entrance to the back room.

The girl called something after me, but I didn't hear what it was.

Before she could so much as catch her breath, I was through the curtain.

The air was cool and dusty.

Boxes about everywhere, all of them in various states of disrepair; scuffmarks all over, and, in some cases, half-squashed.

I glanced about me, noted the corridor leading deeper into the store, and headed for it.

That was when I felt fingernails becoming embedded in

my skin.

I tried to shrug her off, but she sunk her fingernails in deeper, refusing to allow me to go free. I just about managed to trudge on with her hanging off me. Already, I could feel blood welling to the surface of my skin.

But I put it out of my mind.

My mission was clear, and the girl's role was obvious . . . because *I* had once played that role . . . the one which involved shaking off anybody undesirable.

Anybody who didn't merit a meeting with Hanx.

"Really," I got out through clenched teeth, "I'm sure that Hanx will be *delighted* to see me . . . I know you're just doing your job, but—"

That was when I felt her bite me.

I let out a yelp, and, acting on impulse more than anything else, I whipped my arm around, throwing her away from me . . .

I heard her hit the wall with a damp *thud*.

Knowing this was my chance, I increased my pace, headed for the staircase leading upwards. It'd been such a long time since I was last here—since I was last at *Hanx's Hoarders' Haul* —that I'd near enough forgotten the layout of the place.

Now, though, it was somewhat coming back.

Once I reached the top of the steps, I took in the many doors —seven or eight of them; on both sides of the hallway. I bided my time, thinking over what I was actually doing here; trying to retrieve all of those forgotten, long-ago repressed memories.

Behind me, I heard footfalls.

A skitter ran up my spine.

I pivoted on the spot.

Turned to look.

Clive's nose—and Clive, too, of course—rounded the corner.

I felt a reassuring, warming feeling enter my bloodstream.

I had to admit that I was glad it wasn't the girl who'd been at the counter downstairs. I've never been much of a fan of scratching and biting . . . give me a good, old-fashioned blaster shootout any day of the week.

Much more hygienic . . .

I noticed Clive was holding something in his fist, down at his thigh.

"What the hell's that?" I said.

Clive brought the device up for me to see.

It was about the size and shape of a blaster battery.

There was a metal contact on one end.

"Stungun," Clive replied, succinctly. "I gave her a jolt—she should be indisposed for at least the next hour."

I jutted out my lower lip in appreciation.

Clive was made of sterner stuff than I'd imagined.

"Keep it handy," I said, turning back to the doors ahead.

———

I waited for Clive to ask something about our ultimate goal; about our mission here, but he had enough sense to keep his mouth shut, and to simply follow on my heels.

Just like a good, little crewmember he's always shown himself to be.

As I perused the doors—exactly *eight* of them as I now realised—I was all too aware that if we opened the wrong one, it was quite likely to be the last thing we ever did . . . at least, I've never heard of humans enjoying much success in any kind of terms after their heads have been forcefully blown off their shoulders.

With that in mind, it was possibly irresponsible of me, when not seeing any obvious direction to head, I chose a door at random.

Well, perhaps that wasn't *quite* accurate; I at least had some kind of an *inkling* that Hanx's office might be located behind it.

And—who'd ever think it?—it *was*.

All of a sudden, I found myself peering in at the quite tight, and fairly Spartan room within. Although I'd heard that Big Jo —and gangsters in general—had been doing a roaring trade on Arkle-4 recently, it seemed that Hanx wasn't prepared to take any aspect of the situation for granted. He hadn't invested in anything beyond the bare minimum.

Chair.

Desk.

A vidscreen.

Besides the bearskin rug thrown across the floor, there wasn't much else.

Hanx himself wasn't there.

I turned back to Clive. "Guess the girl was telling the truth after all."

"She did feign she didn't know who he was."

"Yeah, good point," I replied, then gave Clive a pat on the shoulder. "And she wasn't looking likely to let us up the stairs here, up into this old restricted area right here."

I trod into the room, wary that it might be booby-trapped,

and keeping half an ear out for any of the other doors opening along the hallway. I knew that all manner of activities could be taking place behind those doors: gambling, prostitution, drug-taking . . . and, from the current state-of-play on Arkle-4, it had to be some pretty extreme kind of any of the aforementioned; something so *reprehensible* that even under literal mob rule it couldn't be practised out in the open. And—it went without saying—blasters were more often than not involved in and around said reprehensible behaviours.

I nodded to the vidscreen, then said to Clive, "You reckon you can get any info off that?"

"What kind of info, Captain?" Clive replied. "Forgive me for saying so, but I feel just a little out of the loop; not got much idea of what's going on here."

I felt my pulse pumping at my temple.

I reached up, caressed the vein with my fingertips, as if that might cool my heart down.

"Hanx," I said, "he was in charge of a bunch of street teams —ran drugs, kidnappings, whatever else, all over this area of town . . . all over Green District." I stared down at the bearskin rug then shook my head. "Even though he might not've had his fingerprints personally lining this, it's not likely that him—or someone within his organisation—wouldn't know just who *was* responsible."

Clive stared back at me, clearly processing this information.

Maybe, as the last member of my crew standing, he was worried that he might be the latest one to get himself snagged by the mysterious bandits.

I could empathise.

He got to work on the vidscreen without delay. His fingers worked busily. Lines of code splurged back and forth across the screen. All of this stuff which, quite frankly, I've avoided all my life like the *goddamn* plague.

As Clive worked away, he spoke to me.

"I've got something which looks like a messaging kit —*bespoke* . . . kind of like a calendar-type deal."

When I looked at the vidscreen itself, all I could see were indecipherable, endless lines of numbers and letters and symbols.

I wondered if I'd even been born with the same *brain* as the rest of humanity.

"Oh, here we go," Clive said, removing one hand from his typing to lift it up in the air and point his finger at the roof.

From the wry smile on his lips, I could tell he was having more fun than he wanted to make out; that he was secretly *enjoying* himself . . . although, of course, he would much rather —*ideally*—be caking himself in oil and grease down in the *Nava's* engine room.

But the *Nava* was out of the picture.

For now.

Clive went quiet for about a minute.

I thought I could hear something stirring out in the corridor.

The fact that Clive paused what he was doing, unfurled his neck, raised his nose as if to sniff the air, told me he had heard something too.

Taking care to move slowly, I trod up to the wall beside the door, flattened my back against it, ready to blindside anybody foolish enough to burst on in without knocking first.

Yeah, and I can just *bet* that trick had never been pulled at all in the back rooms of *Hanx's Hoarders' Haul* . . . but it was such an old trick that nobody would suspect.

I held myself still, then, dropping my voice to a whisper, spoke to Clive.

"You getting anywhere with that?"

Clive continued to stare at the door for another moment or so before turning his attention back down to the vidscreen, and to whatever he was doing with those strands-upon-strands of code. "Just did a search for their names—for the *twins* . . ."

"You might wanna have a go with Milky and Foy, too, while you're at it."

Clive smirked. "Yeah, already did; think I've got a lead on them."

Outside, I couldn't help but notice the sound getting louder still.

It sounded, at least to my ears, like marching boots.

Already, I could feel my previously soaring spirits begin to taper off their ascent.

I knew we could be angling for some Deep Trouble now.

I couldn't help but feel something like an idiot for having thought this a good plan; for having thought that breaking into a well-known front would go unnoticed by the current political administration of Arkle-4.

. . . Maybe I was being hard on myself . . . perhaps it just demonstrated the passion I secretly held for my crew; how closely I cradled them to my chest. That I would do anything for them; put my *neck* on the line for them.

Yeah, something along those lines would read pretty nice on

my tombstone.

It might even convince a few of the uninitiated that Arkle Wright truly was a not-too-bad-at-all sort of a guy.

The stomping got so loud that I couldn't hear myself think any longer, and, as has often been the case, my mouth became divorced from my brain.

I turned to Clive. "Come on," I said. "Time's up."

"Just a second," Clive replied, quickening his typing at the vidscreen.

There was a pair of *thumps* at the door.

A brief pause, as if we were about to open on up.

Then, with an enormous *crack*, the door split open.

Wooden splinters going everywhere.

Dust clouded up about the room. It slowly drifted downwards.

I had enough good sense in me to hold my hands up, in surrender.

Despite the debris, I could very clearly make out the many blasters pointing at me and Clive—Clive, I then noticed, was still working away at the vidscreen, apparently none too surprised by the sudden disruption.

"Step away!" one of the blaster-toters bellowed.

Clive swept his fingers across the vidscreen for a final time, and then, as requested, he stood holding his hands up above his head.

When the dust had cleared a little more, I caught sight of the girl from downstairs; the one who'd 'greeted' us at the counter . . . and who had clawed and bitten me.

She didn't seem too pleased.

10 BIG JO'S PLACE - ARKLE-4

BACK WHEN I WAS A KID, I'd get told all these stories about Big Jo—mostly from other kids at school. They used to tell me how he had this mansion *way* out of Bomberlee City; with all these swaying pine trees, a walled garden, a grand, sweeping drive with a fountain, you know, all of those stereotypical gangster trimmings.

But, as I soon discovered, if I hadn't already suspected, those kids were full of shit.

For one, Big Jo most definitely *wasn't* based outside of Bomberlee—oh no, he was *most definitely* right at the very centre of the place. Just not where most people would think to look.

i.e. *Underground.*

Although none of the armed guards so much as informed me and Clive that this was Big Jo's lair, I'd decided to draw that conclusion by myself.

Who else would go to the trouble of digging out a huge network of tunnels beneath Bomberlee City?

Who else would've had the *funds* to do so?

People on Arkle-4 weren't just broke. They were *flat* broke . . .

The uniforms were all of the same sleek, black variety I'd witnessed back on the *Nava*, shortly before she'd been hijacked, or impounded, or whatever the hell these mobsters wanted to term the wide array of kidnaps they were performing.

I thought, at some point, the guards 'escorting' us through the underground tunnels might holster their weapons; you know, give us a bit of a break from being held at gunpoint. But, nope, they were either under strict instruction to remain armed at all times, or else they had a perverse *liking* for holding guns on unarmed prisoners. Well, nearly unarmed . . . I didn't suppose that Clive's stungun-thing quite qualified as a weapon in this company . . .

We were taken down several floors, and through several corridors, the goal of which—I supposed—was mostly so that we might become disorientated.

So that we might *get lost*.

Be unable to find our way out again . . .

Eventually, we were brought through what I could only really describe as a subterranean courtyard. There were a few abstract marble statues dotted about, all of them crawling with what was either extremely convincing *fake* ivy, or ivy which'd been so genetically tampered with that it resembled almost *nothing* of the original plant.

And then—as if it solely existed to prove me wrong—there was a fountain, water tinkling down from its spout pleasantly.

False daylight flooded down from above; tangerine-coloured and pleasantly warming.

It was almost as if we'd arrived on a different planet altogether.

"Sit," one of the armed guards said.

I did as he suggested, lowering myself down onto one of the painted metal benches at the periphery of the courtyard.

Clive, wisely, followed my lead.

All the guards but one left us. There had only been three, I realised, and felt a touch ashamed that I hadn't attempted a daring escape from our captors. Then again, considering that Big Jo was now very much seen to be the legitimate administrator of Arkle-4, it probably would've been one of my more *rash* ideas. And, well, to be honest, I've had some *pretty* rash ideas through the years.

Sometimes I wonder how I ever managed to end up as a captain of my own crew; often I wonder why those people, apparently of their own free will, continue to follow me around.

Clive leaned into me, dropped his voice to a whisper. "Captain," he said. "I need to tell you what I found out from the vidscreen, just in case we're separated—or they choose to *execute* me."

I detected no sense of humour in Clive's voice.

As usual, his tone was completely plain.

Unshakeably informative . . . no *irony*.

Before Clive could tell me anything at all, however, the

guard declared, "The captain will see you now," apparently having got word through some unseen earpiece.

I glanced to Clive, and then to the guard. "What *captain?*" I replied, wondering if he was trying to be funny, or if he was trying to initiate some kind of scuffle . . . so that I might—*foolishly*—get myself shot whilst being 'uncooperative'.

The guard stared long and hard back at me, and then, without another word, trod his way to the other side of the courtyard. I only completely caught the idea that we were supposed to follow when the guard pulled his blaster from its holster and started shaking it around.

I got up.

Clive did too.

It seemed that the two of us valued our lives on some level.

We followed the guard through the doorway.

———

On the other side, within what I could only describe to be a 'distasteful' room, I came across a familiar—but not particularly *welcome*—face.

The man who had been responsible for the *Nava's* capture.

Captain Norbortwitz.

I took in his leathery face again, the thinned-out grey hair.

And how he wore that same cap as before, drawn down, rendering his eyes in almost impenetrable shadow.

As me and Clive were instructed to sit down on the—not particularly comfortable—wooden chairs before his desk, I caught sight of him flicking his tongue past his pert lips.

I eyed the large chunk missing in it.

As if acknowledging where my attention arrived, Norbortwitz gave a sly smile. "Do you know how I lost that part of my tongue, Captain Wright?"

"How'd you know my name?"

Norbortwitz smiled wider. "Registered to your ship, of course."

Somehow, I couldn't quite bring myself to believe that this was the truth.

But I let the matter drop for the time being.

I did have an armed guard standing right behind my head.

Norbortwitz dialled his smile down a few notches. "Now, as for my *tongue* . . . it may surprise you to know that, in another life, I was an *addict* . . . I had a brain *hopelessly* addled by various substances. Held captive to the outside world." He shook his head, then brought a hand up to cup his forehead. "No *control*—none at all."

For several moments, Norbortwitz remained curled over himself, as if he was having some sort of an introspective moment. I had time to slip Clive a sidelong glance to see if he was just as weirded out by this display as I was.

However, before we could suss out a means of sending any sort of silent message between the two of us, Norbortwitz started up speaking again.

"It was at the end of one of my *longer* manic episodes; one of these periods of time which could last anything from a matter of hours to several days or *weeks*." Norbortwitz shook his head, as if reprimanding his past self. "I would go *out of my mind* to raise the funds to get my hands on whatever I happened to be munching on at that time. Robbery, *muggings* . . . even, I'm quite certain, a murder of a fellow addict who just happened to show his back to me at the wrong time, too soon after he'd picked up." He shrugged. "I was a mess, quite frankly." He allowed himself another few seconds of pity party, and then glanced back up at me and Clive—*his captive audience*—and shone us a grin. "Until I found my feet—until I made a friend of *Big Jo.*"

Although I'd only been sitting on the wooden chair for, at best, a few minutes, I could already feel pins and needles making themselves felt in my buttocks; cramp beginning to settle in over my muscles, starting to wear me down.

I shifted my feet beneath the desk.

Slipped Clive another glance.

Wondered when Norbortwitz was going to get through with talking about himself, and get onto talking about what was to become of *us.*

"You forgot about your tongue," I put in.

But Norbortwitz was already holding his palm up for me to stop talking.

If there's anything I hate worse than a ship thief, it's a ship thief who genuinely believes that all the world's a stage for them to act out—over and over again—their personal history to all willing to put up with it. Or, failing that, all of those *forced* to put up with it.

"My tongue," Norbortwitz went on, turning his attention up to the ceiling above our heads, which, I saw, was some kind of faux marble. Then he revisited his focus on me and Clive. "My *tongue* came about as a result of one of those sessions I was relating to you; when I had gone into a maniac craze, attempting to get my hands on whatever drugs I possibly could." He shrugged. "Who knows *exactly* what I stuffed into my system, the only thing I can say for certain is that—a few hours later; after I'd administered myself whatever dose it was—I began to shudder all over . . . this then graduated into a *seizure*, and"—he poked his tongue out for us to better see the notch then retracted it—"as you can see, I bit *clean through* my tongue in my fit."

A silence settled over the room.

I shifted a glance to Clive, sitting beside me.

"You don't recognise me, do you, Captain Wright?"

I switched back to Norbortwitz.

He was eyeballing me, as if I was in some way an idiot.

"Perhaps if I gave you my first name." He paused for what seemed like a dramatically significant time. "*Henry*."

" 'Henry' ?" I repeated, again glancing in Clive's direction, hoping that his off-the-wall thinking skills might be able to help me out here.

Clive shrugged.

"Or," Norbortwitz continued, "you might know me by my street moniker, the name I went by for many decades, before the revolution came to pass." Another of those dramatic pauses, then, " 'Ernest Harry'."

My chest tightened up.

Blood ran hot to my temples.

That hole in my skull throbbed.

Of course, now that I looked beyond the wrinkled face, the leathered, almost *distinguished* features, I could just about make out the facial profile of the gangster who had terrorised Green District . . . the one who had personally employed my parents.

And that was when sense deserted me.

I leaped up out of my chair. When I bunched my fists, it felt like the knuckles would slice clean right out of the skin. I loomed over Norbortwitz, and Norbortwitz remained totally still, apparently unmoved by my show of strength.

"Now, *Captain* Arkle," Norbortwitz stated, staring back into my eyes. "I'd think long and hard about what you've got to lose before doing anything rash." He nodded to Clive, sitting beside me. "Think about your beloved crew. Wouldn't it be terrible if anything happened to them?"

I continued to loom over Norbortwitz, determined to rain fury down on him if he gave me so much as an inch to do so. It would truly be an ass-kicking. But, somehow—call it *my brain*— I held off . . . perhaps if they hadn't taken away my space blaster and ship I wouldn't have felt so tied down. Slowly, I sank back into my chair.

"That's it, Captain," Norbortwitz said, his voice almost a purr.

He gestured off in the direction of the doorway.

I had hardly any time to realise that one of the security guards had appeared there.

In fact, it was the same one who had escorted us here in the first place.

Now, though, instead of leaving his blaster pistol where it had been, nice and snug in his thigh holster, he had drawn it and was holding it at a steady chest height.

Pointed at me.

Norbortwitz got to his feet. He gave a nod to the security guard.

The security guard approached.

Still sitting in the chair, feeling pinned down by the blaster pistol, I eyed him.

The security guard reached out, took a firm hold of Clive's shoulder, tugged him up to his feet with a strength that can only be summoned with the cool, familiar feel of a gun in hand.

"What're you doing?" I just about got out, turning in Norbortwitz's direction.

Norbortwitz, though, was already pacing for the other door, opposite the one we'd arrived through. He didn't so much as make a motion to answer.

He kept on walking.

Something inside me snapped.

All my past.

My parents . . . their dosed-up, docile faces . . .

How I'd had no choice.

No choice but to *leave* Arkle-4; and here I was . . . back all over again.

Once more, I leaped up out of my chair, but this time there was no cool-headed restraint—if there had truly been any before.

I rushed Norbortwitz, arms outstretched, reaching for his throat.

He saw me coming, went for his blaster.

But I was too quick.

I batted it out of his grip.

Barrelled into his chest.

As Norbortwitz tumbled to the floor, I heard him shout out, to the security guard, *"Don't shoot! Don't shoot him!"*

It wasn't till I was pinning Norbortwitz with my kneecaps to his chest that I realised he meant the security guard wasn't to shoot *me* . . . that he wasn't referring to Clive.

But I didn't much care.

Once I got my hands on Norbortwitz's throat, I could feel all those muscles there, like tightly coiled steel cables, flexing and struggling, fighting to get free, to just get a puff of air.

But I wouldn't give him so much as a sip.

He could *die* for all I cared.

Just like he had driven my parents—and surely so many others—to their deaths.

I was half aware of the hands as they grasped hold of me.

The fingers, like socket wrenches, digging into my skin.

I tried to resist, but I knew it was futile.

There were too many of them.

Too many hands.

Soon enough, they hauled me back, off Norbortwitz.

They dragged me to my feet.

There might've only been a pair of them; or there might've been half a dozen.

But I swung my fists, all the same, till they pinned my arms behind my back.

Then I kicked my feet.

Till they seized hold of my ankles.

I squirmed and squirmed in their grasp, unable to get free.

"Captain . . . *Captain*," Norbortwitz said, sounding impatient now, "I really wouldn't waste your strength—there's a long road ahead of you, I believe you'll find."

I twisted about in the security guards' hold, tried to catch sight of Norbortwitz, but I only received a punch to the temple for my trouble. I started to see stars. Neat, purple pinpricks scattering my vision. My whole body felt lighter.

Somehow, maybe it was because I allowed my muscles to go a touch slacker—perhaps I somehow made my bones less rigid. I managed to catch a glimpse of Clive.

I observed him now, standing stock still.

Something was wrong.

Something felt *off.*

He had no guard on him.

That guard, the one who'd pulled him to his feet forcibly, had been called in to help with the others.

I stared lightning bolts at him.

Felt the anger frothing just beneath the surface of my skin.

I wasn't sure what I expected; if I wanted him to leap to my defence; to show some sort of futile 'loyalty'.

My attention shifted onto Norbortwitz, who was smiling widely.

He even had a *twinkle* in his eye.

My heart skipped a beat.

What the hell . . .

However, instead of Norbortwitz saying something, it was Clive.

"I'm sorry, Captain—I didn't have a choice."

My attention snapped back onto Norbortwitz.

Clive shook his head. "They got to me; months ago." He

seemed to be having trouble swallowing. There was a slight twinkle in his eyes, too. Rather than 'glee', though—as it was in Norbortwitz's case—I could tell the twinkle was tears. "The whole crash, it was all planned. I led you into it." He pointed to my forehead. "That hole . . ."

But then he trailed off.

Whether it was because he could say nothing more, or because he'd received a fierce glare from Norbortwitz, I couldn't quite tell. Despite whatever intervention there might've been, Clive started up again. "There wasn't enough time—not enough time to help . . . to put things right. Please, Captain, if you only knew—"

"Shut up!" Norbortwitz cried out.

Another security guard arrived to lead Clive from the room. As he went out the door, I heard his defeated voice. "Captain. Please *forgive me*. . . . There just wasn't any *time*."

All I knew was—in that moment—my strength simply deserted me.

What Clive was saying slowly penetrated my thoughts.

Betrayed.

That was it.

What'd gone down.

And by a member of my own crew.

There was nothing left to strive for.

My body went limp.

11 BOMBERLEE - BROKE - ARKLE-4

I WOKE UP with a freezing drizzle spitting across my cheeks.

My whole body was shaking, but I couldn't feel a thing.

On impulse, I reached up, touched my forehead, feeling the hole there . . . the hole that'd been *filled* in . . .

I thought on Brian, and how he'd patched it up good. Then I thought about that girl on the counter at *Hanx's Hoarders' Haul*, who'd had a similar hole to the head.

Was there some kind of connection here?

One I just wasn't seeing?

I couldn't help but feel racked by confusion.

Why . . . *why* would Clive do that?

What'd driven him to lead my crew to kidnap?

What'd led him to—*presumably*—lead the rest of my crew, the *Nava*, back here, to Arkle-4?

I wondered if I should feel angry.

If I should feel like I wanted to rip him limb from limb then toss him straight out of the airlock . . . once I got my ship back, that was . . . *if* I ever got my ship back . . .

Slowly, as if it might cause me untold pain, I cranked one eye open.

Then the other.

Daylight was just about leaking onto the scene.

Yup, even without my vision reaching its standard, fairly sharp contrast, I could make out the grisly grey concrete which surrounded me on all sides. The rusted-iron puddles scattered about. And the other slouched-up, collapsed bodies which lay on the same plane as my own . . . For the longest time, I stared at their blanketed forms, at how they would move, almost like a single organism, their breathing somehow synchronised.

An organism *I* was a part of now.

I drew in a breath, and caught a great deal of exhaust fumes with it.

Arkle-4 never really had bought much into the Cleaner Energy for Cleaner Lives craze which'd swept the universe about the time I was a kid. Not that all that many of us had noticed since anybody with half a stick of sense would find some high-rising apartment to hide out in; way above the smog and dust of the everyday.

But I was very much down and dirty now . . .

I took care as I propped myself up, as I straightened my back and somehow regained a sitting position. I used the storefront—sealed with a retractable steel netting—to ease myself up.

Every scrap of meat, which I could collectively term my body, ached.

Actually, it did more than just *ache* . . .

It was a stomach-piercing pain.

So overwhelming that I had to squeeze my eyes shut several seconds.

After I'd taken a moment or so to recuperate, I found my feet once again, using the wall to help myself up. It was a shaky start, but it was a start nonetheless.

The next task soon became getting my vision straight.

I worked out a compromise, allowing my eyelids to droop down to half conceal my pupils. That way I didn't have to figure out too many details of the world; not all at once, in any case. *One thing at a time—just one thing at a time*; that became my mantra.

I staggered along the street, picking my way as best as I could through the homeless all sleeping there. Inevitably, though, both because of the body density-versus-floor space conundrum, and due to the state of my vision, some of them did get stepped on.

I got myself free of the sleeping zone, and back onto the main street of Bomberlee:

Fryer Street.

I took in the vendors, all of them, without exception, tinkering away at whatever deep fryer they'd been commissioned to take a look at that day.

I breathed in the heady scent of oil and it seemed to calm my stomach somewhat.

And then, because I had no crew—no *ship*—I went the only way I knew.

Back home.

———

I wasn't quite sure what kind of expression I'd expected my brother Mertinon to wear when I turned up on the doorstep of good, old 3 – 18. Maybe I thought he'd be surprised to see me again; perhaps I expected him to throw me out on my ear . . . most likely the measure of what I deserved.

Instead, though, like he'd been expecting me, he thrust a moiser into my hand.

After about the ninth or tenth one, I got to the point where, if I was still in pain, I at least didn't feel any . . . not any longer.

I don't recall much of what we talked about, but I remember going to sleep with a big, broad grin on my face for precisely no reason at all. When I finally came to, I caught sight of my brother, sitting up by the window, staring down out across what passed for *countryside* surrounding Green District. I came up rubbing my head.

"Whole place is a prison," Mertinon said, staring out the window.

At first I wondered if he was speaking to himself, if he hadn't realised that I'd stirred at all. But then he glanced back at me. He gave me the loosest of smiles.

I gently eased myself up into a sitting position on the futon which'd somehow appeared beneath my bulk. Strangely, it felt like I'd got the best rest for about a week. I dragged my knees up into my chest, though they couldn't physically get much further than my belly.

"How come . . ." I began, then thought better of it.

"How come *what?*"

I gathered my wits—my *courage*. "How come you never turned out like Ma and Pa? How come you never ended messed up in all the Big Jo business?"

Mertinon gave a shrug then a shake of his head.

I noticed he was still gripping his moiser.

He turned to look back out the window.

"Guess you could say that I was," Mertinon replied. "That we're *all* tied up in it."

I thought about how Big Jo was now in charge of the whole of Arkle-4, and I couldn't help wondering about who might be held responsible for allowing that to happen.

"When Ma and Pa died," Mertinon continued, "Ernest Harry himself—"

"Captain Norbortwitz?"

Mertinon smirked. "Yeah, guess that's what he's calling himself these days." He took a swig of his moiser, swallowed, then spat some residue on the floor. "He came along personally and told me that he felt just *awful* about what'd happened to them." He flashed a glance at me. "That they'd *overdosed*."

It sent a shudder through my gut.

I couldn't believe Ma and Pa had got wrapped up in all this.

When they'd held out for so long.

After a lifetime of poverty—a lifetime of *disappointment*—the Easy Button just gets far too difficult to resist.

"Said that Big Jo'd take care of things; that he'd pay off the mortgage for this dump." He smirked wider, shook his head. "And that I'd get *compensation* for Ma and Pa's lost earnings, as if I needed hand-outs . . ."

I decided it wasn't anywhere near my place to say anything

about his current situation; about how, to my eye, all Mertinon did all day was sit about slugging moisers. Then again, I don't suppose my job was all that much different, excepting for the fact that I did all that up in space.

"You never did think of heading off-planet?" I put in.

This comment got Mertinon's attention.

He stared me down.

I wondered if I'd gone and dragged up some kind of painful memory; if I'd somehow stoked a fire that would've been best left to ember away into soot.

Mertinon seemed to retreat back into himself, as if he was consciously shoving the anger down the same way some guy might smother a rabid dog to death with a damp quilt.

"Nah," he finally settled on.

A silence draped over the room.

A chill crawled up my spine.

It felt as if the warm rapport we'd forced upon ourselves had somehow become ripped; almost as if it'd been nothing but flimsy tissue paper fit for tearing.

It'd torn now.

Deciding there was nothing to lose, I broke the silence.

"You know, out there, in space, there's a whole bunch of opportunities, not just in the FSA, or, you know—"

This time Mertinon rushed up from his chair.

He tossed his half-empty bottle of moiser.

It hit the wall and shattered into hundreds of shards of glass.

I breathed in the hot, steady—*sharp*—stink of moiser on the air.

Perhaps I expected Mertinon to attack me.

I might've welcomed that.

Even if he'd *killed* me then surely I would've deserved it.

But he held off.

He showed far more restraint than I would've . . . if some-body had effectively come clean out and told me that I'd wasted my life.

I always have been the bastard of the family.

Mertinon settled for stalking back and forth by the window as drips of moiser rolled slowly down the dilapidated wallpaper. He threw a glare in my direction every couple of moments, and it was surely the least of what I deserved.

He shook his head wildly, as if trying to get free of some nigglesome thought in his brain. "There was no option, Arkle, you have to understand that." He came to a halt, glared long and hard at me. "Don't you think I looked into it? Don't you think I wanted to see what kinds of options might be open to me? Don't you think the FSA would've accepted me with open arms?"

I remained silent.

This was an onslaught which'd laid dormant for decades and decades . . . now, though, it was coming pouring out . . . quite simply it *couldn't* be stopped . . .

Mertinon finished pacing. "You do realise that Ma and Pa, that they weren't addicts, don't you?"

I thought back to school, to that rudimentary drug education we'd all got.

And I couldn't stop myself before I was parroting one of those messages they'd—*apparently*—so efficiently and so profoundly drilled into our group brain:

"An overdose can happen at any time—even the first time." I

gave the dramatic pause, just as we did in school. *"Especially* the first time."

Mertinon wrinkled up his nose. "Yeah, right," he said, "it *would* be wonderful to believe that, wouldn't it? It *would* be a wonderful way for the world to be . . . for you—*Arkle Wright, Captain of the Navaplastas*—to be totally blameless for the death of your parents."

Although I knew I had to give Mertinon this time to vent, I couldn't help myself.

Sure, I'd been absent—*neglectful* even—but I wasn't about to accept the deaths of two people, and much less my parents, just because my brother was all jilted about how I'd taken on all life had had to offer me while he'd—literally—pissed moiser all up the wall.

I rose to my feet, held my finger out to the tip of his nose. "You listen, you ain't got *no* right . . ."

This time, though, Mertinon cut through me.

There wasn't so much anger in his voice now as there was a kind of vulnerability—a kind of *hurt*, even . . . his voice had lost its edge, as if his strength had deserted him.

Or perhaps the moiser was just starting to hit.

"Big Jo had them killed, Arkle, because you went off with the FSA; because you joined forces with their *enemy* . . . they waited, wanted to see if you'd come back, and, when you didn't, Big Jo decided to take his revenge . . . he *knew* that if he wanted to take his revenge then he had to take it *right then*." Here Mertinon shook his head, over and over again. "Nah, Arkle, they killed Ma and Pa because you didn't come back, then they made me into a prisoner . . . like they used to do in the Olden Days.

Leave one alive to tell the rest; to serve as a *warning*." He met my eye again. "But they got you back, didn't they? They got you back here *in the end* . . ."

It takes a great deal to render me speechless, but Mertinon had managed it.

There was nothing for me to do.

Nothing except for me to say, from the back of my throat, but from the bottom of my heart, ". . . Sorry."

————

We passed the rest of the day in the apartment without saying much—without *drinking* . . . I was at a loss as to what I should do next.

As to how I should proceed.

Really, though, I had to come to terms with the truth; that unless I wanted a couple of shades removed from all-out-war with one of the most notorious gangsters in the history of mankind, then I was up shit creek without the proverbial paddle.

And never mind a ship . . .

"You know," Mertinon said, "I would've *loved* to get out there—into Big Black—go see just what the hell was what; jump from planet to planet." Here he smiled—a much-needed mood lightening. "Sounds like you had a great bunch of adventures up there."

I couldn't help but smile. "Sure have, wouldn't have it any other way, that's for certain."

"And that crew of yours," Mertinon said, jerking his thumb

out of the window. "Seem like a great bunch; like you've built your own family about yourself almost."

I waited out the silence, reading the unspoken subtext.

Then, feeling kind of warm and fuzzy inside, though not just from the moiser, I found myself saying, "You know, if I ever do get the *Nava* back then yours'll be the first name on the ship's log." I paused for a moment, then added, "After mine, of course, but, you know, I *am* the captain."

Mertinon slipped me a sidelong glance and I was certain, for several moments, that he was just going to burst right out into tears. Instead, though, he only reached out his hand, and shook mine, then said, "Thanks, brother, I appreciate that."

It seemed strange that I'd take so long in getting around to explaining just what'd transpired after I'd left the apartment behind. I suppose, there had just been so much on the table—so much for the two of us to deal with personally—that the present had just had to wait. But, in the end, when I'd updated him on everything that'd happened in the past twenty-four-plus hours, it was Mertinon who whirled us back to the current year; current time.

"You know," he said, "when I saw you leave, I couldn't help noticing one of your crewmembers tossing something into one of those bins out there."

I followed his finger, caught sight of one of the bins where I'd left Clive and the twins—in retrospect, *unadvisedly*.

I pouted, then glanced back to him. "You didn't follow what I said, about how Clive *betrayed* me, how he's been in Big Jo's pocket all along."

Mertinon met my eye, then gave a slight shrug. "Really,

Arkle," he replied, "you of all people should know just how powerful—how *persuasive*—Big Jo can be when he decides it that way . . ."

Although I followed Mertinon's argument, I couldn't say that I much agreed.

He could sprout off whatever he liked from this place—from this location so far removed from the rest of the universe—but the thing was he could never *truly* know what it was like to be betrayed by someone you had lived beside, who you had *served* beside, for months.

Years.

Just a fact.

One of those things you can never truly know hiding out in the backend of beyond.

Still, I had to admit that he'd piqued my interest with this talk about the bin.

Perhaps it was a bomb.

Maybe Clive had contrived it so I'd hook up with my brother, get the info on what he'd seen, and then go pawing about in the rubbish like some racoon.

Then it'd be *ka-boom!*

Lights out forever.

Would that really be such a bad idea at this point?

Worse than the prospect of never being able to leave Arkle-4 behind again?

I turned to Mertinon.

If I was going to put myself out of my misery then I might as well do my brother the same favour . . . otherwise it might turn out to be something else he would be able to blame me for . . .

"Show me where," I said.

————

Night was beginning to fall as Mertinon—the star; not the brother—was dipping behind the horizon. Although I would've been happy to dig my meat hooks into the bin, to get up close and personal with all that rotten, sweet-smelling crap people threw away, Mertinon—the brother; not the star—seemed glad to be the one to get his hands mucky.

Perhaps it was the absence of excitement in his life.

Or maybe he saw this as some sort of *Navaplastas* crewmember training ground.

Whatever it was, the fact of the matter was that, after a brief rummage in the rubbish, he came up with a fistful of something wrapped in a small, plastic bag; about the size of a coin purse, no larger. It was held together with an elastic band.

It was surprising that when Mertinon turned on me he was grinning from ear to ear.

And that he had a sparkle in his eye.

It might've been that he just enjoyed digging through other people's rubbish . . .

"Let's go get this washed off, huh?" he said, leading me back to the apartment building.

Up in the old 3 – 18, at the kitchen sink, I watched over Mertinon's shoulder as he washed off the tiny black plastic bag. Several layers of green-brown muck slid off with the warm, steaming water. It all congealed and then swirled its way down the drain.

The bag now dripping-wet, Mertinon shook off the drops then went about unparcelling the contents. He'd already got well over halfway through this action before he glanced up to me, as if asking my permission to open whatever my faithless crewmember had left behind.

Not all that interested in touching the thing, I nodded my assent.

Brow furrowed, Mertinon worked to undo the package.

Soon, within, I made out the object.

It took me a second or so to realise what it was.

An earpiece.

Just a standard *earpiece*.

I looked to Mertinon.

He looked back at me.

"What'd you reckon?" Mertinon said.

I shrugged. "Search me, I'm still just about getting my head around the technological innovation that liquids can be served in glasses . . ."

Mertinon held the earpiece up to the harsh, electric strip lights of the kitchen and squinted as if this was some sort of alien technology that he hadn't come across before.

Now, Arkle-4 might be backwards, but they *do* at least have earpieces.

All the cool kids do . . .

Without another word, and this time without a glance to ask permission, Mertinon thrust the device into his ear. He cocked his head to one side, then shook it a couple of times, trying to find the perfect fit . . . to be fair to him earpieces *are* always a nightmare to get correctly into place, and then it's something like a lottery to actually get them *working* on a consistent basis.

Mertinon closed his eyes, listening intently to something.

He squinted harder still.

Then glanced to me, shaking his head.

"No good," he said, removing the earpiece. "There's a message, but it's in some language I don't understand. Not Basic."

I took the earpiece from him, feeling just a shred of pride that he was—on some level—trusting that I *would* be able to make out some sense from this foreign language.

I jabbed the earpiece in, and, almost immediately, felt as if my brain was being drilled with some sort of a pneumatic device. I yanked it free, scrunching up my nose. "The *hell* is that?"

Mertinon nodded back at me. "Sounds like *hell* that's for sure."

I stared at the earpiece another few seconds and then dropped it on the kitchen counter.

"Well," I said, "maybe we should sleep on it—nothing good ever comes from puzzling over some problem too long."

Mertinon remained fixed on the earpiece, as if—if he just stared hard enough and long enough—it would give up all its secrets.

Maybe he *had* been around Arkle-4, and, more to the point, Big Jo's operation, for far too much time.

"Come on," I said. "Another moiser ought to do the trick."

———

It must've been nearing midnight when I heard the *scrub* of footsteps out in the corridor.

I would've thought nothing of it if it hadn't been for Mertinon's reaction.

Although he'd seemed to be out cold for the night—it'd taken something in the region of twenty and thirty moisers to achieve that effect—he immediately snapped out of his doze, padding about himself manically.

I just about managed to hoik myself up into some sort of sitting position when he'd already made it clear across the apartment to the front door. "What?" I got out. "What *is* it?"

My eyes dipped, to the blaster Mertinon had produced from somewhere and which he now held down at his side.

"Shh!" Mertinon replied, not so much as turning to look at me.

He stared into the spyhole, apparently trying to work out just who it was in the corridor. He might as well not have bothered considering that the hallway lights had been out even when I'd been a kid.

I shifted myself free of the sofa, and the lure of sleep, and arrived beside him.

"Anything I can do?" I said, my voice at the level of a whisper.

Mertinon turned to me.

Eyeballed me.

"Someone's at the door," he said.

And—sure enough—just as soon as he'd said it, the doorbell rang.

It sent a jangling sensation through my whole body.

Almost as if somebody had kicked me in the head.

"What'd we do?" I said, still whispering, and surely being overheard by whoever was standing on the other side of the door . . . I guess that moiser and covert stealth operations have hardly ever gone hand-in-hand; not traditionally, anyway.

Mertinon leaned into me. He whispered husky, and low, and without so much as a missing detail. I could tell that he'd built up quite a tolerance to the old moiser to have the ability to think—let alone *speak*—lucidly in such a short time.

"Under the kitchen sink," he said, shortly, succinctly.

I'd like to say that I sprang into action, but it was more of a lurch.

It felt as if something was trying to crawl its way out of my stomach. And it was taking its own sweet time when it reached my throat. I ducked down, flipped open the kitchen sink cabinet, almost catching myself in the eye with one of the corners as I did so.

I perused the gloom for precisely one second before seeing what it was Mertinon had wanted me to fish out from within.

Blaster rifle.

Even in the darkness—even for somebody as drunk as I was —I could make it out clearly.

Before I really knew what I was doing, I was arming the thing; watching on as the go-green shifted to danger-red . . . signalling that it was armed and deadly.

You don't set weapons to stun on Arkle-4; and much less in Green District.

Not if you know what's *good* for you . . .

Back at the door, Mertinon turned into me, apparently decided.

"All right," he said, his voice strained, husky still, "I'll count to three, and then we break this mother open. Clear?"

I nodded.

"One . . . two . . ."

I waited for the count of three, feeling my heart up in my throat, accompanying whatever it was that had been attempting to escape my stomach. Before Mertinon could reach three, though, the door, apparently of its own accord, blasted free of its hinges.

12 FORMER RESIDENCE - DOWN AND OUT - ARKLE-4

I LANDED with a spine-shattering *thunk* across the room.

It was to the moiser's great compliment that I hardly felt a thing; nothing much more than a dull and distant *sensation* . . . not *pain* exactly, but not entirely pleasant, either.

The whole world spun about me, and dust poured into the apartment.

Bits of wood, too, hailed down.

A couple of splinters became caught in my skin.

Embedded there.

My mind got stuck.

I realised I was lying on my back.

I padded about, hoping my blaster rifle would've landed nearby.

Nope, no luck there.

Realising I couldn't do anything useful, I stared into the dust which constantly plumed into the apartment, trying to make out a form; some sign of something *human* . . . perhaps, too, some sign of my *brother* . . . but there was none to be had.

And then, because my brain seemed to be approaching overload, I closed my eyes and forced myself to go somewhere else; to simply let go of this present, unbecoming reality, and embrace another one entirely.

It sort of worked for a second or so.

Before I heard someone call out to me.

"Captain? Captain?"

Deeply aware that I might be about to let myself in for a world of pain, I cautiously opened a single eye. Stared out. Saw someone standing over me; *looming* over me. And then, from out of the dust, I spied the hand.

Unable to think straight, I reached up and took hold.

Clutched it tightly.

I was on my feet before I realised who it was.

Terry.

One of the twins.

My brain was caught in a whirl for several seconds.

I was trying to reconcile what was going on.

When I glanced about the apartment, though, I had my answer.

I caught sight of the bushy afro which confirmed Terry's brother—Brian's—presence.

I was struck with confusion for a little longer.

And then Terry cut through it with a sharp tug at my jacket sleeve. "Come on. There's no time."

I reached up for my aching head, feeling myself being

dragged towards the door, and not much liking it. "Why . . . what's going on?"

"Later," Terry put in, displaying yet more unseen strength as he guided me out of the apartment.

I managed to switch a glance about me, searching for my brother—for Mertinon. I noted that he was unconscious, and that Brian was lifting him; apparently unperturbed by the fact that Mertinon was, at the very least, three times his size and weight.

He didn't seem to be having too much trouble.

I wondered if Brian's medical studies had taught him techniques on how to lug about unconscious or unwilling patients.

As Terry urged me onwards, towards the door, I caught hold of myself.

Remembered what'd happened before me and Mertinon had set our minds to getting slaughtered.

"Over . . . over *there*," I just about got out, wildly wagging my arm in the direction of the kitchen, and the earpiece on the counter.

Terry somehow grasped the thrust of my panic, leaving me for a moment to flail about on my feet. He returned faster than my mind could quite handle. He was bearing the earpiece. "That everything?" he said, and I didn't have a chance to tell him about the blaster rifle before I heard something giving way in the building's foundations.

Terry had already got me halfway down the hall, away from the apartment, and lagging just behind the apparently super-human Brian, lugging along Mertinon, when I thought to ask for some kind of explanation.

"Just what the hell did you do?" I said. "You planning on bringing the building down?"

"Sort of," Terry replied, and I couldn't help noting there was something like a smile in his voice.

We got back down to ground level, though I could still feel the floor shaking.

The twins had got me and Mertinon all the way across the muddy ground—perhaps fifty metres from the building—when I started to hear big bits crumbling clean off.

When I turned, overcoming Terry's not-insignificant hold on me, I was just in time to witness a hunk of concrete slip free of the building and tumble down through the air.

It landed with an almost celebratory puff of dust.

Others soon followed.

More insistent grabbing and guiding later, and I found myself being whisked away from Green District, back towards the not-so-bright lights of Bomberlee City . . . that location used so frequently in more bad folk songs than I'm of a mind to name

. . .

As if the twins were making use of some intuitive link they shared, they both stopped at the same time, bringing me and Mertinon—as a consequence—to a stop also.

We all stood and stared as we watched the building which'd been my home crumble.

As it crumbled, it fell at an angle, tumbling into the building alongside.

And then the building alongside that.

It was all over in about ten seconds.

Just flattened rubble.

Nothing more.

"Oops," Terry said from beside me. "Hope there wasn't anybody else in those other buildings."

"Don't worry, youngster," Mertinon said. "I was the last man standing—only person stopping the whole development from getting hauled down for whatever they'd prefer to put up there instead." He shook his head, a slight smile clinging to his lips. "Well, if it'll do one thing for me, it'll give me the long-awaited kick up the backside to get up and make something of myself."

Though it might sound corny, I couldn't help but feel a steady, warm glow swill up from my gut to think that, if we could just get *through* all of this . . . if we could *just* find some way to survive . . . then it'd be a great privilege, and a pleasure, to find myself serving on the *Nava* alongside Mertinon. My brother.

Or, perhaps from my perspective, being captain and all, serving *above* him . . .

It'd be a pleasure all the same.

The twins, again seeming to operate on some unspoken plane—one which was impossible to measure by any human means—dragged me and Mertinon onwards, closer into Bomberlee City.

When we reached the edge of the city, they took us in through a narrow doorway which led to a staircase. At the top of the stairs—as there had been at *Hanx's Hoarders' Haul*—there was an array of doors to choose from. Any would've been a decent place to hide out, but, in the end, they took us all the way to the end of the hallway, to the very last room.

It was only when they brought the door shut, and showed me and Mertinon to a pair of mattresses, that there was a chance to draw breath.

It was Brian who spoke up then.

He dusted his hands off as if he'd just finished up some regrettable task.

"That's better," he said.

———

The room was just about as inconspicuous as could be usefully imagined.

It was kind of like the apartment—what'd been my childhood home—only about a quarter of the size. I supposed that the administration of Arkle-4—Big Jo, whoever—had cut back on square metres in new residential developments.

There was a kitchenette, the two mattresses—one of which me and Mertinon occupied one each—and then there was a vidscreen, switched to a static channel.

It was Brian who took it upon himself to explain.

And he did it in a way which suggested that I would throttle him if he didn't get the story out in the minimum time possible.

"Clive told us to hide," Brian said. "So we ran off . . ."

Already, I found myself getting lost.

My thoughts becoming muddled.

But I forced myself to see this through.

To wait until I had a full—if not entirely *satisfying* —explanation.

Brian continued, "We tailed the two of you, while you were

searching for us . . . Clive told us to keep our distance; that we might be in danger, he said something about how the 'net was closing in'—something about how our biggest job was to stay safe." He paused for a long time. "And to wait until you returned to the apartment, then blow the door off, make it look like there was a struggle . . . pull the two of you out."

"Well, mission accomplished," I replied, unable to quite keep the snark out of my voice.

Brian either misread my tone, or thought it was funny that he'd riled me—his *captain*. "So," Brian said, "we staked out the building, waiting to see when you would come back; and, when you did, we went to work right away." He paused. Glanced about. "There was one other thing."

"What?" I said.

"Well, Clive said there was a *device*—something he was leaving behind close by . . . he said that we'd know it when we saw it . . . that it was a message intended for you, Captain."

I felt my heart clench.

Just to hear Clive's name again sent a shiver through my blood.

To hear the name of a *traitor*.

I jerked my thumb in Terry's direction. "Told your bro to grab a hold of it—but I wouldn't waste your time. It's all garbled. The message doesn't make any sense to me . . ."

For the first time following the rescue, Brian looked a touch dejected.

I almost felt bad for having brought the feeling to bear on the kid.

He really did look like he was *crushed* . . .

"Captain?" Terry said, from somewhere near my elbow.

I could see that the habit Terry and Brian had of popping up just about anywhere on the *Nava* had transferred here to planetside. "Yeah?" I replied.

"Could I take a look at the device?"

"Knock yourself out, kid."

Terry held up the earpiece for inspection, in the same way that Mertinon had done the night before. He used the rapidly dawning daylight to get a better look at it. He turned it over and over, holding it about an arm's length away from his body as if he was afraid it might explode . . . and that him holding it at an arm's length might keep him safe if it did.

As if he was some kind of monkey making sense of a human tool for the first time, he carefully prodded the earpiece at his eardrum, working it over until he had—apparently—achieved what he believed to be a good fit.

A second or so later, and he was fluttering his eyelids, as if he'd caught sight of some teenage heartthrob . . . whatever that looked like to teenage boys these days . . .

Then he squinted hard.

Focussed in on what he could hear.

I shifted a glance at Mertinon, and then at Brian.

Brian, though, was concentrating on Terry, who beckoned him close.

"Come listen," Terry said.

Brian arrived at Terry's side, and Terry flipped the earpiece free of his ear so that the two of them could listen into the message.

I was reaching the point where I wondered if they were

having me on; if this was some kind of a misplaced—not to mention *mistimed*—joke. But, if it was, then the two boys played their part perfectly, remaining thoroughly entranced by whatever message was being spewed out through the earpiece. The two twins now engrossed by the earpiece, I shot a look over to Mertinon.

He gave me a shrug.

Despite everything—despite the fact that our childhood home was now nothing but rubble; despite the fact that we were both *surely* battling through a pair of brutal hangovers—we shared a broad grin. Finally, Brian spewed some of the beans.

"It's Foy," he said.

"Huh?" I said, shifting my attention back to the twins. "What'd you mean? I didn't recognise her voice . . . I can't understand a *damn thing* she's saying . . ."

Terry took up the slack this time. "It's because she's speaking in our language."

I thought about the twins and their cousin, Foy . . . how they'd all—once upon a time—come from Trivus-3. Before it'd been blown out of existence.

I wasn't quite sure how to feel about them sharing their own secret language; at least they'd never attempted to try it out as a secondary communication method on the ship . . . if I'd known about this little secret at all then I would've been *certain* to account for it . . .

"What's she saying?" Mertinon asked.

"She says," Brian continued, "that she wants to tell the captain that she's . . . uh"—he pulled away from the earpiece—"'Sorry'," he finished.

I shook my head. " 'Sorry' for what?"

And then, before either of the twins could reply, I put the pieces together—realising that it hadn't been only Clive who'd been in on this whole deal . . . that Foy, and, it seemed, Milky had been too.

I turned my thoughts back to my conversation with Richard 'Ricky D' Hernandez on that planet I'd done everything in my power to forget. How he'd made this whole big *deal* about how he hadn't *really* 'kidnapped' Foy and Milky . . . and there I was believing he was just being cute; that he was trying to do what *all* gangsters—without exception—attempt to do . . . make themselves out to be legitimate. Although I was beginning to feel a numbing sensation crawling its way through my body—from my toes, all the way up my back, and beyond—I did my best to listen in to what else Foy, and Milky, apparently, had to say.

This time Terry picked up the slack.

"Sorry that she had to accept the job—that she deserted the *Navaplastas* . . . but she hopes that you'll understand."

I tried to process this information.

And failed.

I pulled myself free of my daze. "Does she say when she's planning on coming back?"

Brian shook his head.

He exchanged glances with Terry, then added, "I don't think she will come back—either her *or* Milky . . . from the sounds of things they're planning on staying with Big Jo for the rest of their, uh"—Brian appeared to be searching for the appropriate word—"*career*."

I felt an almost ticklish sensation making its way up from my gut.

My lungs seemed to pinch in on themselves.

I had to sit down on the mattress.

That felt better.

I felt more secure.

Grounded.

But, still, without so much as a clue on how to proceed.

Or *if* there was any way to proceed.

13 ANONYMOUS HIDEOUT - CLICKING INTO PLACE - ARKLE-4

W E SPENT the best part of a week in the hideout as I put all the pieces of the puzzle together. It took me a while to sort through the jumble; to work out what might be paranoia, misinterpretation, or whatever else. In the end, it all began to look much the same.

I traced back how Clive had been the one to set up the job which'd led to that fateful hit-and-run kidnap. I wondered if Milky and Foy had known anything about *anything*.

As I sat slumped up in a chair, staring out through the apartment window, into the deserted, dejected streets of Bomberlee City, I noted Terry out of the corner of my vision. I paid him little attention, trusting he would come out with whatever it was he felt he had to come out with.

"Clive programmed the earpiece from a remote location," Terry said.

I continued to stare out from under glass, feeling the chilly air coming off the surface.

I said nothing in reply.

Terry continued.

"It seems that he managed to get in touch with Foy and Milky planetside, here, and he managed to set the message to automatically run on the earpiece."

I felt a sigh raising my shoulders.

I puffed it out.

Somehow managed a "That's great, kid."

Terry held back.

I wondered if he was hoping for some kind of kudos; a fatherly pat on the head for his good work. But, quite frankly, I just wasn't in the mood. How'd I ended up being the father of a pair of orphans? . . . Hell, a *trio* if I counted the missing Milky . .
.

"Captain?" Terry said.

"What?"

"There's something else."

My stomach sank slightly.

I turned away from the window.

Faced him.

"What is it *now?*" I said, unable to keep the coiled-up tension out of my voice.

Terry backed up a couple of steps. His eyes swivelled about their sockets, meeting mine for a fraction of a second before darting off to somewhere else, across the room. "With the earpiece," he said, "I managed to patch it into the *Nava's* systems."

I near enough fell out of my chair.

Thankfully, though, I caught myself before I hit the ground.

Before I knew it, I was up on my feet.

Approaching Terry.

Shoulders hunched, features no doubt all pinched as I bore down on him.

"What you say?"

Unsure of himself now, Terry backed up several more steps, until, with a *thud*, he made contact with the apartment wallpaper. From the looks of the soiled material; the damp oozing out from beneath the surface, it was advisable to spend as little time as possible in contact with it.

"The *Nava*," Terry got out, managing not to babble or stutter, "I got in *touch* with her."

Losing control of myself now, I reached out and grabbed hold of Terry's shoulders.

Gripped them tightly.

His cute little face filled my vision.

"Where?" I said. "Where *is* she?"

Terry blinked rapidly. "She . . . she . . ." He took a gulp of air, gathering himself together; trying his best to placate his overexcited captain. "*She's* at the terminal."

Realising how tightly I was gripping Terry's shoulders, I let off slightly.

I backed up from him.

I reached for my forehead, feeling for the filled-in hole there. As it had done ever since it'd got patched up, it ached a great deal. This last week, though, it seemed to have started to ache even worse than before. I knew in my heart of hearts that

I'd be best served getting some proper medical attention—rather than from the kid who'd hung out a shingle as Ship's Doctor—but, being the hardened space smuggler I am, I didn't see the point.

Just more wasted time.

And it wasn't like it was a *vital* organ, or anything.

Not in my line of work.

The boundless enthusiasm was tapered slightly.

Although it salved me to know her location, it wasn't much comfort to know that she was at the terminal; a place I would have little to no chance of infiltrating.

I glanced back up to Terry. "Any more info?" I said.

He started to shake his head, then stopped himself. "Well," he replied. "There was *one* thing."

"What?" I put in, my tone sharp.

"She's being staffed by Clive Wodd—he's been appointed captain."

Right then it felt as though an enormous, yawning gulch was opening up right beneath the soles of my boots. I thought I would take a tumble and just keep on going . . . right down to the core of Arkle-4.

I couldn't help uttering, "The man has no shame—no shame *at all.*"

———

"So," Mertinon said, "you fancy running me through the plan another time?"

I glanced up to Mertinon, away from the vidscreen we had

projected across the bare wooden floorboards of the apartment. Then I looked to the twins, to Brian and Terry, the two of them wearing an expression stuck somewhere between apprehension and excitement.

To be honest, I supposed I looked pretty similar.

There's something about adventure—a sense of wonder—in boys, in men, which can never quite be knocked out of them . . .

I looked back down to the vidscreen.

Fancy, complicated plans have never really been my bag. I much prefer to Keep It Simple Stupid, or, even more often, to just Keep It Stupid . . .

The vidscreen showed a virtual, real-time blueprint of the terminal.

Through the earpiece, Terry had managed to access one of Milky's programs on the *Nava's* systems. One which was designed for hacking into terminal computers and getting any information which might be required.

This particular blueprint showed off the entrances and exits to the terminal building. It also showed the people moving about the terminal; each of them represented by a tiny blue dot. Their personal identifications were available at the touch of a fingertip. Although it was only a number, Terry explained that he'd hooked up another program which'd cross reference any of their personal identifications with a database of names, places, occupations, etcetera.

What interested me the most, however, were the flight paths of delivery drones, constantly streaming in and out through a service entrance.

Indeed, when I put my mind to it, when I turned my attention out of the apartment window, and in the direction of the terminal, I realised that I could make out the unending stream of drones all humming through the air; each of them with their package clasped in the grappling hook beneath.

That was our way in.

I suppose it must've been the knowledge that Clive had commandeered *my* ship for himself which'd really kicked me into gear; which'd proven to me that we'd sat back and *watched on* for long enough.

In fact, when I summed up what'd befallen me these past weeks, it started to truly piss me off:

First, they'd pinched, arguably, the two most valuable members of my crew.

Second, they'd lulled me into a trap; stolen the *Nava*.

A truly unforgiveable transgression.

Third, they'd brought me back here—to Arkle-4—and trapped me for what seemed to be Forevermore.

Well, no way—*no fucking way*—not if I could help it.

I decided that if this was my time to get greased then so be it.

I could only get greased once, so what the hell was I afraid of?

I turned my attention back to Mertinon, gave him the slightest of smiles—somewhere between exhilaration and hysteria—and explained.

"This drone, here," I said, "it'll be big enough for all of us . . . after studying its patterns over the past few days, running that, whatcha-call-it—"

"Flight-path scan," Terry put in, obviously wanting to be helpful.

I snapped my fingers in his direction, recognising his contribution, just as any pseudo father figure surely should. "Yeah, that," I said, then turned back to Mertinon, and the vidscreen. "It makes a drop at this place; *Fryers-4-All* . . ."

"Yeah," Mertinon replied, scratching his head, "that place is known throughout the universe—get deep fryers for repair from all over the place there . . . from what I hear, they get calls from as far as Fritten, too."

"Terrific," I said, realising we were getting side-tracked. "So, the plan will be to intercept this drone, when it arrives for the drop-off . . . we all jump inside, and it takes us into the terminal building."

"Then what?" Brian said.

"We take back the *Nava*."

Brian screwed up his features. "Didn't you say Clive's the captain now? What if he's shifted all the security systems about, made it so that nothing's how it was?"

I glanced across the vidscreen, to Terry, then gave a smile. "You know, I think we'll be able to wheedle some sort of a Trojan horse . . . what'd you think, Terry?"

Terry just beamed back at me.

Hell, I was glad the kid could be put to *some* use.

———

We waited till dark.

It probably comes as no surprise that the busiest time of day on Arkle-4 is right after Mertinon slips below the horizon, and night comes to bear on everything. Since the majority of business on Arkle-4 is somewhat clandestine—and the clandestine prefers as little light as possible—it kind of makes sense.

Still, just because we were in good company, when it came down to people up to no good, it didn't mean we took no precautions.

Each one of us got hold of a pair of jet-black overalls—kind of similar to those which the security detail Big Jo employed used—and we snuck through the back streets.

After the experience of waking up in the street myself, I took as much care as I could manage not to step on anyone. But, in the end, it proved somewhat impossible to miss *all* the hunched-up bodies lying massed together.

I caught a couple of drug-addled, "Heys!" and "Watchow!"

. . . But, from the tone of the voices—from their defeated nature—I couldn't quite see any one of them angling for a fight.

Especially with someone who still possessed a—*mostly* —fresh mind.

We got to *Fryers-4-All* after about an hour of sleuthing.

I gathered all the others behind me as I pressed myself up against a nearby wall, peering around the corner to get a sense of our surroundings.

I watched on as droids filed in and out of the building, through their specific doors.

Then I turned my attention upwards, sure enough seeing the endless file of drones humming through the air, passing through the upper-storey doors; each of them carrying their cargo; cardboard boxes of some sort, no doubt filled with deep fryers for fixing.

More importantly, I spied the other file of drones.

The ones headed back to the terminal.

I glanced back at my team . . . over my *crew* . . . and shot them a toothy grin. "All right, gang, any last words?"

Nobody said anything.

If they'd wanted to pull out that was their chance.

————

The back entrance to *Fryers-4-All* was poorly guarded—which was to say that it wasn't guarded at all. And some careless, unintentionally generous soul, had left a blaster rifle hanging off a wall; no doubt for some human foreman to deal with any of the homeless who might attempt to take shelter in the warehouse during the night.

I tossed the blaster rifle over to Mertinon.

He always had been the best shot of the two of us.

We skipped along through the factory, dodging the endless deep-fat fryers gathered on the warehouse floor. Droids constantly saw to the fryers; carefully lifting them up and laying them down on the appropriate conveyor belt. I glanced about, catching sight of a couple of security droids across the warehouse. I hadn't so much as raised a *squeak* before the two of them blew up into approximately a thousand bits and pieces.

I turned back to Mertinon, finding myself on the other end of his wide—*wild*—grin.

"Oops," he said.

I gave him a good-boy pat and we moved on, rushing up the staircase.

Headed for the drone bay.

———

I glanced back to Terry. He was wearing the earpiece—our direct link to the *Nava*. I asked him for an update on the progress of the drone.

Actually, what I *really* asked him for was the time.

Thankfully, his standards of humour were higher than responding, 'Time you got a watch' . . .

We had approximately half a minute to wait.

I looked over my crew, wondering if there was anything we were missing. Well, we were still two members down—minus our *traitor*—but we'd hopefully take care of that before too long. We'd even managed to snag ourselves a weapon, too, so things weren't looking too bleak.

Then again, it'd be a whole different matter dealing with whatever security measures were in place at the terminal, than a pair of two-bit security droids at a deep-fryer repair warehouse.

When the droid arrived—like some sort of whale when compared to its sleeker brethren—I eyed up the cargo hold, and then, having deposited its load, it hovered right over our heads. I leaped up and grabbed its sides. Yanked it down towards us.

It let loose a *howl* which would've made any cat proud.

Lots of flickering danger-red lights, too.

With the twins' help, we got the cargo bay doors open in a manual fashion—which is to say that we dug our fingertips into the gap and tugged them wide open. Like the gentleman captain I am, I helped all the members of my crew inside before deigning to add my bulk to the drone's weight.

There was a fairly hairy moment when I convinced myself —perhaps the drone even convinced *itself*—that we wouldn't be able to get airborne again.

And a hairier moment still when the drone continued to make a ruckus with all its alarms and lights. Before long, though, I felt that joyful, weightless feeling which it seemed I hadn't felt for *such a time* . . . us taking to the air.

Headed for the terminal.

———

Using the earpiece, his finger sticking in his eardrum, Terry updated us on our progress; on the current location of our flight path as related to the terminal. We didn't need Terry to tell us that the drone was slowing down, though; that we were closing on our destination.

Mertinon, for one, the way he'd been fawning over the blaster rifle—cleaning this; grubbing that—seemed like he was *raring* to go.

That was the sort of spirit we needed.

Even if we died, we'd do it with a roar on our lips.

The drone cranked to a halt—apparently struggling with our *larger-than-usual* weight—and the cargo doors wound open.

It was only when I looked out through the doors that I realised an issue with our plan.

A drop.

A *long* drop.

Four . . . *five* storeys?

I looked back to the others within the drone. "Go round again?" I said, searching for something to contribute.

It was then that Brian arrived beside me.

He peered out of the drone.

Pointed.

"Up ahead," he said. "You see that?"

I followed his finger.

Watched on as the drones, in their distinctive, neat file— following the invisible waymarks in the air—passed through a large, stainless-steel loop.

Realising what it was—that it was a *steriliser*, designed to get the drones nice and *fresh* for their next shipment—I turned back to my crew, and said, loud and proud, "*Shit.*"

I estimated that we had about twenty seconds to make up our collective mind.

It came down to a choice between death from falling —*quick; instantaneous even*—and death from radiation sickness —*long; drawn-out.*

Somehow, I couldn't help thinking that all the life choices I'd made to that time had been leading to a decisive point just like that one.

Well, at least I had a *choice* of how to die . . .

"Over there!" Terry called out.

I followed *his* finger—identical to Brian's.

He was pointing out a ladder.

Currently it was attached to a ventilation duct.

We were about to pass by it.

There was no time to think.

I looked to Mertinon, who looked back at me. He shouldered the blaster rifle, took a couple of steps back and then hurled himself out of the side of the drone.

For someone of his size and bulk—superior even to *mine*—it was a wonder to watch him flop through the air, and somehow grab a hold of the ladder rungs. If the fact that he made it at all was a minor miracle, then it was a real god-buster that he managed to hang on and swing himself up.

I suppose that fat bodies can be deceptive.

Who's to say there aren't at least some muscles beneath those rolls of flab?

The twins were next, the two of them jumping at the same time.

And catching onto the ladder at the same time too.

I spent a good while thinking things through.

I wondered if I really—*really*—wanted to go on living in a world where I was both kept apart from the *Nava* and forced to reside on Arkle-4.

In the end, I chose life.

I knew something had gone badly wrong from the moment my foot left the drone behind.

Perhaps the drone, pleased to be relieved of our weight, was in the process of restabilising itself—of trying to level out with the other drones. The upshot of whatever it was that was going on was that the drone dipped in the air.

When I leaped free of the drone, I clawed above me, for the rungs of the ladder attached to the ventilation hatch. But it was in vain.

I tumbled down.

It's times like those when I wonder if some kind of feline gene doesn't run in my family.

I felt myself turning in the air—not significantly, but at least shifting myself around so that, instead of being stomach-down, I was now side-on.

The last image which filled my brain was of my crew, all of them stopped in their advancement up the ladder. Hanging down, their eyes fixed on mine. Mouths latched open.

Somehow I managed to formulate the words:

"Do it!"

It was either a mumble, or a cry.

Maybe I was the only one who heard it.

"Do it for the *Nava*!"

14 TERMINAL - ARKLE-4

I CAME TO with the sound of machination all around me.

My head throbbed harder than I'd ever felt before.

When I angled my elbow around, attempting to prop myself up into some kind of a sitting position, pain racked my body. It blinded my thoughts. Made me bite down, into my tongue.

Until I tasted blood.

I breathed in quickly, and then, realising that wasn't going to be all that effective if I ever wanted to settle into a normal respiration pattern, I eased my pace.

I took in deep breaths.

Allowed my shoulders to flex backwards, even though it sent shudders of pain across my abdomen; seemingly through every single one of my muscles.

My heart leaped up to my throat.

It beat hard, as if in its death throes.

Sweat was dribbling down my face.

. . . But I was lying on something soft.

Something . . . *unsubstantial.*

I padded about me.

Realised I had my eyes closed.

I opened them.

Took in the scene.

Black.

I was surrounded by *black.*

I might've thought there was no light if it wasn't for the dazzling strip lights which hung above me. I reached out, realising that it was black material; that they were overalls.

Those same overalls which Big Jo's security detail wore.

I switched my mind back, thought about what'd happened.

There I'd been, flopping through the air with all the grace of a banked salmon, when it'd suddenly got dark. I wondered if it was because I'd blacked out.

But I had no recollection of closing my eyes.

No, the blacking out part had come a little later.

As I'd fallen, I remembered the long waiting for the body-breaking *crack-thud* as I hit the cement floor. But it hadn't come. And I recalled seeing the land all rising up about me—*continuing to rise about me*—as if I was somehow on an express train to Arkle-4's own brand of hell.

Was I in hell now?

Some kind of hell of my own making?

Well, if I was, then the devil surely knew how to punish me without mercy.

He kept me in my same, earth-dwelling body.

The same, flubbing, good-for-nothing model . . .

With this revelation sketching my mind, I rocked back onto my knees, manoeuvring myself into a sort of crawling position. I felt my hands and knees becoming buried in the overalls. As if I might be on the verge of sinking.

Keep moving . . .

I *had* to keep on moving.

So I did.

It took me another few moments to actually find somewhere to aim for.

A black doorway.

It looked just as likely as anything else here to be an exit.

Maybe I spent the best part of a day trying to reach that blackened doorway, it certainly felt as if it was some kind of an epic journey. As I made my way across the discarded overalls, I couldn't help but bring to mind my crew, and what might've become of them.

I reassured myself that Terry had the earpiece.

He had contact with the *Nava.*

He was the most important for the time being.

Me?

Right then, I felt like nothing but an extra . . .

I reached the exit, realised that it was a tube.

It took me another second before I registered an other-worldly *swish-swoop,* and another one still before I got hit— square in the nose—by a fresh batch of laundry.

More uniforms.

They hit me with all the force of a wet flannel dropping off a washing line, but, all the same, in my condition, they managed to knock me from my feet.

And back into the main pool of black overalls.

I gathered my thoughts for a moment, told myself that I was being nothing short of a sissy, and that it was about time for me to get my *man* on.

So, sucking in my chest, and prepping my muscles, I set about the task—again on my hands and knees—of making my way slowly up through the tube.

The incline was nothing too steep, and when a few fresh consignments of overalls came tumbling down, I had the good sense to treat them for what they were.

Just clothes.

They brushed past me on their way down.

It was only when I'd nearly reached the top of the tube that an idea dawned on me.

The idea which—*surely*—must be as old as time itself.

When another one of the overalls slid past, I reached out and grabbed hold of it.

On impulse more than anything else, I gave it a quick sniff.

I was surprised to discover that it had a zesty, *fresh* smell.

As if it'd been recently washed.

More than just washed . . . *laundered.*

With the purloined overall bunched in my fist, I set about clambering my way up the tube. Soon enough, I reached the top. The tube levelled out and I eyed a hole, through which a droid was stuffing the overalls.

Acting quickly, I got myself changed out of the black clothes I'd thought would be perfect for this night-time raid of the terminal, and I put on the overalls.

It was tight, but I *made* them fit.

Hell, I wasn't going for any sort of *fashion* prize.

This was a purely functional garment.

All zipped up, and ready to go, I slipped down the tube, finding myself—immediately—surrounded by what I could only describe as a *factory*.

My mouth surely latched open of its own accord.

Since there was nobody around to shut my jaw for me, I reached up myself, and gave my chin a firm shove upwards.

Droids ... perhaps *hundreds* of them ...

It was difficult to reconcile exactly what they were doing at first.

That they were all busying themselves about sewing machines; that they were, each of them, overseeing the creation of clothing; precisely the black overalls worn by security, the ones which *I* was wearing right now.

I suddenly felt somewhat shifty, to be in a place like this; kind of like when you stumble across a secret which somebody has surely kept closely guarded for a long, old while.

When you're the only one privy to a secret.

I thought back to the *Fryers-4-All* warehouse.

To compare the activity there with the activity I saw here and now, it was almost like another world . . . or, maybe more accurately, as if this industry was all being exerted in the interest of *creating* another world.

I managed to get myself up against a wall before I found myself in any real trouble.

And, to be honest, when I did get myself tangled in trouble, it was Fairly Major Trouble Indeed.

"Halt!" came the eerily neutral, synthesised voice.

———

In my experience, when you're the one burgling into someplace —the one who's *quite clearly* in the wrong—then it's better to just fess up if you're caught.

You're on someone else's territory, after all . . . even if that *someone else* is a droid.

Actually, *especially* if that someone else is a droid.

Droids have never been renown for either flexibility or mercy.

If they were then they might as well just hire a human for half the cost . . .

I stared back at the droids—two of them—as they fixed their blasters on me.

I looked into their tinted camera lenses, wondering just what might be going on behind that blacked-out glass. Were they running my numbers—my personal identification?

Undoubtedly.

"Error," the droid said, as far as I knew the same one who'd first spoken. "Personal Identification Read Error. Prepare for arrest."

The other droid, too, moved in on me; its mechanical joints whirring and whining as its articulated limbs prepared to pull the trigger if at all necessary.

I noted the handcuffs which'd been produced, thought long and hard about freedom, and then, seeing the gap, decided to run.

Several times I stumbled.

Almost fell flat on my face.

Those stumbles, though, as it turned out, worked in my favour. Each one of them seemed to perfectly sync with the laser blasts burning through the air; brushing up against my skin . . . singeing my beard in several places. Finally, I got myself clear of the room.

But it was only to hear a flat, flatulent claxon and to see many blinking red lights.

I also made out the sound of grinding gears as the whole place was churning into lockdown.

I needed to get out of here, and I needed to get out fast.

As I thrust myself onwards, I couldn't help but think about all the trouble I might've been able to avoid if I'd only thought to make a habit of keeping my earpiece in *ear* while I was down planetside. But, then again, I'd hardly got the chance to do so before Big Jo had snatched the *Nava* out of my grasp.

That's my excuse and I'm sticking to it . . .

Up ahead, I eyed a fire shutter rolling down to block the hallway beyond. I drew on just about every single muscle in my body—and bent several bones—to throw myself onto my front and soar in beneath the gap as it closed behind me.

When I dusted myself off, got to my feet, I heard the dull *thump-thump* as a pair of laser shots hit the blast door at my heels.

I stepped away.

And into a welcome crowd.

I took my bearings, realising that I'd made it back into the main terminal building of Arkle-4. People bustled about me, all of them apparently trying to get somewhere or other. All of them, I noticed, wore the same black overalls that *I* wore . . .

and, as I got closer to them, I couldn't help but see that they all had hastily patched-up portions of their foreheads.

Before I got a proper chance to consider this detail, I heard somebody call out to me.

Well, actually, it was more of a *"Psst!"*

I turned to look.

Saw who it was immediately.

Mertinon.

My good old, good-for-nothing brother.

Just like before, he had his blaster rifle slung over his shoulder.

I had to admit that the fact he didn't have either a pair of overalls on or a hole in the head meant that he stood out.

Mertinon grinned at me, called me closer. "Thought you were a goner, brother," he said.

"Yeah, me too," I replied. "Where're the others?"

Without speaking anything in reply, still grinning, he reached up, and, with two fingers spread, indicated an area out ahead . . . it took me a second to realise that he was indicating the landing bay; the location of the parked-up spaceships.

I turned back to Mertinon. "And what're you doing here?"

"Giving covering fire."

I screwed up my eyes. "Don't look much like it to me."

"Ah," Mertinon said, smiling wider still, "it's all in the brain, brother, *all* in the brain."

Unsure what he was precisely getting at, and, to be honest, not all that concerned to discover the truth, I shifted my attention to the landing bay; trying to pick out Brian and Terry, who, apparently, in my absence, had taken it upon themselves to lead this raid.

Cheeky buggers.

My heart near enough leaped free of my throat and right into my mouth when I laid eyes on her . . . and this time it wasn't the *Nava* . . . no, it was *Foy*.

I took in her honey-coloured hair, the peachy eyes I could make out, even from here, and the rosy cheeks. Even in such a drab piece of clothing as the black overalls Big Jo had his boys wear, Foy stood out. But, I supposed, her appearance hadn't been the leading factor in Big Jo wishing to recruit her. No, I was certain that it was for her gunner skills.

My attention shifted across the bay.

Again, my heart lurched.

Petur Hgun.

Or, as I knew him, *Milky*.

Despite being placed in Big Jo's service, he hadn't been made to part with the plait which bounced down off his lower back.

Like Foy—like everybody else about the terminal—he was wearing the black overalls.

Although it weighed my heart down to do so, I shifted my glance across the crowds, over to the others wearing the black overalls, searching for the twins.

I spoke low to Mertinon, still crouching down, his blaster rifle over his shoulder, as if he was some space marine just waiting to be called into action.

Perhaps this was all he'd ever dreamed of . . . the *adventure* he'd dreamed of.

"Can't see them," I said.

"Who?"

"The twins."

Mertinon met my eye. "Leave them be," he said. "They'll get the job done, I bet. Just got to give them a bit of a loose rein." He grinned wide and toothy—again, it seemed out of place given the perilous situation. "Might surprise you."

Although I didn't say it to Mertinon, the last thing I wanted right then was a surprise.

Not *unpleasant* surprises, in any case.

As we stooped down there, half-hidden behind a concrete pillar, I wondered what was going to come next. When I'd first arrived beside Mertinon, I'd felt almost overwhelmingly para-noid about the droids turning up—lasers blasting—searching for the One Who Got Away. Now, though, I'd got past that fear. I'd moved onto a far more *solid* fear . . . I was concerned that the twins were going to get themselves captured.

That, like Foy and Milky before them, they would be kidnapped.

And it'd be all *my* fault.

I turned back to Mertinon, shaking my head. "Come on," he said. "It's been too long—they might be in trouble." I rose from the hiding place, expecting Mertinon to follow me.

Instead, though, he grabbed hold of the sleeve of my overalls.

Jerked me back down.

If I'd really tried, I might've been able to overwhelm his hold, but, in the end, I couldn't quite bring myself to break away from him.

I suppose, though it pisses me off even to *think* it, that I was just a smudge afraid.

I was, more or less, in the belly of the beast, after all.

"Just give them a minute," Mertinon said, his voice firm, unshakable. "Give them a minute—for Ma and Pa."

I held myself very still, silently cursing Mertinon for bringing personal stuff to bear on this. Just what *in hell* could Ma and Pa possibly have to do with the situation we currently found ourselves embroiled in?

Nothing, that was what . . .

But it didn't make his tactic any less effective.

I remained where I was.

Watching.

Waiting.

I kept my eyes trained on Foy and Milky.

Studying them for any sudden movements.

They didn't seem to be in any rush.

I was nearing the end of my tether, and I was ready to break away from Mertinon, this time for real, when I heard an enormous *whoosh* filling the air. I felt an extreme heat up against my cheeks. It felt like—if I so much as allowed it—it would be capable of melting my skin right off my bones.

But I had no *intention* of allowing it . . .

When I stood this time, Mertinon made no motion to stop me.

In fact, he rose to his feet too.

The two of us stared at the sight facing us.

The ship—the *Navaplastas*—hovering about the terminal.

People lay on their bellies; it was impossible for them to

remain in a standing position. They pressed themselves flat against the ground. The material of their black overalls flapped with the gush of warm air pouring through the terminal.

Somehow, perhaps it was just some divine *strength*, me and Mertinon remained standing.

Although Mertinon might've been doing his best impression of a space marine, I'm the one with all the experience of these stressful situations. And so I guessed that was the reason why I was the one to grab hold of him; to jerk him clean off the spot and towards the *Nava* . . . and the ladder which was stretching down to collect us.

Transfixed by the ladder dangling down, Mertinon almost made it to the rungs before I called him back. He turned to face me, his expression sketched with a kind of delight I'd never expected him to show . . . all those moisers, all of those years of solitude, had they been a means for suppressing his inner-most desires?

For suppressing the kid in him?

He wanted nothing more than to get up into the spaceship.

To fly away.

But we couldn't leave just yet.

Having caught Mertinon's attention now, I gestured towards Foy and Milky, who, like the others, were lying flat on the ground; knocked over by the power of the reverse thrusters. Mertinon seemed to snap into action, realising what it was that had to be done. The two of us dashed for Foy and Milky; me jerking Foy to her feet, while Mertinon took care of Milky.

Together, we did our best to get to the ladder of the *Nava* as quickly as we could manage.

I helped Foy's near-senseless fingers to feel the rungs.

I eased her up the ladder.

And then I stood by at the base of the ladder, watching on as Mertinon got Milky up there.

I was the last to look out about the terminal, to all the faces sketched with total surprise at what they were witnessing . . . people breaking free of Arkle-4.

I took one last—*deeply aware*—breath of the Arkle-4 oxygen, and, with a definite exhale, blew it right out of me.

I would never come back here.

Not in a million years.

15 THE NAVAPLASTAS - DESTINATION UNKNOWN

I T FELT GOOD—*really good*—to slump back in the captain's chair.

I listened to the springs slinking about beneath my weight.

I slowed my breathing, no doubt experiencing the kind of inner peace which Yoga enthusiasts toil away for years to achieve.

When me and Mertinon had arrived on the bridge of the *Nava*, it'd been to discover Terry holding the ship's position, at the controls, while Brian busied himself plotting a course away from Arkle-4 . . . that must be the sweetest phrase in the *whole* history of human language:

Away from Arkle-4

I had to admit that the twins *had* surprised me.

I'd never thought they'd manage to single-handedly burgle into the *Nava*, let alone have the nous or knowledge to fire up the engines and send her to Outer Space.

Maybe my brother Mertinon was onto something.

Perhaps I *should* give people a chance to surprise me . . .

Content with the rest I'd given myself, I glanced about the bridge.

Terry was present, having taken over from his brother at the navigational screens; while Mertinon was seated in the co-pilot's chair, just as I'd promised him.

Brian was seeing to Foy and Milky in the medbay; seeing just what kind of damage Big Jo had inflicted upon them.

I realised I could hear footsteps sounding in the corridor leading to the bridge. I turned in my chair to see Brian darkening the doorway.

"Everything okay?" I said.

"Captain," Brian replied, a touch red-faced. "You need to come see this."

With a deep sigh, I turned control of the ship over to Mertinon, who eagerly took up his place in my captain's chair. His style was delightfully enthusiastic . . . there was none of this slouching in the chair and kicking his feet back onto the control board. Nope, he perched himself right on the very edge of the cushion and gripped the stick as if we were navigating an asteroid field; rather than just drifting about in open space.

No job.

No destination.

I left the bridge behind, following Brian to the medbay.

When we got there, I immediately noted the pair of examination tables; and one patient lying on top of each.

Brian shifted a nervous glance at me.

I saw for myself just what the trouble was; just what'd

necessitated pulling the captain from where he was quite content—not to mention *comfortable*—on the bridge.

Foy and Milky, I saw, like me, had holes in their heads.

And just like the hole in my head, their holes had been patched up.

I glanced to Brian who looked just as clueless as I felt.

I moved closer to Milky, deciding to examine him first.

Yep, sure enough, it was a *hole* . . .

"I gave them each a sedative," Brian said, from my heels. "When the two of them got up here, into the ship, they seemed disorientated, and then . . . well . . ."

"What?" I said, now examining the hole in Foy's head.

"They got *angry* . . ."

" 'Angry' ?" I replied, turning to Brian as if it was his fault for simply stating the facts.

He nodded back at me dolefully.

I shook my head, turned my attention back to Foy and Milky. "Jesus, why'd they get *angry*? We've just saved their skins —just *liberated* them from kidnap . . ."

I just stewed there for several minutes, not really sure what to make of all this . . . of all these *holes* in people's heads . . . of the hole in my *own* head . . .

"Captain?"

"What?"

"We're still missing a member of the crew—we left someone behind—"

I felt a flash of anger.

I turned on Brian. "Who?" I said, voice thick with fury. "*Who'd* we leave behind?"

Brian went for the smart option.

He pressed his lips together.

Remained silent.

With a nervous smile, he slipped from the medbay.

I turned back to the patients—to Foy and Milky—glancing over their sleeping faces.

I drew in a steady breath, then gave a shake of my head.

There're some things which're just beyond me . . . just *totally* beyond me . . . and this was one of those.

————

We were perhaps half a day's journey out of Arkle-4 when I heard the proximity alarms pinging away. I glanced over my shoulder, to Terry, still at the navigational screens . . . where he might end up staying now that Clive was off the team . . . he looked back at me, then said, "Incoming, Captain."

Despite the gravity of the situation, he wore a slight smile.

I could tell, like my brother Mertinon, he was greatly enjoying his new role.

Having *something* to do on the ship.

"How many?" I said.

Brian shook his head. "Pretty sizeable fleet, I'd say."

"Port of origin?"

"Unknown," Brian replied, and then looked up at me again, "but I'd bet anything that they're coming at us from Arkle-4."

I twitched my nose. "Yeah," I said, "you're probably right."

I rose to my feet, not because there was anything I could

immediately do to help with the situation, but more because it *felt* the right thing to do.

I ran my hands through my hair.

"Got any IDs on those ships yet?"

Brian was halfway through shaking his head, when he stopped himself.

He locked his gaze on the navigational screens.

"What?" I said, moving towards him. "What is it?"

But I was soon close enough to see for myself—to see the ID tags as they popped up above the dots which represented the ships.

To see the one which most struck my imagination.

Ghost Wave

On impulse, I turned back to Mertinon, who was looking extremely attentively at his co-pilot's controls. "Listen," I said, "does anything about *Ghost Wave* chime with you? Sound familiar to you at all?"

Mertinon turned away from his useless twiddling for a moment.

He met my eye.

"Sure," he said, a slight smirk on his lips.

Feeling like I was being an idiot somehow, I prompted him further. "What? What does it mean?"

Mertinon gave a shrug. "It's Big Jo's flagship—everybody on Arkle-4 knows that." He arched an eyebrow. "Surely *you* know that."

"His flagship," I repeated, mostly to myself. "Yeah, Big Jo's flagship. Now I remember."

"How come?" Mertinon put in.

"Because," I said, turning my attention back to the navigational screens, "it's heading right for us—it's *pursuing* us."

That was when Mertinon went pale.

He looked—very briefly—like he might be about to faint.

"Bad reputation?" I said, testing the waters.

When Mertinon spoke again, his voice was weak, like it might give up on him at any given moment. "You could put it that way," he finally replied.

———

There was nothing to be done, of course.

Without Clive on board to work his magic on the engines, we were stuck maintaining the same pace. One of the kids— maybe it was Terry, again—had the bright idea of switching power from the weapons into the thrusters . . . and that succeeded in only flooding the engines; and allowing the fleet to get even closer.

Watching the navigational screens, I was reaching breaking point, knowing that there would be nothing for us to do—that we could only surrender ourselves again and hope that they'd show us mercy . . . ask them *nicely* not to swipe the *Nava* out of my hands again.

Talk about wishful thinking . . .

Since there was nothing else to be done, I turned to Mertinon again.

For whatever reason, I'd allowed him to sit in the captain's chair.

And, despite the oncoming peril, and that revelation I'd

dropped about it being Big Jo's flagship closing on us, he again wore a wide, old grin.

I spoke almost to myself, though my words were loud enough for Mertinon to hear. "What does he want?" I said. "What does he want *with me?*"

Mertinon remained focussed at the controls of the *Nava*, as if I might take them off him if he showed even a momentary lapse in concentration. "Like I said, Arkle, he doesn't like that you sided with them—that you went with the FSA." He turned his attention full onto me now. "You're like the little fishy that got away." He shook his head, turned back to the controls. "Just think—someone with your aptitude; with *your* talents, and, to them, you went right on over to the dark side."

"Yeah," I replied, my brain hitting some kind of automatic gear. "The *dark side*."

Brian soon joined us on the bridge to witness the closing fleet of ships, and everybody got to their feet. I could tell that not one of us had any interest in dying while sitting down. We wanted to face our enemy and die with something approaching bravery.

"How many are there?" I asked Terry, my lips almost making the sounds without any intervention from my brain.

"Over thirty," Terry replied. "At last count."

"Jesus," I said, "they're sending the entire fleet after us . . ."

This time it was Mertinon who spoke. "They don't just want you, Arkle—they want your crew . . . they want your *ship* . . . Big Jo, he wants everything back; as he sees it, he wants *everything back* that you took from him . . ."

I stared at the navigational screens.

Watched on—*powerless*—as the approaching fleet, as *Ghost Wave*, locked onto the *Nava's* proximity systems, and, without so much as batting an eyelash—in spaceship terms—overrode the hack protection . . . drew the *Nava* towards it with the tractor beam.

All of us shifted our attention to one of the portholes, and we watched on as *Ghost Wave* towered above us, like an enormous, all-encompassing submarine placed against . . . how had Mertinon phrased it? . . . a little *fishy*.

16 BANGED UP ON BOARD
GHOST WAVE

PERHAPS I EXPECTED another one of those blasts from the past, like when we'd arrived on Arkle-4 . . . how Captain Norbortwitz—*Ernest Harry*—had arrived to give me a special welcome home. But not this time. All we got this time was an extremely well-armed squad of security and droids; all of them bearing no-nonsense blasters, and looking like they were awfully twitchy individuals, especially when it came to their trigger fingers.

I mostly put my hands up in the air and went out of my way not to piss anybody off.

I held out some hope that the intruders wouldn't think to search the rest of the ship; that they'd, for some reason, stop themselves once they'd found the best part of the crew standing on the bridge.

This was extremely mistaken, though, of course.

On the contrary, they were very thorough with their search,

going onto the medbay, where they located both Foy and Milky; bringing the two of them along on a pair of hover stretchers.

Whatever it was that Brian had dosed them with, the marketing campaign behind the drug could quite comfortably say that it'd allow the patient to sleep right through a hijacking . . . whether or not that'd be a selling point they'd pursue, who's to say . . .

Ghost Wave was a nice enough ship, in the way that enormous, great big battle cruisers are *nice* ships. I couldn't help but speculate as to how I'd missed the thing when Foy and Milky had first got themselves kidnapped . . . my best guess was that it remained out in space, sending down shuttles to whatever terminal was nearby.

It was certainly too big for any terminal around *these* parts. And that bumpkin place where the kidnapping had taken place surely had none of the capacity to house such a ship.

As was standard procedure for a crew capture, I found myself being separated, almost immediately, from the rest of my crew. I was led off at gunpoint by a pair of guards, with a droid walking out ahead of me; one walking behind, for good measure.

It was a short walk to the sliding door that I was soon to discover led to Big Jo's cabin.

I was surprised—though not unpleasantly so—when the guards and droids let me walk through the doorway myself. This, I knew, was one of those macho Mafioso moves; a kind of confidence trick to make it look like they weren't intimidated by anyone on their own ground. The irony would be that Big Jo's cabin was completely *plastered* in all types of surveillance equipment; that if I so much as sneezed the wrong way, those droids and those armed men would be down on me like a shot.

I took in Big Jo's cabin.

It reminded me of something out of a retro science fiction movie; those ones from the eighties with the minimalist black backdrop, broken up only by geometrically correct sweeping neon white lights. For a couple of seconds, I was rendered pretty much stunned by the sight. Even I—a hardened, well-travelled space smuggler—was impressed.

When I glanced back over my shoulder, it was to see the door to Big Jo's cabin sliding shut, and the security detail, plus the droids, slipping from sight.

I allowed myself to breathe freely for the first time.

Thing about having a gun pointed on you is that it's not really any good for exercising normal human functions. Tends to have the effect of stiffening up your whole body; making it so you become hyper aware of every last twitching nerve.

After taking this time out to fulfil my respiration require-ments, I trod onwards into the cabin, several times becoming hypnotised by the neon lights which swept about me; over my head, beneath my feet . . . and then disappeared into the dark-ness out ahead.

I finally caught sight of Big Jo, or, at least, his crouched-over form, in a chair ahead.

The seat itself simply seemed to grow out of the fabric of the cabin.

And more of those neon lights swept over and around it.

Big Jo, although I couldn't quite make out his features due

to the lack of light, rested his chin on his fist, and appeared to be eyeing me as I approached.

I couldn't help but think back on what Mertinon had told me.

About how Big Jo thought of me as the one who *got away* . . . as if I'd betrayed my planet—*myself*—in some way by joining up with the FSA.

When I felt a thrill enter my stomach—something like shame—I scolded myself.

There was no reason for me to feel that way.

I had done nothing wrong.

I had done what was right for me.

Because, let's face it, a man isn't defined by his planet any more than a planet is defined by a man.

I squinted through the gloom, doing my best to make out Big Jo. As if the room itself was responding to my own motions, there was a sudden flash of lightning. It momentarily lit up the entire room. It lit up Big Jo, and where he was hunched over himself. Even though the lightning effect lasted less than a scattering of heartbeats, I managed to catch sight of those black eyes.

And to feel Big Jo's gaze enter mine.

"Arkle Wright," Big Jo said, his voice throaty, as if he was perennially on the verge of coughing. "It's been some time . . ."

I wondered if he was referring to some meeting we'd shared before.

If he was then I couldn't think of it.

Not right now.

Of course, I'd run a few jobs for old Hanx—nothing major;

and I certainly hadn't much of a handle just what I was getting into—but I'd never got anywhere near anything that Big Jo might be interested in . . . at least, I thought *not* . . .

"Big Jo," I replied. "I've heard an awful lot about you."

"As I have about you, Captain."

A steady, uneasy silence settled over the cabin.

I kept expecting another flash of lightning.

For the gentle, fleeting strips of neon lights which whipped about the room to suddenly congeal into a single, blinding, flickering mass. My eyes still stung from the last time.

I sucked in air, taking it right down into the pits of my lungs.

I knew that I needed to stand up, that I needed to show myself to be the captain I'd always dreamed that I could be if I just put my mind to it.

I stared through the gloom, doing my best to pick out Big Jo's eyes. "What's your game, Big Jo? What beef've you got with my crew?"

" 'Beef' ?" Big Jo repeated, his voice still throaty, but now with an audible smile entering his voice. "Mm," he continued, almost a purr, "I haven't got a *beef* with anyone . . . the only reason someone like me—someone as *successful* as me—is able to remain a relevant influence in the universe is because I know what I *need* for my own business; for my own affairs."

"You took them, Milky and Foy, because you think that they'll help out your business?"

"Absolutely," Big Jo replied, now rising out of his chair.

It felt as if an invisible hand caressed the back of my neck, raising up every last hair.

Acting on instinct, I glanced behind me, as if I expected to find a ghost there.

But, of course, there was nobody . . . *nothing*.

When I turned back to Big Jo, he had arranged the room so that one of the neon strips had come to a standstill and now lit up the lower half of his face; his muzzled mouth, and those full lips. "See something, Captain?"

"No," I replied, though my voice croaked.

This brought out a fresh smile from Big Jo. "It's perfectly fine—perfectly *understandable*. This whole ship, you see, is infested with my own brand of virtual reality; my own legion of *ghosts* . . . sort of goes back to the name, I suppose: *Ghost Wave*."

I looked back over my shoulder again, and this time I realised that I did see something.

Nothing more than a vague outline of a person.

A *phantom*.

I blinked, and it was gone.

I turned back to Big Jo.

He laughed. "Oh, Captain, you really *are* a little jumpy . . . the truth of the matter is that I don't quite understand what it is you have to be jumpy *about* . . . I only want to talk to you; only want a frank meeting of minds; to see whether we might be able to find some mutual interest; some mutual *goal*."

Somewhat preoccupied by the mention of digital ghosts, I allowed the panic to enter my voice once again. "What're you . . . *talking about?*"

"Well, through the years, you've built up certain skills— certain *valuable* skills—the kinds of skills which would be eminently useful for someone with an operation such as mine."

"And what kind of operation is that?" I replied, managing to take my mind off the ghosts for a few moments.

Another smile. "A purely *legitimate* one, that's what."

I thought the matter over.

Thought through my options.

Once more, Big Jo had captured my ship—*my crew*—and here we were, out in the middle of space, no means for escape.

If ever there was going to be a time to talk then, surely, now was it . . .

Decided, I pressed my lips together and then gave a firm nod. "All right," I said, "why don't you tell me what it is you have in mind."

———

I have to admit that I was fairly disappointed with what Big Jo had to offer.

To begin with, there's a certain pride which goes along with being an independent operator—which, when it all comes down to it, a smuggler really is. What Big Jo was proposing was to put me on one of his contracts—with all sorts of benefits, and all—in exchange for doing whatever it was that he had to say. Oh, don't think I wasn't tempted when he got to the part about 'entertainment expenses', which, I read, from his raised eyebrow, meant ever-flowing moiser among other perks which, for the bog-standard, independent smuggler, were clearly elevated up to a luxury somewhere close to those partaken by royalty.

And, to be honest, I was—and *am*—a long way off royalty . . .

He explained to me how, most likely, the days of the free-wheeling space smuggler were reaching their end; about how, soon enough, only those smugglers protected by a larger 'organisation'—as he chose to put it—would be able to feasibly survive.

I'd heard that yarn just about a million times before, but, I had to admit, the way that Big Jo put it, with all these statistics and stuff, made him sound far more convincing than anything I'd heard before. By the end, I had to admit that I was coming around to believing him.

In the end, when Big Jo had finished his pitch—because that was what it was—I stopped him dead, deciding that now wasn't the time to beat about the bush.

I actually held up a palm, as if I was some sort of planetside police officer, in charge of keeping the traffic running through a busy junction.

"Big Jo," I said, feeling somewhat surreal to actually speak his name aloud, "I've just got one question for you, okay, let's see if you can answer me it."

Big Jo inclined his head.

As it had been throughout out meeting, his face was obscured in shadow, save for the light which illuminated his mouth.

"I wanna know why you didn't just come to me, like a proper *businessman*, and put this to me like a *real* proposition." I shook my head. "Why'd you have to go to all the trouble of that *kidnap*? Am I really that big of a wheel? Am I really worth all *that* effort?"

Big Jo pouted here, apparently considering his response.

Finally, he broke out into his familiar smile all over again.

"Well," he said, "you did come after *Ghost Wave* . . . you *did* pursue your crew—I suppose that would count as a kind of *determination* . . . something which would separate you from the standard space smuggler. Almost like a proper *captain*, wouldn't you think?"

I had to admit then that he had my emotions kind of stirred up.

I tried to resist the twisting feeling in my gut.

I didn't think to mention that, if I'd known just what kind of a ship *Ghost Wave* was, that I would've thought twice about pursuing it . . . I suppose it was more out of an interest of keeping the *Nava's* capabilities secret than any matter of foolishness. Even though, most likely, Big Jo having had the *Nava* in his clutches twice over by then, I didn't suppose there was really any mystery remaining about the ship's capabilities.

Still, a man's got his pride . . .

I thought about another issue. "Well, then," I said. "what was with the kidnapping? What was with the holes in their heads?" I reached up and pointed to my forehead. "What's with the hole in *my* head?"

I half convinced myself that Big Jo would pass this off as he had just about everything else in the conversation; with some kind of a wide, wry grin. One of those exceptionally *annoying* grins which tells you—unequivocally—that someone knows what you *don't* know.

Instead, though, his expression remained largely neutral.

"Captain Wright," Big Jo said, "I would've thought you'd worked it out by now."

I hunched my shoulders; something like a shrug.

I guess that Big Jo was still learning the lesson that you should never—*ever*—not under any circumstance, overestimate the ignorance of a space smuggler. And don't get me started on the lack of critical thought or pragmatism . . .

"As I'm sure you've noticed," Big Jo went on, taking a few steps across his cabin, with the light above him, shining down on his mouth, following him, "my most loyal employees all have one feature in common."

My heart dropped. "A hole in the head?"

Big Jo nodded. "Exactly." He smiled now. " 'A hole in the head'."

"Mind control. Neural implant."

This time Big Jo snapped his fingers. "Attaboy . . ."

It took me a moment to realise I was blushing—yeah, *actually* blushing; like I was some kind of nineteenth century biddy with her corset too tight . . .

Big Jo turned back to me. "But, Captain Wright, as I'm sure you will have noted, the hole in your own head hasn't had any effect."

I prepared myself for the explanation; hoping that Big Jo was going to inform me that it had something to do with my higher-than-average IQ; or an *exceptionally* uncommon makeup of my brain. Instead, though, he explained, "It's common that those who suffer from the Hydgrea Virus develop an immunity; a hard *shell* over the very centres which the neural transplant acts upon."

It was time for more blushing.

Because, as is known throughout the universe—by adults of a certain age and condition—there's only one way you can get yourself stuck with the Hydgrea, and it ain't from holding hands
. . .

"So," I replied, finally catching on, "I'm immune from mind control?"

Big Jo laid on a thick smile again. "Yes." He paused for a moment, and then added, "At least from my own *personal* brand of mind control."

"Well, that's good to know."

With a sigh, Big Jo continued, "When my employees went to work on you and your crew—when we got the *kidnapping* all fixed up—they did manage to drill a hole in your head, but, it seemed, you simply wouldn't be controlled . . . you *refused* to be controlled." He shrugged. "And so we left you there."

I thought about this some more.

"I didn't notice a hole in Clive Wodd's head."

Big Jo looked back to me, though his eyes could've been just about anywhere . . . they were still draped in shadow. "No," he replied, simply. "As we've gathered through the years, the implant tends to be ineffective on those from his home planet. We needed to go through another route."

I stumbled for a moment, thinking about just what Big Jo was saying—the slight which he was casting in the direction of Hortenine-6 . . . having said that, though, I could say with fairly decent certainty that that was where I most likely picked up the Hydgrea myself.

I turned my attention back to Big Jo.

"What did you offer him?" I said. "What did you *say* to him?"

"That remains between me and him."

"Did you threaten to destroy his planet?" I said. "That old fig?"

Big Jo just smiled wider. "As I said, it will remain between me and him . . . all that I can say is that he and I very much see things in a similar fashion; we see the *world* in a similar fashion."

For a long few moments, I allowed my brain to fly back over recent past events—some not-so-recent events included. There must've been something I'd said; something that I'd paid no attention to at the time. Something which'd sown the seed.

Something.

And yet, I could think of nothing.

I glanced about, seeing a pair of virtually rendered ghosts standing off near one of the walls. They were eyeballing me. It sent a shiver down to my gut.

I turned my attention back to Big Jo.

Big Jo himself was fixed upon the ghosts also. "Whenever we take in a new employee, whenever I have them fitted for an *implant*; I'm sure to take an impression of their brain, as it stands." He gestured to the ghosts staring at us. "Then I download them to the ship, allow them to wander about my cabin." Here Big Jo twiddled his fingers in mid-air, as if to illustrate some point that I just couldn't grasp. "A way of remembering past adventures—of keeping people's *faces* in mind . . ."

Only now did I realise that the pair of ghosts were a rendering of Milky and Foy.

The two of them staring back at me.

Almost as if their souls were walking free about the ship.

The very idea of this sent my brain spinning and sizzling.

If there's one thing I've learned to fear in the universe, it's a scientist that goes unchecked by morals or ethics . . . as if the

whole plane of existence is just some damn *playground* to them
. . .

"So," I said, turning back to Big Jo, "if you want me as your own employee then you're going to have to make me sign the dotted line of my own free will?"

"Yes," Big Jo replied. "It seems that way. And, if you think about it logically, it would be a *great* shame to break up the crew of the *Navaplastas*, don't you think? You've surely spent such a great effort in assembling them, in bringing such a *talented* collection of individuals together."

"Don't really matter *who* they are if they're just gonna be zombies after everything."

" 'Zombies' ?"

I jerked my thumb back in the direction I'd come, and so, I imagined, by extension, the direction of the docking bay. "My Ship's Doctor told me that the two crewmembers we recovered were having something like a flash of bad temper . . . that they got all het up and angry as soon as we slugged out of Arkle-4 orbit."

"Ah," Big Jo replied, his mouth latched open, "I can *imagine.*"

"How? *How* can you imagine?"

With another shrug, Big Jo simply said, "The implant is constantly speaking with my own systems. Those fitted with the transplant shall be nothing except for *nice, obedient* employees. Ones who would have *no intention* of stepping out of line." He threw up his hand, as if to dismiss this as a minor matter, hardly worthy of his time and attention. "However, the same can't be said for the ones they leave behind. For want of a better word, their *loved ones*."

I wondered if Big Jo was including me in that category.

And, if he was, I wasn't quite sure how I felt about it.

He went on, "To mitigate for this *issue*, I have the implants programmed in such a way so that if an employee happens to leave orbit without the acceptable permissions, they will flip out and do whatever is necessary to return."

That seemed to explain it; at least to my Neanderthal brain.

"But," Big Jo continued, taking a few steps towards me, "it's fair to say that I wanted *you* Arkle . . . I wanted *you* to return to Arkle-4." His smile thickened. "And though it might've been preferable that you'd have come back of your own volition, or —*better*—with a fully functioning neural implant, I'm glad to have you here now. To be able to talk *sense* into you now."

It was as Big Jo got out these final words that I found my attention slipping, as it's wont to do whenever I'm trapped in some conversation. This time, though, it was a good thing my attention did slip. Otherwise I might not have seen the ghost.

It stood just at Big Jo's shoulder.

Whether or not Big Jo himself was aware of it, I have no way of knowing . . . aside from asking him, of course.

All I knew was that it was a virtual representation—a *carbon copy*—of Big Jo himself.

And then, all of a sudden, everything clicked right into place.

I shifted my attention back to Big Jo.

To his face—now partially illuminated by his own ghost.

And I could make out the filled-in hole in his head.

17 GHOST WAVE

BIG JO made no mention of the ghost which'd cropped up at his shoulder—that perfect rendering of himself in virtual form. Even just thinking about how Big Jo and his ghost had stared at me sent a tingle coursing up my spine. My blood ran impossibly hot. I'd hardly been able to process the parting words which Big Jo had dealt me.

That I'd have twenty-four hours to consider his proposal; the contract he wished for me to sign, or, quite simply, he would take what was mine by force—my ship; my crew—and then blast me out into space on a shuttle. But, as I trudged the corridors with my armed guards, I could hardly bring myself to concentrate on the offer itself.

My mind wouldn't budge from that hole in Big Jo's head.

That ghost standing at his shoulder.

What did it mean?

What *the hell* did it mean?

Big Jo—or whoever was controlling him—was kind enough to allow me to return to the *Nava* for the duration of my decision. Apparently he believed that I'd be better equipped to make a sure and steady decision if I was surrounded by home comforts.

When I returned to the *Nava*, I found the twins and Mertinon there.

No sign of either Foy or Milky.

It seemed that they'd been taken off somewhere in the flagship; no doubt to be seen to by some of Big Jo's very special, personal doctors . . . one who would, most likely, make sure that those neural implants were still very much in place.

When I returned to the bridge, I wasn't expecting a surprise party—complete with a welcome banner and cake—or anything; but, having said that, I *was* expecting to be greeted by something more than grim-faced expressions all around.

Really, it looked as if somebody had just died.

Couldn't my crew muster just the *slightest* enthusiasm for having their captain home?

. . . Then I reminded myself that I'm a hardened space smuggler and such matters really couldn't bother me in the slightest.

I butted Terry out of the captain's chair, folded my hands behind my head and kicked back, resting my ankles up on the controls.

I closed my eyes.

"Captain?"

Irritated, I peeled back an eyelid, peering out.

It was Brian.

Know-it-all, Ship's Doctor *Brian.*

"Mm," I just about got out through my lips, closing my eyes again when I realised that there wasn't a fire or something to attend to.

"We had a word with Clive—with Clive *Wodd.*"

This did get my attention.

I snapped back from the precipice of whatever doze I'd been close to achieving.

I sat up straight in the captain's chair.

Eyeballed Brian.

"And what'd *he* have to say for himself?"

"Uh," Brian replied, shifting his attention off over my shoulder; apparently exchanging glances with his twin brother.

I snapped my fingers at him. "Hello, short stuff? Over here?"

Brian immediately twitched back onto me. He bumbled out a "Sorry, Captain", or something like it, and then got to the point. "We were escorted off the ship like you were. But, once they'd got through with relieving us of our weapons, they brought us back here. To the *Nava*; said that further instructions would follow."

I shot Brian a fiery glare.

The two of us *all* too aware he wasn't getting to the point.

Answering the question which'd been asked.

As was often the way with the twins, Terry picked up where his brother had left off. "We didn't authorise him aboard, captain, he just *arrived*—he turned up on the bridge." He shook his head. "I don't think I've ever seen anybody look as ashamed as he did . . . you should've seen the big black bags beneath his eyes."

Here I reached out into thin air and snatched my fist closed, as if snuffing out a fledgling flame. "Cut the emo shit, okay?"

"Okay," Terry agreed. "All I wanted to say was that he looked run down, as if he'd been suffering himself; as if he'd been going through some tough times."

Another glare from me, and Terry got to the business-end of things.

Apparently having lost his nerve, Terry allowed Brian to pick up the slack. "He came along to inform us that if you, Captain, chose to reject Big Jo's proposition—something about signing a contract with him—then he would be the next captain of the *Navaplastas*. He explained to us that while Big Jo held the *Navaplastas* impounded, he had been nominated interim captain; and that it'd been with a heavy heart he'd accepted."

"Well, then," I said, unable to help interrupting, "perhaps he shouldn't have *accepted* then . . ."

"That wasn't it"—this time Mertinon broke into the conversation from where I'd believed him to be dozing away in the co-pilot's chair—"he wanted to say that, once this is all over, everything will make a whole lot more sense . . . that everything will fall into place. He said that he could *promise* that."

I tried to break in, but Mertinon was having none of it.

I guess sometimes it pays for the crew to have someone on board who's unafraid to interrupt the captain . . .

"Look here, Arkle—"

"*Captain*," I butted in, feeling nothing but a prize dick to interrupt my own brother in such a way.

Mertinon, though, was apparently taking the high ground, making an effort to appear unbothered by my manners. "*Captain*," he said, with great emphasis; with just a *hint* of sarcasm. "Although I've never met the men—never once in my life—I couldn't help coming away from the meeting with him with a great deal of respect."

"And why was that?" I said, feeling—if anything—all the more furious because Mertinon was being so reasonable; because *I* was the one being made out to be some kind of an indulged *brat*.

Hell, if a captain can't be a brat on his own ship then just where can he be?

"Because," Mertinon replied, his tone becoming a little more pointed; his patience with me apparently beginning to wane, "he told us that he's done some tweaks to the *Nava's* engines, unbeknownst to Big Jo . . . and not just that . . . he's made it so that *Ghost Wave* won't be able to give chase if she so wishes. He also says, that if we *do* choose to go, that we shouldn't worry about either Milky or Foy . . . they'll be taken care of, all being well."

I shook my head, then cast a glance over the twins, certain that this was some kind of a wind-up; that Mertinon was playing some sick joke . . . and at a time like this.

But, if the twins *were* playing this for laughs, then they remained utterly stone-faced.

I shifted back to Mertinon. "I don't get this," I said. "I don't get this *at all* . . . we can escape?"

Mertinon reached down to his side, and, from within his boot, he retrieved what looked to me like a simple remote control; just a single, red button on it. "Just got to jab this and we'll release the *Nava* from anchor, allow her to fly on out into space. *Ghost Wave* will see that we've gone, of course, but they won't be able to do anything about it."

I shifted from the device Mertinon held, to Mertinon himself; now suddenly extremely interested. "What about the other ships in the fleet? Won't they catch us up?"

Mertinon gave a wry smile this time. "Not with the modifications Clive Wodd performed on the *Nava* . . ."

I shook my head a ton of times—so many times that I was certain I was on the cusp of saying no . . . of telling what remained of my crew to forget about the whole deal . . . and yet, I just couldn't let it go. I couldn't let the hope of *escape*—just *one more* escape—free of my mind. It seemed to be the only thing I could focus on anymore.

"You think we can trust him?"

I was met with a chorus of "Yes" from the entire crew.

I wondered if they'd practised the response it was so on point.

Oh, I tried to put off making up my mind for the longest time.

I stood over my captain's chair, staring at no spot in particular, wondering if this whole situation might just vanish if I stopped thinking about it.

But, no.

Still very much there.

Finally, with a heavy heart—but with a strangely optimistic

buzz in my veins—I gave the order for us to fire up the engines and pull out.

Hell, the way I saw it, it'd be far better to get ourselves blown clean out of space than to have to sign some contract which'd turn my crew—*quite literally*—into zombies.

18 THE NAVAPLASTAS

NOW, I am not what you would call a Nervous Flyer, and yet, those minutes as we shot off, leaving *Ghost Wave* in our wake, I had been rankling for a moiser to loosen me up.

I kept my eyes fixed on the navigational screens, looking over eager Terry's shoulder to see smaller fighters flying on our tail, attempting to catch us up to haul us right back where we'd started. But, true to Clive's word, one by one, they all fell back, vanishing into the depths of space . . . relegated to some forgotten cabinet of memory.

"Okey doke," I said, with us clear of the fleet, and me doing my very best not to show any sort of emotion. I couldn't help but notice feeling *pretty* hot under the armpits. "Where to next, gang?"

Mertinon popped up again with the answer.

I saw that he held something in his fist.

A portable memory stick.

He looked to me, and I nodded him permission.

He slipped it into the *Nava's* control board, and we watched on as the navigational screens all lit up like some kind of non-denominational winter's celebration.

I was on the cusp of spinning about in my chair, demanding that Mertinon whip that stick out of there *right now*—that Clive had somehow managed to get a virus installed on the *Nava*, and made us do it—when the navigational screen settled.

I watched on as various colourful lines swept over the screen, finally settling into a pattern; one which I recognised as a flight path.

Clive had given us someplace to go.

I eyed the flight path, frowned, then turned back to the twins. "You know where we're headed?"

Brian looked blank.

But Terry, from the way his eyes near enough seemed to burst from their sockets, looked like he had the answer.

"Shoot," I said.

"That planet—the one where they kidnapped Foy and Milky."

There was a long pause.

And then I decided it came down to me to say its name.

"Karsedguron-17."

———

I have to admit that I've never been so excited about heading to as dull of a planet as Karsedguron-17 than I was right then.

It was like I had this weird—possibly *illegal*—substance bubbling away within my veins.

Driving me onwards.

Onto . . . well, that wasn't entirely clear right then, but I had faith that the Mists of Fate would clear before too long.

Once we'd got within about a day's journey of Karsedguron, I couldn't help but begin to feel anxious. I thought back on the accident, on all that *weirdness* which'd gone on; and, though I hadn't yet informed my crew, I thought some more about that hole in Big Jo's head.

And what it might mean.

He had told me and told me straight, that, whenever he activated the neural implant in somebody's mind, he would take something from them; a kind of impression of their brain, turn it into a ghost for his cabin. And I'd seen Foy and Milky with my own two eyes. There was little doubt that he could back up his Big Talk.

My mind tripped over so many possibilities that I was afraid I might be coming into danger of losing my senses. Some brains are made for thinking, and others are made to be ignored; or so I've heard many a smuggler say.

"Captain?"

I turned around, looked to see that Terry was standing there.

He wasn't at the navigational screens any longer; there seemed little point since we were moving faster than anybody could catch us . . . and even if somebody *did* happen across the screen who might be able to give pursuit, the proximity alarms would give us fair warning.

"Can I have a word?"

I slipped Mertinon—in the co-pilot's chair—a look.

He gave me a slight smile, as if to suggest that *he* might have an inkling of just what this was all about. Well, he might've helped a brother out.

Literally.

"Go ahead," I said, turning my attention back front and centre, checking over the engines. While Clive had done *some* job with these modifications of his, I couldn't help noticing that several of the engines were running pretty hot.

"In private?"

I flinched.

Thankfully Terry didn't see . . .

With a quick glance back to Mertinon, and seeing him sitting all smug and the like, I lifted myself up and free of my captain's chair—more easily said than done considering how *comfortable* it is—and I followed Terry off the bridge and along the corridor; into one of the smaller cargo bays that he'd, apparently, already marked out for our would-be impromptu chat. Because it felt like the situation demanded it, I brought the door shut behind us.

Perhaps it was just my brain going wild, but I couldn't help thinking that Terry's hair looked a lot *flatter* than usual; like he'd spent more than the minute-or-so morning visit to the bathroom which being a member of my crew required.

"I've been doing a lot of thinking, Captain."

"Uh-oh," I replied. "Never a good idea."

A smile tweaked the corners of Terry's mouth. But it was

gone by the next instant. "I've been thinking about my role on board, you know, the *Nava?*"

Seeing his sneaky smile, I raised him a smug grin.

Folded my arms across my chest.

"Going too tough for you? All this to-ing and fro-ing . . . all this capture, escape, recapture, *escape again* getting to you?"

Terry shook his head. "No, Captain, that's not it."

"Then what, boy? You know, all things going well, we'll be planetside in the next few minutes—out-of-the-frying-pan-and-into-the-fire time."

I couldn't help but note how my own mood was pleasantly warm. Almost as if danger—the *prospect* of danger—cheers me right up out of any funk I might've slipped into.

Perhaps it does . . . perhaps *that's* the explanation.

"Really, Captain," he said, "I thought it was my duty to let you know." He paused for an impossibly long time, and then said, in a quiet, husky voice, "I'm *leaving* the *Nava.*"

I actually got it into my brain that I hadn't heard so much as a sound escape his lips. "You *what?*"

He looked me in the eye this time, instead of out the port-hole. "The Nava, I'm *leaving.*"

Once I'd caught my breath back, I furrowed my brow. "Whoa, whoa, whoa . . . let's back this up a little first, shall we? When did you make your mind up on this? Before or after we got ourselves trapped by *Ghost Wave?* Before or after we got crewmembers kidnapped?"

"Actually," Terry said, looking awfully bashful all of a sudden, "I've been thinking about it for a long time . . ."

"About what?"

"About how I don't *fit* on board, Captain."

" 'Don't fit' ?" I repeated back to him as if he was speaking some alien language.

He nodded.

It wasn't the best start to a reply considering that I couldn't instantly think of a way in which he did fit on board the *Nava*. And he seemed to note my silence. I decided that I had to say something—*anything*—to bolster the boy's mood. "Look," I said, "you're still young—still learning your trade . . . you've been getting about the ship, working out where you should belong." I sucked my teeth. "I think you just need to be a bit more patient, all right?"

I could hear someone calling me from along the corridor; from the bridge.

I got the impression we were closing on Karsedguron fast.

"Look," I said, turning my full attention back to Terry for, perhaps, the very first time in the entirety of our relationship, "take it slow—think about it some more . . . once this is all through, once we know where we all stand, then you can make your mind up." On impulse, I reached out and gave his shoulder a squeeze. " 'Kay?"

He nodded back at me.

Flashed a smile.

But I could tell that I'd done a piss-poor job of convincing him.

Ah, well, some of us have got the Gift of the Gab, others haven't.

Most of us don't have any *gift* at all . . . hell knows *I* don't . . .

With the closest thing to an emotionally charged chat on board the *Nava* over, I bucked my way back onto the bridge and saw that, indeed, we were closing on Karsedguron.

What a *fricking* treat.

19 ROUND-AND-BACK - KARSEDGURON-17

I T WAS ONE THING to be pummelling our way through space at speeds which would've made Einstein blush, but it was quite another to arrest said speeds in preparation for our descent to the planetside terminal.

I went to work, as best as I could, with Terry helping out, patching one of Milky's programs over the engines; apparently cross referencing—or whatever the hell you call it—the mechanical with the theoretical. The upshot of the whole deal was the *Nava* slowing herself down considerably.

While we weren't back to anything like normal speed, we were certainly puttering along at a far more manageable velocity. As I brought the *Nava* in through the atmosphere, I took care to engage well over twice the strength of reverse thrusters I thought we'd need. And, even then, the landing was a mite bumpy. But I landed her just fine.

The terminal staff could see to all those gut-wrenching *squeals* of metal; all that unpleasant jangling of screws.

With my crew out of the *Nava* and smartly marching along in my wake, we cleared the relevant landing authorities and got ourselves back out onto the terminal road.

And then, I have to admit, I was somewhat stumped.

In actual fact, I was *well and truly* stumped.

Just what the hell were we supposed to do next?

With that thought on my mind, I eyed Mertinon and the twins, hoping that ideas might spring forth from their mouths. But, no, *nothing*.

"Uh," I started out, somewhat unconvincingly, "Clive didn't say what we had to do once we reached our destination, did he?"

They all shook their heads.

Again, it was like some kind of prearranged gesture.

Maybe it's time that I get some sort of surveillance set up on the *Nava* so I can keep an eye on what the crew gets up to when I'm not around; not that I'd ever be able to shrug off my natural laziness for long enough to actually *review* the tapes . . .

I glanced back to the terminal.

And then to the city surrounding us.

I couldn't help but feel my attention drawn to the building; all white with those silvery windows. Like some kind of goddamn ivory tower. Then I found myself thinking about Ricky D; about the man who I'd been to see at the start of this whole affair . . . the one who had, inadvertently or not, turned me onto Big Jo . . .

Perhaps it was with the idea in mind that the best means of

fighting a mobster was with another mobster which set my feet moving out from underneath me. Even if said mobster was the victim of someone else's Machiavellian manipulations.

With the others in tow, I ran the gauntlet through Ricky D's building another time, all of us traipsing our way up to the top floor: the thirty-third.

And, like the time before, Ricky D was very much available for a chat.

Maybe it was because of the previous experience that I was so presumptive; that I simply burst right on in on the slickly groomed young man, as before curled up at his desk, hard at work on something or other. I barely registered the trio of moons shining through the skylight as Ricky D worked away.

"Need some information," I said, without so much as a greeting.

Slightly startled, but, aside from that, apparently not too bothered about the interruption, Ricky D glanced up from his desk. He cast a quick glance across the rabble which I called my crew, finished up whatever he was doing and rose up. He rounded his desk and approached us, adjusting his glasses over the bridge of his nose as he did so.

"What can I do you for, Captain?" he said, sounding like he genuinely wanted to be of help.

I guess, all things considered, it was much to his credit.

A big credit to his manners; his upbringing.

Kudos to the mother, I say.

I jerked my thumb upwards, to the skylight, indicating space. "Got on the trail of Big Jo—went to go search for my crew, you know, the ones you helped kidnap?"

Again, Ricky D did nothing but smile at my choice of words.

"Well," I continued, this time pointing at my forehead, "I worked out just what the hell these holes in the head are all about—*finally* . . ."

Ricky D looked over my crew another time, resting his attention on Terry for longer than any of the others before turning back to me. "And what are they all about?"

"Mind control," I stated, simply, as if it was all elementary.

Ricky D pouted. "Interesting," he said, and then, indicating the chairs which sat before his desk—somehow there were now *four* whereas before there'd been only one—he added, "Please, come in and sit down. I'm sure you've had a long journey."

"Actually," I replied, taking a seat of my own, while the rest of my crew nervously took *their* seats, "we've had something like a goddamn funky getaway. Not all that much *long* about it. We whipped ourselves out of there just as quick as we could; when Big Jo got his hands on us."

"Huh," Ricky D replied, consulting something on the vidscreen before him.

He turned his attention back up, to us.

"And where's 'Big Jo' now?"

"Oh, he's *way* back there . . . off on another plane, almost, I'd say . . ."

"You sound confident."

"Goddam right," I replied. "I've got just about the greatest engineer in the business working my ship—he knows just how to tickle the machines right; to get them chuckling and humming along so that nobody can catch her."

"Where's your engineer now?" Ricky D put in, squinting as he regarded me through the lenses of his glasses.

"Oh, uh . . . back on the ship . . . along with another pair of crewmembers." I paused, drew some breath, then continued, "Actually, that's the reason we're here—why we thought we should come to you . . . I was wondering if you'd be able to do anything to help us get them back."

At this remark, Ricky D gave a wry grin.

I guess there's not many things a gangster likes more than a challenge.

"I'd pay, of course," I said. "Or recompense you, you know, however . . ."

Ricky D seemed to consider this for a long moment. He drew in a pensive breath, as if he was doing the thinking with his entire body, right down to the pit of his stomach. He leaned back in his chair, turning his attention upwards, to the skylight; and to the trio of moons shining down on us.

"Big Jo," he said, attention still fixed on the moons, "has really been a *wonderful* client of mine—a *really* reliable earner." He brought his attention away from the celestial and back down planetside with a *bump* of the front legs of his chair. "You would need to offer me something which would give me an equally good return on my investment."

I glanced across the faces of my crew and decided that, if I was going to tell someone what was going on—what I'd *discovered*—then it might as well be Ricky D. And, quite frankly, there seemed no reason for me to keep what was going on a secret from my crew for a moment longer. It wasn't like I had planned on *not* telling them; more that the subject hadn't had a chance to come up in normal, everyday conversation. To be quite honest, there hadn't been any 'normal' let alone any 'everyday' for what seemed like a very long time indeed.

"Look," I said, "I think somebody should tell you this . . . you seem to be an on-the-level businessman, I mean, in gangster terms."

Realising how this sounded, I held up a hand in apology, but Ricky D—the gentleman he was—had nothing of it, and dismissed the matter with a shake of the head and a wry smile.

"It's just, I don't want you to tie yourself in knots further down the line, and if somebody doesn't tell you what I've found out . . . what's *really* going on . . . then you could, quite frankly, find yourself getting screwed."

"And what is it?"

I held myself still for another second; for some reason actually *quite enjoying* the sense of suspense I'd created. "Big Jo," I said, "he's being manipulated by someone." I wagged my finger in a way I was sure some detective—at some time in history— had done. "The holes in the head, *Big Jo* has one . . ."

Silence billowed up in the room.

Because it felt like somebody had to break through the utter stasis, I put in, leaving subtlety at the door, "Somebody's controlling his *mind*."

I studied Ricky D's reaction.

His face remained plain.

And then, very slowly, he brought his hands up together.

He touched his fingertips in a gesture which—I could quite easily imagine—might suggest him holding the whole planet in his grasp; ready to do his bidding . . . if he really wished he could crush it with a single motion.

"Interesting," Ricky D said, and then went quiet.

I half expected him to throw us from the room; or, failing that, to go all rapid-fire on his vidscreen, beginning to make provisions for this dynamite piece of information I had just dropped directly into his lap, like some obedient hunting hound.

But, as I was quickly learning, Ricky D wasn't like most mobsters.

He seemed to have got over his lust for power at a *very* early age.

Allowed it to be displaced by cool, hard, infallible *logic*.

"Okay, Arkle," Ricky D said, turning his attention back to me. "If I may call you that?"

I nodded my assent.

In that moment, with all the tension racking the room, I was fairly certain he could've called me just about anything and I would've responded in the affirmative.

There were still two . . . *three* lives in my hands.

People in desperate need of rescue.

People depending on *me*.

"I think we can strike a deal."

"What?" I said. "Tell me what you've got in mind."

———

Fury blazed right through me.

I felt as if my heart was twisting in my chest, doing its

goddamn best to sink all the way down to my stomach. To get itself some of that freedom it'd heard so much about.

How the hell . . . *just how the* hell?!

I felt my crew pattering along quickly in my trail.

I knew that Ricky D hadn't tossed them from his office, and that, most likely, they'd just been rendered stunned by my reaction; by my *anger* surrounding his proposition.

"Arkle! Arkle!" Mertinon called after me.

For some reason—must've been *nostalgia*; his being my brother and all—I ceased my escape bid and stared back at him. *Glared* back at him.

Mertinon drew closer to me, slowing his pace. "I mean, *Captain Wright*."

I waved this confusion away with a hand, and watched on as Brian and Terry caught up with the escape. My attention, though, focussed in on Terry; the subject of Ricky D's proposition. He had been simple and final with his offer; he had announced that, in return for Terry entering his business, as an apprentice, he would aid me in recovering my lost crewmembers; in bringing them back to the *Nava*.

Of course, I had delivered him a flat no.

There was no question about it.

Even with that talk Terry had cornered me with.

If he *was* going to leave the *Nava* then it sure as hell wasn't going to be so that he'd be taken under the wing by some *gangster* . . . no matter how pretty his office; or how well-kempt his outlook.

Mertinon was eyeing me very closely now. His eyes were sharp, and I only then realised that he'd taken hold of my forearm; that he was squeezing it tightly . . . so tightly that he'd near enough cut off my blood flow.

It dawned on me that he was afraid I was going to run off again.

That I was going to leave them behind.

That I was going to leave my *brother* behind.

Why *couldn't* it happen again?

What would *I* care?

"Arkle," Mertinon began, "why didn't you stay there—hear the man out." He flipped a look over his shoulder, to Terry. "Why didn't you hear your own *crewmember* out?"

I jabbed my tongue up against the backs of my teeth.

I cast a glance over Brian, then Terry.

The two of them staring up at me with wide eyes; like a pair of baby deer caught in the headlights of my wild anger.

I turned back to Mertinon. "You of all people should know how it is—someone like you who grew up on Arkle-4 . . . who spent half their life trying to avoid the Easy Button; all those options which Big Jo threw out about the place." I gave a firm shake of my head. "Why didn't you ever take him up on his many offers? Why didn't you work for Big Jo?"

This time Mertinon stared hard back at me.

At the last moment, just as he was about to reply, he looked away.

"Because," Mertinon said, "Big Jo wouldn't have me . . . didn't see any need for me."

For a long few seconds, I felt the entire surface of my skin tingling. Anger continued to throb through my veins. My mind got stuck on something or other—*nostalgia* again?—and I felt as if somebody had pricked me with a pin; set about deflating my lungs.

I turned my attention back to the twins.

Back to Terry.

That poor, lost lamb.

No direction.

No sense of *purpose.*

Christ, did I know how *that* was like . . .

"Look, Arkle," Mertinon continued, "you really think he'll have a better life serving under a space smuggler than working for some upscale mobster?" It was his turn to shake his head. "If you think that—if you *really* think that—then, quite frankly, you're deluding yourself. Please, Arkle, why won't you see sense on this one? Allow the boy to have somewhere he can set down his two feet; where he can grow up in peace, huh?"

That tingling feeling continued to pass across the surface of my skin.

My heart hummed in my throat.

Damn, how much I wished that I could be a droid in that moment; something unfeeling and *estranged* . . . just how in *hell* had I managed to get myself a crew of my own on the *Nava* after spending so much time bumbling about space on my lonesome?

How had I lost sight of the great, innumerable benefits of solitude?

The funny thing was that it wasn't a case of benefits vs. drawbacks . . . it was just the simple matter that I couldn't imagine life without one member of my crew—not a *single* one of them. I guess it was kind of how people feel about their families; not that I've ever allowed myself to get too drawn into that sort of deal . . . or maybe it's just because my ma and pa are dead.

It could be that just as easily.

And yet, what was that thing about 'if you love something, then you let it go'?

Was that what applied in these circumstances?

Who the hell really knew?

I looked to Terry, said, "This what you want, kid?"

Terry shifted a glance to his twin brother Brian.

Something passed between the two of them.

Something which I couldn't rightly describe.

But it sure as hell was there.

Getting a nod off his twin brother—whatever it meant—Terry turned his attention back to me, then said, clearly, unambiguously, "Yes, captain. This is what I want."

"Okay then," I said, already turning away from the boy.

I'd almost made it clear out of the building before I thought to turn back.

To check that Mertinon and Brian were following me out.

They were there.

But Terry wasn't.

Something about the picture didn't compute, and the tear which threatened to sneak out of the corner of my eye didn't compute either.

I gave Brian and Mertinon my back.

Headed us back to the terminal.

20 RESCUE PLAN - THE NAVAPLASTAS

E VERYTHING was sorted out with Ricky D.

In fact, Ricky D was so efficient that I already had a message waiting for him. A set of coordinates which we were supposed to follow. I searched for any mention of Terry in the message—even something subtle, easy to miss—but there was nothing at all.

Business had been conducted.

The deal struck.

Nothing more to say about it, I suppose.

I got Mertinon—my Co-pilot—working at the navigational screens while I handled the fiery pieces of the machinery. All the systems had reset, of course; all of those tweaks which Clive had made to the *Nava's* engines were back to their factory setting . . . whatever that really meant seeing as the *Nava* was just about one big mesh of parts from one area of the universe or the other.

As we whistled along the flight path Ricky D had set us, we received another message, telling us to arm our weapons. To prepare to do battle.

I couldn't help but feel perplexed by the whole deal.

By just what was going on.

But, then again, I've never been much of a master planner.

Plans just tend to get in the way; make you blind.

In my humble experience, I've found you can do just as well by hurtling into the unknown on a wing and a prayer. I'm not dead yet if that's any measure of the thing.

"Captain?"

I glanced back, saw Mertinon with his brow furrowed, looking over the navigational screens. "What's up?"

"Nobody around to lock onto . . . nothing in range . . . we're just way out; in the middle of *nowhere* . . ."

I froze up for a second, expecting the worst.

I wondered if—for whatever reason—Ricky D was trying to trick us.

If he was planning on shooting us out of space now that he had his prize.

An *apprentice* of his own.

"Standby," I replied, sounding far surer of myself than I felt.

From the engine room, I got a message from Brian, informing me that he'd drawn back on the thrusters so we could get more power into the cannons.

I ordered him back up to the bridge.

I checked over the messages, wondering if there might be another one waiting there from Big Jo.

But there was nothing.

Every heartbeat which pounded at my temple—at that hole in my forehead—was like agony. It felt as if we were somehow wasting time; if there was something which we were missing. If Ricky D had given us enough clues to know what was really going on.

What danger we were putting ourselves in for.

With Brian back on the bridge, sitting in the co-pilot's chair since Mertinon was over at the navigational screens, I was on the cusp of ordering him to return to the engine room; to get us out of this sector just as quickly as he could manage.

But then Mertinon caught my attention.

"Captain? We're not alone."

I glanced over to him; to the navigational screens.

And, sure enough, I took stock of the entirety of Big Jo's fleet.

I felt a layer of sweat prickle across my forehead.

A single bead drooled down my cheek.

Well, if this was Ricky D's idea of a deal—him arranging for us to face off with an entire fleet of ships—then I'd got well and truly shafted.

I thought back to my behaviour; how I had surely come across as presumptive; *over confident*. Maybe I'd inadvertently managed to make Ricky D believe that I had a fleet of my own. Perhaps he had simply *assumed* that someone as unsubtle as myself *had* to have the goods to back it all up.

Nope.

"Captain?" Mertinon said, this time sounding a touch panicked. "What'd we do?"

Brian was slumped back in the co-pilot's seat, his hands

gripping the arms so tightly that all the blood had left his complexion. His skin had turned an unhealthy blue about the edges.

I knew that we had no option now.

That we'd gone past the point of no return.

I wouldn't have time to so much as utter the order for Brian to go back down to the engine room; to get his hands dirty turning us around.

In a way it was comforting to know we had nowhere to go.

That we had to either put up or shut up.

And—either way—we were most likely going down in flames . . . not literally, of course, since there *aren't* any flames in space . . .

"Arm weapons," I said.

I waited for the cautioning tone of either Brian or Mertinon.

But neither of them spoke up.

I suppose I must've spoken with more authority than I felt I possessed at that moment.

The authority to lead not just myself but two others to their deaths.

I watched the laser cannon gauge fill up to its danger-red, and then I sat back in my chair, as if this was something I did every day of the week. Yeah, facing off with a fleet of ships —*dozens strong*—nothing to it . . . with the flagship, *Ghost Wave*, slap-bang in the middle.

And yet, something told me that I had to trust Ricky D on this.

That he hadn't read me wrongly as I'd first assumed.

Above all else—above being a *mobster*—Ricky D was a shrewd businessman.

And it wouldn't be any good for business to stiff someone on a deal.

Word would get around.

Eventually.

For one, Terry would know that Ricky D had reneged on his deal.

That he'd sent all of us—including his own twin brother—to his doom.

And, let me tell you, there aren't many worse things than finding yourself on the pointy end of a life-long vengeance; I've heard it straight from the mouth of other smugglers who managed to dig themselves in deep because of a 'misjudgement' of some situation or other.

"Ready to go, Captain," Brian said, from where he now manned the cannons.

I drew in a deep, cleansing breath—*breathed it out*—then said, "Fire."

———

Even as I uttered the word, I was certain that I wouldn't live to see a single laser blast stream towards the fleet. That the fleet would note the attempt at a laser lock and we'd be on the receiving end of an unstoppable counterpunch. As it was, though, not only did I live to see the laser blast flying through space, but I also got to see it neatly penetrating the hull of one of the outer ships in the fleet. Nothing bigger than a scout. But it was a start.

Mertinon was merciless on the cannon.

With another couple of direct hits, the ship blew into pieces.

And then he held off.

All of us—all *three* of us on the bridge—waited to see what the reaction from the rest of the fleet would be. I fully expected nothing short of a barrage of laser cannons to make themselves felt on the hull of the *Nava* . . . but there was no response.

I cast a glance about the bridge.

If there's one thing which makes me greatly uneasy about space melees, it's when the enemy puts up no fight whatsoever. It gets me antsy; makes me wonder if they've got some trick up their sleeve. If they just want to draw me into a false sense of security.

Readying the counterpunch.

But, even for Big Jo, it seemed a touch extreme that he'd given up a scout ship.

Why would he give up *anything* to me?

Unless . . . and, well, perhaps I should've seen it before . . . he wanted to take me, and what remained of my crew, alive—for his own business purposes.

Mertinon awaited the order, but I gave him none.

I wanted to see what Big Jo was planning.

Sure enough, the fleet continued to approach us; not one of them so much as locking their lasers onto the *Nava*. It was as if the fleet realised how comically they overwhelmed us. That to shoot the ship down would be akin to stomping on an ant which happened to cross its path; even if that ant had given you some mean, fiery bite, it was still only an ant . . .

Again, I checked my messages, wondering if there would be anything from Ricky D.

But, nope, nothing.

Nothing at all . . .

Realising that there was only one thing to do now, I had Mertinon dish through the information on the navigational screens; flip through until he uncovered the location of *Ghost Wave*. He did this without any fuss, and I sucked in my stomach as the *Nava* increased speed, heading deeper into the fleet.

It could happen at any moment.

They could fire on us.

Blow us clean into nothingness . . . or whatever happens to ships when they get all shot up.

Still, though, the *Nava* was given a free reign to journey through the fleet at the wit and whim of her captain; of Arkle Wright.

"Still nothing?" I put out.

"No, Captain," Mertinon replied. "No tractor beams . . . no contact." He glanced at me, giving me what must've been a nervous grin; or perhaps this was what space-adventuring was all about, and he was having the time of his life. "It's eerie, isn't it?"

"Just a touch," I replied, then looked to Brian. "Got any ideas?"

"Who? Me?" Brian said, jerking his thumb at his chest.

"Yeah, you."

Brian glanced up to the navigational screens.

To all the colourful dots and lines swirling about.

All of those graphical renderings which seemed to attempt to deaden the horror of the situation we found ourselves in.

"I guess, Captain," Brian said, "that we've won."

I held Brian's gaze for the longest time.

I was unsure why, but I couldn't help believing that he was right.

When I turned back to the vidscreens—saw we were almost in touching distance with *Ghost Wave*—I was overwhelmed by a sense of awe at the size of the ship.

Just who the hell were we messing with?

And could I really get my crew back?

Could things *really* ever be as they once were?

21 RETURN - GHOST WAVE

G IVEN THE SITUATION, I wasn't too bothered about being met with Captain Henry Norbortwitz—or 'Ernest Harry', as he'd been in another life. He was professional, hardly blinking an eye at me. As if something had suddenly come over him . . . as if he'd decided that it was time for him to buck up and show me how he'd firmly placed his 'sordid' past behind him; where, I suppose, all pasts—sordid or otherwise—truly belong.

He led us through the labyrinthine corridors of *Ghost Wave*, not pausing once to detail what our ultimate destination was going to be.

In the end, though, I guess I should've known.

I should've known that we would end up at Big Jo's cabin.

At the *captain's* cabin.

Just as it had been before, the room was set in pitch-blackness which was broken up only by the odd twirling, fizzling neon-white line.

I kept an eye out for any of the ghosts, but couldn't see any.

That didn't mean they weren't there, though.

There was no sign of Big Jo this time.

I glanced about my crew—to Mertinon and Brian. Both of them looked somewhat intrigued by this setup, and I had to admit they had a right to be surprised. They hadn't been asked into the cabin the first time, after all.

I noted that Captain Norbortwitz hadn't come in with us.

Perhaps I should've taken this show of trust as a grand compliment.

But, more than anything else, it just seemed to be slightly negligent.

We waited.

And waited.

Those white lines zipping past our noses.

Slipping beneath our shoes.

When I finally did make out a form in the cabin, I realised that it wasn't Big Jo at all.

It took me a moment to figure out just who it was.

And, like the lunkhead I can often be, I jabbered it out loud. "*Clive!*"

Clive remained still, not responding right away. Just like everybody else on this ship—in this *fleet*, I gathered—he wore black overalls. He remained grave-faced, apparently apprehensive about approaching us; about coming closer to me, in particular.

Probably with good reason, too, since he might've been understandably concerned that I could easily be in the mood to rip his head off . . . but, and this surprised me too, on some level,

I didn't feel anything like anger. It took me another second to pin it down exactly, to realise what it *was* that I felt. And then it struck me.

Gratitude.

Goddamn, we never would've got away from the fleet in the first place if it hadn't been for Clive and his delightful molestations of the *Nava's* engines . . . and he was the one who'd steered us back to Karsedguron-17; back to Ricky D.

Still, being a captain—if not *his* captain—I had to keep a cool exterior.

"Wodd," I got out, this time scaling back the surprise; and hopefully coming across as the more formal, grounded individual I often imagine myself to be.

"Captain," Clive replied to me, and then looked over the others. Here was the first time he did anything but squeeze his lips together in a pout. He gave off the lightest of smirks. "I see the crew's been dropping like flies."

"Seems so, don't it?" I replied.

Clive turned back to me. "I have to apologise for all of this, Captain . . . in truth, I don't really know *where* to start—"

I couldn't resist cutting him off.

I'd waited this long for him to interface with me and I'd be *damned* if I was going to wait so much as a second more.

"Why not start with the bit where you decided to master-mind a crash-and-kidnap, huh?"

Clive's features darkened.

For a second, I believed he was going to flip out on us; or else he was going to do some kind of reversal shit . . . reveal that he'd been on Big Jo's side all the time . . . that he'd been nothing but a *sleeper* agent biding his time; awaiting his opportunity.

"Captain," Clive got out, "I know this is all hard to take in . . . as if you haven't got the foggiest about what's going on."

"Got that right, goddamn."

Here Clive glanced about him, as if he'd seen one of the VR ghosts himself . . . though why he wouldn't expect that—seeing how deeply he apparently was in Big Jo's pocket—remained a mystery to me. He shifted his attention back to me and the abridged crew. "Listen, I'm going to do my best to explain—to let you know what's going on . . . but first—*really*—it's for the best if we get hold of Milky and Foy. Get them back to the *Nava*."

In all the excitement, I had to admit that I'd forgotten about Foy and Milky, and that they had been recaptured by Big Jo. And, as if it was a foregone conclusion, I couldn't help wincing when I considered the prospect of Foy finding out that I'd handed one of her cousins over to a gangster.

"This way," Clive said, turning his back to us, and leading us deeper into Big Jo's cabin.

I cast a glance back to Mertinon and Brian, as if I needed their assurance that this was the right thing to do; that we weren't all about to fall for some elaborate trap Big Jo had decided to set.

Neither of them communicated anything like confidence to me; but if there's one thing I've learned in all my time of being a captain and a smuggler, what makes leadership in a man—or *woman*—is the willingness to put your neck on the line when everything looks like it's going to shit. Like it was then.

With a quick shrug—mainly to myself—I led us off on Clive's heels.

Deeper into the ship.

———

Clive brought us to an abrupt halt outside an inconspicuous-seeming room.

He glanced back at me, meeting my eye.

I could tell he was feeling me out, trying to work out if I was back to trusting him; if our relationship was back to some shadow of its former self.

Whatever my positive feelings about him setting us free from *Ghost Wave* for the first time, I couldn't help but hold myself back. No way was I going to leave myself open. If he intended to get my defences down and attack then he was going to be gravely disappointed.

"What's this place?" I said.

Clive gave a slight smile. "You'll see."

He activated the door with what I supposed to be a near-invisible earpiece.

The door swept out of sight—sliding sideways into that most mysterious of hidden realms.

I took in the scene facing us.

It was awash with activity.

All those people in black overalls.

All of them one large fabric of activity.

I absorbed the machinery parts—the plastic tubing, the electrical wires, and who knew whatever else. Droids stumbled along; their articulations jerky and machinelike. Their operators stood nearby like proud parents watching the toddler they'd sprogged out take its first steps.

My gaze slowly moved upwards, to the ceiling.

To the drones which hummed about there.

And then my gaze drifted back down again, to those standing on the floor, clearly operating the devices; reeling off silent instructions.

Perhaps I should've known to trust my instincts; to allow my eye to sweep about the room looking for the largest, most impressive example of technological innovation.

Beyond the grinding droids—the ambling *drones*—I made out something entirely unique.

The other droids and drones all seemed to be standard-issue tech, perhaps with the odd modification here and there—this mostly meant a welded-on blaster of some kind. But the one which stood out the most resembled neither droid *or* drone.

For a second, I was rendered stunned.

At its sheer *size*.

And then, again, when it dawned on me what it was.

A great, honking mechanical—manmade—*dragon*.

It stood on its hind legs, paws—*claws?*—held penitent at its chest. Its head was bowed, too, and I could tell that it was currently powered down. Just to absorb the craftsmanship present in the dragon was enough of a wonder to behold. How the dragon had scales beautifully carved onto its gunmetal-grey body.

Its head almost touched the ceiling of the expansive room.

A *warehouse*, really.

It took me a moment for my attention to slither free of the mechanical dragon, but I managed to pick him out eventually.

Milky.

Just as the other figures, all dressed in their black overalls, he looked studious about his project; jabbing at the dragon here and there, correcting this or that . . . making sure that everything about his design was as he wanted it to be.

That perfectionist attitude I'd learned to *love* about him.

Especially when the *Nava* was the focus of such an attitude.

I made to tread towards Milky and was surprised to find Clive's hand extended over my chest, apparently in an attempt to prevent my advance.

I looked to Clive.

"Captain," he said, "you might want to consider . . ."

"Consider *what?*" I said. "That he might be *happier* here? That he might somehow be better off just being some kind of zombie puppet?"

Clive gave a shake of his head. "That's not what I . . ."

But it was too late to reason with me now.

Although I hadn't had time to think about it, the wounds from Terry's departure—from handing him over to Ricky D— were still very much raw . . . they *stung* . . . no way in hell was I going to allow another crewmember to slip through my fingers; to suffer because of my personal negligence. And it was with that thought in mind that I stormed through the others.

The others all determined to tinker with their own devices.

With their own drones and droids.

"Captain!" Clive called out after me.

But I ignored him.

I guess I must've made it about halfway across the room before I noticed something change about the atmosphere. It was almost as if the air had suddenly turned cold; or as if somebody had just decided to pipe sulphur into the ventilation systems.

The effect was significant enough to make me stop dead, right where I was, and peer about.

Everybody—*everybody*—in the room was staring at me.

And, I couldn't help noticing, every last drone that'd been hovering—every last droid that'd been otherwise occupied—was now focussed squarely on me.

None of them looked especially pleased, either.

In fact, I could honestly say they looked damn *slighted.*

I cast a glance back to Clive, Mertinon and Brian.

All of them were staring after me, as if I'd just gone and stepped on a landmine, and they were somewhere safe in the distance waiting to see what the fallout would be.

From the looks of things, they wouldn't have long to await the outcome.

I drew in some very conscious—very shaky—breaths.

There wasn't all that much manly—nothing *macho*—about them, that was for sure.

I reached for my thigh holster. Found it empty. It was then that I realised I'd long ago lost my blaster, and that there seemed nothing to be done about it; not for the time being.

Everything happened so fast from then on.

All the mouths around me seemed to yawn open.

Ready to bark out orders to their mechanical charges.

To send them barrelling towards their target.

Me.

So I did the only thing that I possibly could at that point.

I shut my eyes.

And waited for the pain.

––––––

. . . But it didn't come.

When I dared crack open a single eye to gaze out at my surroundings—to no doubt witness that my aggressors had only delayed their attack, wanting to pad out time so as to make my last waking moments just as insufferable as possible—I was stunned that everybody around me, all of the puppet-zombies . . . or whatever the hell their official name might've been . . . were frozen in their places. Each and every one mid-scream.

Their droids and drones stuck in the midst of their programs.

I saw that many of them bore blades. Others had been stuck in the middle of priming laser blasters. Milky's dragon, I noted, now stretched its winged arms up to the ceiling, and had its jaw latched open in a silent roar. Milky, too, as with the other operators, had been rendered frozen.

With just about a million questions on my mind, I shifted my attention onto Clive, who was still standing off close by the door with the remaining two members of my crew.

As if nothing at all had just happened, Clive wandered through the frozen droids, drones and operators, and approached me. "Captain, if you'd allowed me to finish . . ."

"What happened?" I said, shaking my head; maybe trying to get my brain free of the almost overwhelming disbelief.

Clive paused his advance. "I shut them off, you see—"

" 'You shut them off' *how?*"

"Using my earpiece."

"Wait," I put in, now feeling *thoroughly* out of my depth, "you have *control* over them?"

"Yes."

"How'd you manage to swing that?"

Clive held up his hand. "It's a long story." He nodded to Milky. "For the time being, let's get the team back together, huh?"

Although I would very much have liked to bleed Clive for the exact reasons behind his 'control' over these zombie-puppets, he had already taken the initiative. He took Milky's forearm in a firm grip and guided him out of his static pose.

Even though everybody within the room *seemed* to be frozen solid—as rigid as statues—it turned out that Milky was really quite malleable. Clive hadn't much trouble in guiding him forwards, making him step alongside. There was something about the situation that I really disliked . . . but I couldn't quite put my finger on it.

Soon enough, Clive had us at the door, and moving back along the corridor, away from the room filled with the drones and droids. As we proceeded along, he muttered to me, over his shoulder, "With all due respect, when we fetch Foy I'd like you to stay back, Captain. Don't want anyone to get hurt."

"Understood," I replied, and sheepishly fell in with the group like some chided schoolboy.

———

It was a much lengthier task to recover Foy, but, as had been the case with Milky, she was located in a room filled with other zombie-puppets—all of them, like her, being controlled by some outside agent. As it soon turned out, the cannons within *Ghost Wave* were all controlled within a single room. Actually, as I took in the vidscreens for the first time properly, I realised that they weren't just the *Ghost Wave* cannons but the cannons for the entire fleet.

When I regarded Foy herself, I saw that—just like Milky— she had made herself out to be prominent among the others. She had, by far, the greatest amount of screens available to her; the greatest amount of responsibility?

As we ventured out, with Milky and Foy both in a semi-comatose state, the two of them able to walk when given guidance, I couldn't help putting the question to Clive. "Is that the reason why the fleet didn't fire on us? Because Foy saw it was the *Nava*? That she wouldn't fire on her good, old captain?"

Clive gave a wry smile. "Be nice to think that, wouldn't it, but, no . . . that's not the reason."

"Then what *is* the reason?" I replied. "How come we could mince along here so nicely—so *easily*—and return to *Ghost Wave* without so much as anybody batting an eyelash?"

Clive again became preoccupied with something or other. Although he was clearly busy trying to shepherd Milky and Foy, I reached out and grabbed hold of the back of his overalls.

Spun him around.

I got right up in his face.

"You tell me what's going on," I said. "And you tell me *now*."

Another beat passed.

I expected either Mertinon or Brian to tell me to stop being all intense with Clive; that there were *far* more important things to get going on. But neither of them put in so much as a word.

"I let you in," Clive replied.

Harnessing a strength which I'd never known he possessed, he tugged himself free of my grip. He turned his attention back to Foy and Milky, guiding them on their way.

Apparently we were all headed back to the *Nava*.

———

By the time we'd got into the docking bay, I couldn't help but feel that we'd got away with it. That we'd managed to extricate ourselves from whatever mess we'd wound up in by setting foot on *Ghost Wave*. But, as always seems to happen—at least when *I'm* involved—things weren't really that simple.

I could smell the *Nava's* particular personal brand of fuel. Of course, I don't use anything other than the standard stuff that any other price-conscious pilot prefers; but there's something about inhaling *your own ship's* fuel that is certainly *particular*.

As my mind began to open out to the possibilities—as my imagination got all plump and round and a gateway was opened which appeared to show off Great Promise—Captain Norbortwitz decided to show his ugly mug.

Like before, his eyes were concealed in shadow beneath the brim of his cap.

Seeing as Clive had a much better grasp on life aboard

Ghost Wave, I deferred to him with a glance. I didn't want to risk breaking anything—or *anybody*—after all.

Norbortwitz stood there.

Like all the others.

Powered down.

A tremble ran through my gut, and I couldn't help considering Clive in an entirely different light. He seemed to be having little trouble slipping into the shoes of some kind of puppeteer; of appearing to be able to hold the world dangling at the end of a string.

I made a mental note never to cross him.

And hoped I'd remember.

As we passed by Norbortwitz, curiosity overtook me.

I reached out for the brim of his cap, then flipped it off his head.

Sure enough, on that wrinkled, well-tanned forehead, I made out the hole.

They—whoever *they* was—had got to Norbortwitz . . . *Ernest Harry*, too.

"Captain?"

When I glanced up, I realised Clive and the others had already boarded the *Nava*.

I bid *Ghost Wave* goodbye about as emotionally as I had first greeted it.

Which was, when it came down to it, little more than a noticeable shrug.

22 HOME AND DRY? - THE NAVAPLASTAS

BACK ON BOARD the *Nava* and with six out of seven crew back where they belonged, I thought I was getting closer to being given answers. But, as Clive quickly made off for the medbay; Milky and Foy out ahead of him, with Brian in tow —clearly wanting to be helpful—I realised that I wasn't going to get a response as fast as I'd hoped.

I retreated to the bridge with my brother Mertinon, guessing that his company was just about as good as I was going to get for the time being.

I slumped down in the captain's chair while Mertinon took up the co-pilot's chair. There was something about the arrangement which just felt one-hundred-per-cent natural; as if it was The Way Things Should Be. Maybe it's true what they say about blood being thicker than water . . . actually, I've probably seen enough blood to confirm that's actually the case.

Mertinon slipped me a glance, smiling away.

I had a brief, fleeting urge to give him a playful, brotherly punch on his upper arm.

But I resisted.

"You really are a noble captain," he said.

I smirked in response, turning my attention back to the navigational screens; and trying to work out just what was coming next. "Not totally sure a 'noble' captain goes about tossing a crewmember into the care of gangsters."

Mertinon shrugged. "It was a three for one offer—and it's not like you don't have another one."

I held off saying anything by way of reply.

I didn't want to get into trouble further down the line.

"Captain?"

When I turned in my chair, I saw that Brian was awaiting me.

That he was standing to attention in the bridge doorway.

"What's up?"

"Foy and Milky. They're *awake*."

I glanced back to Mertinon, and before I knew it, the two of us were leaping up out of our seats and heading on after Brian to the medbay.

———

As we bombed into the medbay, I immediately saw Clive standing off to the side. He looked a touch sheepish, his brow furrowed. He glanced to me and Mertinon. He opened his mouth but no sound came out. Sure enough, when I looked upon Foy and Milky, I saw that they were both sitting upright on their respective examination tables. And, besides their slightly dazed expressions, they appeared to be unharmed.

I looked back to Clive. "What'd you do to them?"

"I disabled their implants; what was controlling their actions."

"And what now?" I replied, turning back to Foy and Milky. "How long till they recover? How long till they'll be back to how they were before?"

"I . . . don't know, Captain . . ."

I waited for Clive to slip something else into the conversation, but it seemed that nothing was forthcoming. He was supposed to be the expert here, goddammit . . .

Rage flashed through me, blood bubbling up to my temples.

It ripped away my sense of perspective for several seconds.

When I finally regained it, my heart tapped out rapidly against my ribs.

I kept my tone cool—*collected*—as if I might be able to reason with the facts.

Whatever *the facts* were . . .

"What've you *done* to them?" I repeated.

"Just . . . just—"

This time, Clive's eyes flickered to Foy and Milky, and I saw there was fear.

He locked his eyes back onto mine.

"Captain, I . . ."

Somehow, everything broke free once more. I swung out a fist and caught Clive flush in the chin. He was as taken aback as I was by the sudden blow. He spun around; first falling against the wall, and then, unable to gain any sort of purchase, he tumbled to the ground, landing on his back. He stared up at me with wide, *terrified* eyes.

I felt Mertinon's hands on me, but I was able to shrug him off for the time being. "What *the hell* did you do to them, asshole? Have you wiped their memories? Will they ever be the same again?"

Clive, understandably stunned by the blow to his chin, took a few moments to come around. Still lying on his back, he squinted up at me. "I don't . . . I don't . . . *know*, Captain."

I got right down in Clive's face this time.

Grabbed hold of the neck of his shirt, yanking him up to me.

Mertinon—wiser than he looked—didn't think to step in.

"Listen, here, buddy, if you don't fix them up right this instant then I'm gonna flush you out into deep space." I paused a beat, as if that would help to drive my point home. "You get it? This isn't a game. Whatever game you were playing with Big Jo, with Ernest Harry, now it's time to come back to the real world . . . *capeesh?*"

Clive was dumbstruck by the whole experience. He tried to look around me, but I could tell that the world was only a fuzzed-up mess; that the universe was spinning faster than usual. When he realised he couldn't ignore me any longer, he focussed in on me. "I thought," he said. "I thought I'd done everything . . . everything that was required . . ."

"Required by *what?*" I shot back.

"By . . . by the ship . . . by the systems."

"What *systems?*"

"The ones which keep crewmembers brainwashed—the ones which keep the entire damn ship *going* . . . the deactivation protocol . . . I was sure . . . convinced that it'd be . . . it'd be . . ."

But Clive didn't have the strength to go on.

He fainted before he got anywhere close to delivering a meaningful reply.

Realising that I was still tightly gripping the collar of his shirt, I released him, allowing him to fall back onto the ground with no kind of delicacy at all.

I straightened up, looked to Milky and Foy, the two of them sitting up on the examination tables.

Both of them with equally blank stares fixed on their faces.

It was difficult for me to even look at them in their current state.

In the end, I just turned my back and walked out of the medbay.

Over my shoulder, I muttered a vague, but just about audible, "Lie them down—lie them *all* down," as I made it back to the bridge.

23 BOURTHNORNE-5

W E DRIFTED ON into space for what must've been about a day or two of a journey.

Neither Foy or Milky made any sort of recovery.

Clive, too, remained knocked out by my earlier swing at him.

It seemed that I'd really clocked him a good one.

I slipped away from the bridge about once every hour of travel, glancing in on the medbay, seeing what kind of state Foy and Milky were in. But the two of them merely remained there, lying on their backs, staring up at the ceiling as if they expected some kind of alien life form to come bursting into the ship. And, for all I knew, that was precisely what was going to happen.

Although I wasn't actively searching out any sort of a job, I noted somebody dialling up the *Nava*, looking for somebody to get a parcel to its destination.

And who was I to resist a quick buck?

A *distraction*.

So I brought us down to this mildewy-stinking planet: Bourthnorne-5.

There were great big pine trees just about everywhere.

A mean, icy fog which draped down across the scenery.

I suppose there was a certain ghostly beauty to the place, but, in all honesty, I just wanted to get my credits and leave. It's funny, I never thought there would come the day when I'd become fed up with smuggling . . . or ever making some cash.

Despite there being a standard, bumpkin terminal, the client specifically requested that we make it further out into the boonies. The package which'd been marked for transport was surprisingly large. When I'd first caught wind of the order, I'd considered turning it down on the basis that it might well be too large for the *Nava's* cargo hold . . . but I had too much pride in my ship—I couldn't think of turning down the offer.

On the vidscreen, there was an image of a run-down shack—standard for somewhere way out on a planet such as this one—but what I saw up ahead on the real-time screen didn't seem to quite fit *that* picture. What I could in fact see was a shuttle—specifically a lander.

From a much larger mother ship.

I glanced across to Mertinon, who, despite his lack of space-travel experience, seemed to catch onto the funny goings-on here. As I slammed down the thrusters, wanting to get us up and clear of the atmosphere just as fast as humanly possible, Mertinon made himself busy updating the crew on just what was going on . . . on just what the trouble was.

Namely, that we were about to get jumped.

That they should brace themselves.

The *Nava* squealed like a stuck piggy as I bent her into all sorts of undignified pitches.

With a small amount of fuss and a great amount of skill—if I do say so myself—I got her nose facing back up into space. I readied the engines, firing them up. Then I got ready to release the safeties. Only, when I brought my hand down, to flush the engines, there was no response whatsoever.

The *Nava* just gave a sad little chuckle.

And I couldn't help from thinking that we were moving.

Not upwards.

But sideways.

We continued to drift away from the upward position.

I tried to flush the engines again.

But nothing.

Not so much as a *tiny* shift in the ship's position or pitch.

We continued sideways at the same pace as before.

There seemed nothing I could do to stop the ship's motion.

My seat straps dug into my shoulders.

If there'd been any prospect of getting up off my ass and giving Clive a big slap about his chops, bringing him awake with a firm *smack*, then I would've done it . . . but, as I've well learned throughout the years, it doesn't necessarily pay to manoeuvre about a ship while it's gravity-bound; while it's playing by the laws of physics of some planet. Or, as I soon realised, while the ship's being *manipulated* by somebody with some extremely expensive technology and no small amount of malevolence.

It only took me a few seconds longer to establish that the

shuttle was the source of whatever was going on with the *Nava* .
. . not that that particular realisation helped much given that I
didn't have anybody sitting in the seat ready to pump them with
the cannons; let alone that the best gunner I'd ever seen was
lying incapacitated in the medbay.

Still, at the very least, it did give me a little time to prepare.

Yeah, like the time to say my *prayers* . . .

Soon enough, me and Mertinon were bracing for impact.

For the *Nava* to hit planetside.

When she did, the entire ship buckled.

Everything around us shook violently.

It felt like my brain rattled about my skull.

And I made a mental inventory of all the potential damages
which might've occurred as a result of our abrupt meeting with
the ground. The client, I decided—*right there, right then*—would
be the one to pay. No way was I going to come out for the worse
in this deal.

All I wanted was profit.

When I attempted to bring the *Nava* in flat, onto her belly, I
realised I couldn't get even that much done. Whoever it was
who was in control of the *Nava*—who was preventing me from
effectively captaining the craft—was some devious so and so.

They wanted to keep us in a compromising position.

Bastards.

It was then that I realised there was nothing for us to do
but wait.

Lying back in our chairs.

Like a whole ship full of numpties.

Of course I expected the advanced party—to find ourselves

on the sharp end of a whole bunch of blaster rifles. That wasn't how it went down, though.

We just remained there, in the ship, floating about on the tailbone of the *Nava*.

If I'd been bothered at all about it, then I might've given the order to have something cooked up; something to keep us occupied before our inevitable capture.

However, what happened in the end was the vidscreen sprouting up.

Spitting static just about all over the place.

When the image came clear, I found myself staring into the eyes of a familiar individual.

Big Jo.

Like plunge pools, those black eyes of his allowed me to lose myself; to draw me down, and down, and down . . . before I really knew what was going on, I'd slipped off into the Land of Snooze.

24 BOURTHNORNE-5 - HYPNOTISED AND HIJACKED

WHEN I CAME TO, my whole body was held in place to an articulated chair, angled at forty-five degrees. My arms and legs kept in place with extremely stretchy straps. I could get some decent enough movement from where I lay; enough so that I could crane my neck and take in my surroundings.

There was another pair of chairs.

One to either side of me.

Both of them, like mine, at an even forty-five degrees.

It didn't take me long to realise just who was strapped onto them:

Brian.

Mertinon.

My Ship's Doctor.

My brother-cum-Co-pilot.

If we hadn't been up the spout by then, we surely were now.

I shifted my attention back to the rest of the room.

Noticed that it was small.

Tight.

How—even through its darkness—it seemed to press down upon us.

To be shrinking.

I wrestled a little more with the straps holding me into place, and was surprised to find that I got enough slack in the elastic that I could worm an arm free.

Using my free arm, I set about liberating the other one.

Soon enough, I got to work on my legs.

Just as easy as the arms.

Before I knew it, I was standing free of my chair.

I turned my attention to Mertinon and Brian, knowing that I had to perform my escapology with them.

From the looks of their faces, they were still out.

Dozing from whatever it was Big Jo had dosed us with.

Outside the room, I could make out the sound of footsteps.

For a quick second, I was caught with panic—not really sure what to do.

I was of half a mind to fight them with my bare hands.

In that moment I couldn't have given two damns if they had blaster rifles, or worse.

I would take them down.

But my logical mind finally took over the wheel.

Talked some sense into me.

I worked quickly to contort myself back into place.

Where they'd left me once they'd blacked me out.

Back beneath the straps, but with the knowledge that I had

enough slack to free myself when the time came, I let my body go limp.

The door slid open.

———

To begin with I didn't want to risk anything.

I shut my eyes.

Made a point of making all the muscles in my eyelids relax.

They couldn't suspect anything.

As they passed in through the doorway, I noted the voices—their words still too dampened to be made out. But I could recognise them instantly:

Clive . . . Big Jo . . .

And then another which I couldn't square straight away.

Then it hit me.

And it was like driving a rusty nail through my forehead.

Terry.

My mind flashed about and—I was sure—my eyelids must've twitched.

If any of the trio noticed this, then they said nothing about it.

Clive addressed Big Jo. "We're having them all fitted for the neural implant—the surgeon should be along in the next five minutes or so."

Big Jo said nothing in reply, but I heard his unmistakeably thick, percussive footsteps as he trod about the examination chairs. I sensed him drawing close to me. I felt his warm breath up against my face. That slightly sour stench of his breath. His rattling, vacuous breathing. And then, apparently unaware of this unexpected moment of intimacy, Big Jo backed away. He spoke to Clive this time. "There was some trouble in fitting Captain Wright here with the implant, correct?"

"It seems the surgeon is confident that she's corrected the flaw."

I heard the rustle of clothing, and I imagined Big Jo wearing an ankle-long, sweeping jacket. "You mean you *will* be able to fit Captain Wright here with an implant?"

"Yes, sir," Clive replied.

It sent a thrill through my gut to hear Clive refer to Big Jo as 'sir' . . . it was almost as if it was the final insult. I'd trusted him *again*; and all the time against my better judgement.

My only mistake with clocking him one good in the chin was not hitting him hard enough. In not *killing* the bastard. Now, though, my mind spinning, it was Terry who spoke up.

"Sir?" Terry said, addressing Big Jo.

Again, this rankled.

Another rustle of jacket as Big Jo, apparently, turned his attention to Terry.

"I was wondering if this is *really* necessary . . . if I really have to . . ."

I imagined Big Jo holding up his palm here, gesturing for Terry to shut his trap. "You will do what you are told," Big Jo replied, sharply. "And you shall not speak out of turn *either*."

Here, the whole room became steeped in silence.

I chanced cranking an eyelid open a notch.

Even though I'd heard their voices—even though I'd

witnessed their conversation—it was something entirely different to actually see them all now.

To see them all standing around Mertinon.

Although I silently screamed at myself to close my eyes, to not show any sort of emotion, I couldn't help but bunch my fingers into fists down at my sides.

I was so sure *I* could show them.

That I could pummel all the bastards.

All *three* of them . . . well, maybe I'd let Terry go free . . . he was the only one vaguely innocent in this whole deal.

Noticing Clive shifting a glance back in my direction, I shut my eyes once more.

Allowed my fingers to go slack.

My mind tuned into their conversation again.

"All this capture and release," Big Jo said, "it's really got me a little giddy . . . but now everything seems to be in place; everything can be performed to our satisfaction."

"Yes, sir," Clive replied. "It seems so."

I held myself as still as I could, but I realised I'd started trembling.

It was one of the hardest things I'd ever done, attempting to remain still while lying on that examination chair. Knowing that I could break free at will . . . that I could get myself out of this mess . . . free the entire crew.

Save those who I *wanted* to save.

"Okay," Big Jo said, in a decided, sharp manner. One which told the listener—without mistake—that he had people to see; places to be. "Inform me when the work has been completed." Again, I could tell from the *rustle* of his jacket that he was glancing back across us . . . his captured bounty. "Then we can start to put plans into place."

"Yes, sir."

As I lay there, strapped to the examination chair, I had to sink my teeth into my lower lip to control the unchecked fury which piled on through me. I felt my pulse pound through my tongue. The blood pump into my mouth. I waited out the long seconds—listening for the door sliding open, and then shut again, as Big Jo left.

Then I broke free.

———

I found myself instantly facing off with both Clive and Terry.

I'd grabbed hold of Clive's shirt before he could so much as utter a syllable.

In my peripheral vision, I made out an open-mouthed Terry.

Apparently stunned.

I couldn't rightly blame him.

I had been *mighty* sly.

As I drew back my fist, ready to put Clive's lights out once and for all, he somehow managed to spit out the only words which would've been able to stop me. "Captain, please! If you kill me then you'll never find them—Milky and Foy . . . you'll never see them again."

I held myself very still.

My heart throbbed against my ribcage.

It ticked along in my throat.

And I held back.

"*Where*," I just about got out of my impossibly dry throat, "tell me *where* they are, and then I'll *kill* you."

Clive's eyes again widened.

He shifted a glance off at Terry.

I followed his gaze, only realising now that Terry held a blaster pistol.

And that it was trained on me.

I met Terry's eyes, stared long and hard into his.

When I spoke, it was almost as if my voice belonged to someone else. "You go ahead now, and you shoot me," I said. "But know this, even if you shoot me down, I don't care how bad you fry me, I ain't gonna get killed till I've taken care of business —till I've freed Milky and Foy. You get that, boy?"

Terry remained still.

All the colour had drained from his face.

He glanced to Clive.

And that was his mistake.

I broke free.

Released Clive.

Dived at Terry.

And a searing pain filled *everything*.

I could smell blood.

Actually, I couldn't *just* smell blood, I could *feel* it too.

Thick, and sticky, and oozing.

At first it was warm against my skin, and then it got cold.

Real fast.

A gradual shudder worked its way all the way up my spine.

It became uncontrollable when it got to my shoulder blades.

And then it was all I could do to keep my teeth from chattering.

From gnashing themselves into itty, bitty pieces.

I was lying on the floor.

I guess—when I'd dived—that was where I'd ended up.

I was staring up at Clive and Terry, the two of them looming over me now.

A single coil of smoke rose from the barrel of the blaster pistol Terry held.

He held the pistol down at his thigh, now.

Forgotten, almost.

As I felt their wide-eyed expressions attempting to make some sense of me, I found some words for them. "Now," I said, "just why in *hell* would you want to go do that?"

Neither of them answered.

But there didn't seem to be much reason for answering.

"And," I said, starting to get delirious, "who's this *surgeon* you keep on . . . keep on *keeping* on about, huh?"

Again, no sound from either of them.

"Captain," Clive said. "I think it's time."

"Time for *what*?" I replied, as if the words were a bitter taste on the tip of my tongue.

"For you to know the truth." Clive shifted a glance in Terry's direction. "The truth about the whole of the situation."

"Well, now," I said, again slipping Terry a glance, "You ain't gonna tell me this has something to do with Ricky D, now, are you?"

Clive drew a deep breath.

His shoulders arched back.

"Ricky D," he said, "is part of it, sure . . . but that's just the beginning . . . you need to know what the big picture is now."

"I'd be greatly obliged," I replied, and then nodded off in the general direction of our surroundings. "And it'd be a wonder if you could give me something for this *damn* pain."

25 BOURTHNORNE-5 - A CONSPIRACY, OR WHATEVER

CAPTAIN, although it pains me to admit it now, I've been keeping up company with other elements in the universe; elements which've helped to illuminate a better idea of what's really going on . . . call me naïve—call me *whatever*— but I did it because I thought that it'd be valuable information for us to have. Some kind of intelligence, I suppose . . . something which would benefit the crew, the *Nava*.

It was about six months before the 'accident' down on Karsedguron-17 that I first caught wind of Big Jo's plans.

One night, in the *Bitch's Leap*, back on Hortenine-6, remember that I left you and the others to have a drink while I went off to go and catch up with family? Well, on my way out of the bar, I couldn't help but notice a pretty shabby group of guys all dressed in leather jackets. Now, that's nothing abnormal for Hortenine, as you know, but there was something about the way they walked—it was so *uniform*; almost like they were *marching* to the beat of some invisible drum—so I decided to follow them.

Don't know clearly why.

But I *did*.

They followed the terminal road, apparently heading back to their ships, whichever they were. All preparing to set their course back up into space. As they went along, as they trod through the terminal entrance, I noticed just what it was that had caught my attention.

The holes in their heads.

Like bullet holes, almost.

You know, just like the ones Foy and Milky, and . . . well . . . *you've* got.

The ones which they'll be drilling into Brian and Mertinon in a matter of minutes.

I'm sorry about how this has happened; how things have come to this, but, as I hope you'll soon understand, there was just no other way of going about it.

Not without setting ourselves up for even greater danger.

Anyway, although weird, I didn't think anything of those holes in the head until about a month or so later. It was when we were back up on the *Nava*, bombing it someplace or other, when we got a job offer in through from one of Big Jo's representatives. As is *Nava* policy, whenever anything comes through with Big Jo's name in any way connected to it—when there's anything with *Arkle-4* connected to it—I made to reject the offer.

But not before I'd got a look at the avatar which was attached to the message.

Oh, the guy looked like your standard-order smuggler—leather jacket, the ankle-high boots, and whatever else—but I couldn't help noticing the stand-out feature.

The hole in the head.

Just like those hoods back on Hortenine.

I didn't act on it then, obviously, I just closed the message.

Binned it.

But it stuck with me.

That image . . . that hole in the guy's head.

And I knew that *something* had to be going on.

I sort of threw all of that onto the backburner in my brain—not really putting much conscious thought into the thing. I'm sure you'll be glad to hear that I take my duties on the *Nava* extremely seriously, and I don't like to channel too much mental bandwidth away from them. And it wasn't until about a month before the accident that I found myself being faced with the holes-in-the-head thing once again.

We'd gone planetside—some job which'd pay us a good few weeks' expenses, if I remember rightly—and I was shifting my way through some market or other alone, while you and the twins, Foy and Milky, all piled along on the mission. As I was making my way through the market, I felt somebody grab me from behind. Just as I always make a point of doing, I whipped out my blaster pistol, and stunned the guy. As he writhed about on the ground, I saw yet another one of those holes in his head. It got me thinking again. I rifled through his clothes, hoping to be able to dig something useful out of him.

Something which'd give me a clue.

And that was when I came across the business card.

Ricky *D's* business card.

Well, I didn't know exactly who Ricky D was, or what he was up to, but I got to thinking that perhaps it wasn't as I'd thought it before; that Big Jo was the one behind these holes in the head.

I shifted my thinking.

Did some digging into Big Jo; hoping to turn something or other up on the guy. As I'm sure you've noticed, he comes across as a legitimate businessman—whatever that counts for—and he'd done a good job of covering his tracks. If it hadn't been for that business card, I wouldn't ever have thought to so much as go looking for Ricky D.

I would've—most likely—let the whole thing slip my mind.

But, with that business card in hand, I had an actual *physical* clue.

Some place I could start my sleuthing.

As we travelled away from the job later that day, I did a whole bunch of thinking; wondering just what the guy had been trying to achieve by grabbing me at the market. I got to believing that it might have something to do with kidnap, rather than robbery. You know how it goes with thieving—with *muggers*— for the most part they don't go about busy places *grabbing* people . . . nah, they'd much rather pinch your purse, or, if they absolutely want to use force, then they get you someplace solitary.

Somewhere nobody will hear you scream.

With that in mind, knowing that it was Ricky D behind this whole deal; and that he'd attempted to jack me—one of Arkle Wright's crewmembers—I couldn't quite get my head around why it would be. Why he would want *me* of all people. Maybe it would've been the thing to do for me to go to Ricky D, confront him with this. But it seemed far too risky.

And, anyway, I had a better plan.

Being a tough guy, Ricky D, what with his office building, and his fleet of neat, swift-manoeuvring ships, I knew that he could easily crush me like a bug if I got too close to his boot heel. So I went with the next best thing—with Big Jo.

Now you know why I asked for time off for a couple of weeks.

I needed to do my ground work.

I needed to bide my time.

Get things straight.

Of course, as it turned out, I soon discovered that Big Jo had one of those holes in his head himself. It didn't take me long to work out who was responsible for putting it there:

Ricky D.

Anyway, once I'd got myself aboard *Ghost Wave*—not too much of a big deal given that all the security was taken care of by neural-transplanted zombies—I found myself able to access the main computer systems where I burgled myself into managing the whole *damn* fleet . . . Big Jo, and his delegates, turned into nothing more than a simple puppet.

Only this time, instead of Ricky D, it was *me* pulling the strings.

Big Jo was all about recruiting more neural-implanted zombies for his fleet, but he didn't have the ability to stop and think; to realise that he *himself* was one.

I had to take care, obviously, I had to make it *seem* like Ricky

D was still very much in charge of all the goings-on of *Ghost Wave* and her fleet, but it meant that I had effectively got myself into a position—Trojan-like—where I could corner Ricky D.

I have to be honest, it took me back a little when I intercepted a request from Ricky D to kidnap the crew of the *Nava* and have them implanted, but I soon realised—I soon *saw*—just what was going on. I'm sure you witnessed for yourself all those black overalls back at Bomberlee City Terminal; on Arkle-4 . . . a set of those was intended for the crew of the *Nava* when they were added to Big Jo's zombie fleet.

I thought on it a long time, Captain, and, believe me, I thought hard about whether or not to tell you this. In the end, I decided against uttering a word. I thought that the fewer ears in on what was really going on, the firmer upper hand we'd have. I'd already gone so far, manoeuvred us into such a strong position, that I couldn't stand the prospect of it getting all thrown away.

I was the head of my own *fleet* for Christ's sake.

And nobody even *knew*.

We had to go through with the job, with the kidnap plan which Ricky D had put in place for us on Karsedguron-17.

And I had to ensure Ricky D believed—*truly believed*—that he was still in charge.

That was the key.

But I managed to keep you, Captain, to keep the neural implant from taking effect.

They could only take Milky and Foy into their midst.

A sacrifice which had to be made.

All that remains now is to think on what we're to do with

the fleet . . . to think on just what we can do with all this power. Ricky D won't stop, Captain, he sincerely wants the *Nava*, and her crew, to fall into line beneath Big Jo's *Ghost Wave* fleet.

And, quite frankly, and I can only speak for myself, that's something which doesn't bear thinking about.

26 BOURTHNORNE-5 - BETRAYED OR BETRAYER?

DESPITE THE PAIN which was forcing the wrinkle lines into my brow, I managed to get out something approaching a smile at Clive. Why, I would even go so far as to say that I was *glad* I hadn't flown clean off the handle and killed him with my bare hands.

And that was quite *some* change of heart.

Seeing Terry and Clive standing over me, both of them looking rightly dour, I sucked up all the captainly strength I held within, and then reached a hand up.

Clapped Clive on the shoulder.

Clive met my eye.

I could see he was close to tears.

"Please, Captain," he said, "you *must* forgive me." He shook his head, then reached up and rubbed his eyes. Whether or not a tear streaked his cheek, I couldn't tell by the time he turned back to me. His gaze was back to being firm, unmoving, *sincere.* "I tried to send the message through Foy, through Milky, to tell you how sorry I was . . . how you had to forgive me. But you have to understand, I was afraid that Ricky D would get to you; that he would manage to get a neural implant popped in place. And then he would know everything. He would know that *I* was really shepherding his fleet. That he had no control. I had to bring you far away from him—I had to bring you *here*—where I could be sure that Ricky D wouldn't be able to stop us." He gave a wry smile; one of those smiles which—if it's not careful—can find itself shortly bereft of teeth. "I had Big Jo knock you out with those *hypnoeyes.* I thought it might work better if you were strapped in while I explained, but, it seems, that wasn't necessary." He stopped to take a much-needed gulp of air. "So, Captain, we need to discuss our next move. We need to talk through how we're going to topple Ricky D."

Maybe it was through the blood loss.

Or perhaps it was the extreme pain rankling my skull.

But I couldn't quite follow what Clive'd just said.

"Come again?" I put in, the words sounding all jangling and distant.

———

Clive and Terry set about waking Brian and Mertinon from their Big-Jo induced slumber.

Brian had hardly blinked himself back to consciousness before his eyes came to rest on the wound I had on my upper arm, where Terry had shot me through with the blaster pistol.

Before I could utter anything at all, he was upon me, wadding up the injury with something or other . . . something *medical*.

I asked Clive about Terry—about how he had managed to prise him away from Ricky D.

With a wry smile, Clive told me that it hadn't anything to do with 'prising away' since Ricky D had specifically sent Terry along so that he could be 'fixed' for his neural implant.

He had placed Terry into Big Jo's care.

But which was, in reality, Clive's sphere of control.

Once I'd got myself patched up by Brian, and we had all shaken off whatever it was that Big Jo had done to us, we set our minds to recovering Milky and Foy.

On our way along the corridor, Clive turned back to me. "I don't want you to be alarmed, Captain, believe me, I was more dubious than anybody about these neural implants—the implications which they have for the individuals fitted for them, as well as the reliability of their pre-zombified skills. But this surgeon—I assure you—is *quite* capable. She'll have the best shot of bringing Milky and Foy back."

We turned the corner, and a door slid clean out of our way.

Beyond the door, I made out the pair of figures lying on examination tables:

Milky and Foy.

Just as me, Mertinon and Brian had been, they were strapped down.

My attention instantly swerved away from my crewmembers, though, and to the surgeon.

Sure enough, she was all garbed up in a sterile, green pinion, with a mask on, a neat skullcap pinning down her black hair, a pair of gloves, and—*I'm sure*—a whole bunch else.

Even from just her eyes I could tell who it was . . . those *sparkling green eyes . . .*

The *biter . . .*

She didn't seem to register me, or, if she did, she made no signal or sign.

Guess that's pretty much the effect I have on all the ladies.

The surgeon—the *biter*—moved from one of the patients to the other.

I turned back to Clive. "Uh," I began, "how long's this going to take?"

Clive glanced to me.

He shook his head.

"Don't know, Captain."

"And," I said, "what about Big Jo . . . might he not come stomping around here; find out that we've all been let loose?"

Clive gave a shrug. "Doesn't matter. He's under my control . . . although it may not seem like it. Guess that with brainwashing you can't quite change somebody's natural makeup— their *personality*."

"Pity," I said.

And meant it.

Just as I was ready to open my big fat gob all over again, the surgeon trudged over to the other side of the room and switched on some loud machine which sounded something like a cross between a hairdryer and a machine gun. When she got through —having taken care of bursting everyone in that room's eardrums—she padded back over to the patients. Rested her palm flat against each of their foreheads in turn, as if taking their temperature. It was almost as if the surgical theatre itself was responding to her own thoughts, although, more likely, she had just trod on some switch or other. The two examination tables arched back into their upright position so that Milky and Foy were more or less in a standing pose.

My heart stuck in my throat.

The biter-cum-surgeon forgotten for the time being, I shifted my attention onto Foy and Milky, and, more specifically, their expressions.

Nothing.

Neutral.

Devoid of emotion.

Personality.

I glanced back at Clive, feeling a shred of that fury which'd not so long ago coursed through me. If either of them had got hurt during this whole sequence of events then I would never forgive myself; that would be an impossibility.

Recalling the story which Clive had told me, and that I was supposed to be feeling more or less kindly towards him, I turned my attention back to the patients.

Back to Foy and Milky.

It happened very slowly. It must've been only so much as the flinch of an eye; the curling of a lip; the twitching of a nose.

Nothing more dramatic than that.

But then they were awake.

Their eyes met mine.

And I knew.

They were back.

———

It felt somewhat odd to have the whole crew together.

And for all of us to be making confident progress along the corridors of the shuttle—the place which'd sucked the *Nava* into its influence. Clive had assured me, by the by, that it wasn't as simple as it appeared; and that it was actually packing a heftily powered shield generator, along with other curiosities. He went on to say that some corps of his zombie fleet engineers had had a hand in putting it together . . . all under Clive's command, of course.

The upshot was that Clive could free the *Nava* from the tractor beam since he was the one in control of it.

With the crew all back on board the *Nava*, it felt strange to have the whole of the bridge filled to bursting. Mertinon, in the co-pilot's chair; Foy at the guns; Milky checking over the navigational screens. Clive had headed down to the engine rooms to see if he couldn't find an extra burst of firepower from somewhere. Terry and Brian were squirrelled away somewhere, in the back rooms, doing who really knew what . . . I just hoped that they weren't going to break anything *important*.

Back to normal.

Once Clive had finished up his jiggery-pokery in the engine rooms, he returned to the bridge to help guide me through the process of patching the *Nava* into the rest of the *Ghost Wave* fleet. We got ourselves up into space, with the shuttle-cum-shield-generator in our wake, before anybody did any serious talking.

"Captain?" Clive said, obviously to me.

I turned in my chair, having got comfortable, and in no real hurry to lug myself up off my lardy buns. "What?"

"We need to think about how we'll deal with Ricky D."

"What do you mean *deal* with him?"

"He's not going away, sir. He'll continue to pursue us . . . and, quite frankly, now that I've gone and got my hands so dirty in his zombie fleet, he'll see us as a great threat. Once he gets the reins back of the *Ghost Wave* fleet he'll hunt us down." Clive gave a shake of his head. "The modifications I managed on the *Nava's* engines will get us out of the odd sticky situation but we won't be able to rely on them always . . . there'll come a time when we will slip up; when we won't see them coming. And Ricky D will have his revenge."

I studied Clive's words carefully.

His *reasoning*.

"So, what you're saying," I replied, "is that you want us to go after Ricky D, right now?"

"Correct, Captain."

I glanced over to Mertinon, in the co-pilot's chair.

He threw up his hands as if absolving himself from any of this.

Perhaps he wasn't aware that demotions could be swung into place just as quickly and easily as promotions . . .

I looked to Milky, and then Foy.

Neither of them appeared to have anything constructive to contribute.

With a sigh, I shifted my full attention back to Clive.

"You reckon *now's* the time?"

"It's the only time, Captain," Clive replied, soundly, and

firmly. "I've set up the *Ghost Wave* fleet in such a way that we can play it like an orchestra."

"That *I* can play it like an orchestra," I corrected him.

Clive flushed slightly, and I felt a touch bad about having chided him.

Mind made up, I glanced about the bridge, and then stared long and hard back at Clive. I rose up out of my chair, an accomplishment in itself seeing as I was lying in what might well have proven to be mortal peril barely hours ago.

I reached out my hand for him to shake.

He took my hand off me.

Shook it firm.

"Welcome back aboard, Wodd."

Clive smiled from ear to ear.

27 GHOST WAVE TO KARSEDGURON-17

ALTHOUGH I WAS OBVIOUSLY the captain of the situation—as was my wont—I allowed Clive to guide us through the basics of the plan . . . a plan which, to be quite frank, I really hadn't the first clue about.

The first stage involved docking the *Nava* in the bay of the *Ghost Wave*.

Despite everything that'd gone on—getting the crew back; and finding out that Clive wasn't a slimy, traitorous bastard after all—I couldn't quite bring myself to *believe* everything would be okay about me slotting the *Nava* into the bay . . . almost like I'd gone and landed on some unseemly planet and decided to leave her behind at the terminal; unsure whether she'd still be there by the time I got back.

But I managed to get past my separation anxiety.

Clive got us to the bridge of *Ghost Wave*, and I felt myself trembling all over as I made to sit down in the seat there. It was irrational. It was almost a *phobia*. Perhaps it was all of the stuff—all of the *baggage*—which surrounded Big Jo coming back to me.

How he had dominated my childhood.

How he would *continue* to dominate my home planet if nothing was done about him.

And his puppet master.

Ricky D.

I glanced over the vidscreens.

Although I was loath to mention it right there and then, it was the first time that I'd taken control of a fleet . . . well, at least one *this* size. There was something about the task itself—just the sound of the word; *fleet*—which brought all the hairs on the back of my neck standing up. But I did what I had to do . . . I pretended that I wasn't some small-time, two-bit space smuggler, and I got myself down to *doing my job*.

I had the assistance of Terry, Brian and Mertinon; the three of them joining me on the bridge, while Clive swept Foy and Milky away, promising that he had—*apparently*—more worthy things for them to do. Things more worthy than serving beneath *my* command, in any case . . .

Although Clive was being very nice about the whole ordeal, I knew that there was very little ambiguity surrounding things; Clive was the one with all the answers, he was the *real* one in charge. At least for the time being.

But I just did my job the best I could.

And waited for all the pieces to fall into place.

As I sat down in the captain's chair, directing Terry, Brian and Mertinon about their work, I felt something cool—*metal*—press up against the side of my neck.

I held myself very still.

Having caught a blaster wound too soon ago to bear thinking about, I didn't make any sudden movements. When Terry called out to me for some help with some insignificant thing or other, and I didn't reply, my whole crew turned to look.

To see me sitting there; a blaster pointed at my neck, and with Captain Henry 'Ernest Harry' Norbortwitz at the other end of it.

I felt Terry, Brian and Mertinon all staring down on me.

All of them equally as stunned.

And all of them—*just as equally*—useless.

"Get up," Norbortwitz said, too close to my ear for comfort.

Who was I to argue?

I did just what he said.

Back on my own two pegs, having left the comfort of the captain's chair behind me, I thought to glance back. And I caught sight of Big Jo for my troubles.

There was something about him which I couldn't quite place.

Something which just didn't *sit* right.

He seemed . . . *lost* . . . almost.

On instinct, my eyes searched out Norbortwitz.

It wasn't too difficult.

I had only to follow the barrel of the blaster pistol.

He gave me a smirk by way of reward.

"Trying to make it all click into place, Captain Wright? Trying to work out what's going on? How it could be that Clive Wodd's not got a handle on me—that he can't control my *mind*?"

It felt like somebody had pinched me in the gut. "Yeah, actually."

Using the hand which didn't grip the blaster, Norbortwitz reached up for his forehead. To where he wore that cap of his held snugly down; the visor keeping the top half of his face in shadow. He removed his cap. Showed me his bare forehead. No sign of the hole from before.

He smiled more widely still.

"No strings now. Reversible procedure." he said, "however much Clive would wish it to be different." Now he nodded over to Big Jo, who still seemed as though he was occupying a different slice of space-time to us. "You do realise that there is something of a grand prize at stake here, don't you? And Clive didn't expect me to simply sit off on the side lines like some hired *goon* while he put everything that's been arranged into place for his own purposes?"

Still feeling the uncomfortable sensation of the blaster pistol sticking in my neck, I eyed Norbortwitz. "What's in it for you?" I said. "What's Ricky D paying you?"

I hoped that name-checking Ricky D would flummox him . . . or something.

On the contrary, though, he only gave a dry chuckle.

"Oh, Arkle," he said. "You really have *such* a small imagination. Do you really think that I suffered by Big Jo's side for so many years just so that I could serve *another* master?" He shook his head. "No, that wouldn't do at all . . . when I possess such a tool as the *Ghost Wave* fleet, and with so many willing and able crew, why would I do *anything* anybody else tells me?"

Despite everything, and seeing the stunned expressions of

Terry, Brian and Mertinon still dominating my vision, I couldn't help but shrug, then say, "Dunno, a conscience?"

This brought along a laugh.

When Norbortwitz had picked up the pieces, he said, "Well, I think I can safely say that neither one of us possesses one of those—not *really* . . . not when it comes down to it." He sucked in another breath through his teeth. "Not when we've got *skin* in the game."

I sincerely believed he would pull the trigger right then.

That he would blow my head clean off my shoulders.

But, for some reason, he held back.

When the blaster did finally go off, I felt the blazing warmth pass too close for comfort to my earlobe. I sniffed the acrid scent of burning hair—my *own* hair—and it was enough to curl my toenails.

———

Feeling numb, I stumbled away from the scene.

Caught my brain back.

Looked over the faces of my crew—of Mertinon, Terry and Brian—all of them fine.

But equally stunned as I was.

Once I'd got over the momentary disappointment of none of *them* coming rushing to my aid, I realised just who it was who had.

Big Jo.

I stared long and hard at him as he wrestled with Norbortwitz, apparently having broken free of his zombielike daze. The blaster pistol, I saw, was lying at their feet; forgotten while they grappled in a hand-to-hand melee.

I shifted a look at Mertinon, Terry and Brian, and then fired myself forwards; again engaging brawn over brains. Before I knew it, I'd recovered the blaster pistol, and held it tightly in my grasp. But it seemed that Big Jo and Norbortwitz were doing a fair job of destroying one another.

Actually, to put it bluntly, they seemed to be ripping the *shit* out of each other.

I stood back with the rest of my crew, and wondered just what my role was going to be here, as decided by whatever celestial gods truly exist. I still held the blaster, of course, and something within me told me that I should shoot one, and then the other. But, having just had that conversation with Norbortwitz which'd touched—at least superficially—on the nature of the conscience, I couldn't quite bring myself to murder these two men in cold blood.

Even if they were clearly blood-thirsty gangsters themselves.

"Arkle . . . I mean, *Captain!*"

I glanced behind me.

Caught Mertinon's eye.

He was nodding in the direction of the melee, clearly imploring me to take the shot; to take the opportunity while it was still there to be taken.

But . . . despite everything . . . I just *couldn't*.

"Arkle! Goddammit, *Arkle!*" Mertinon screamed, this time in my ear.

Before I knew what was happening, he had peeled the

blaster free of my fingers, and he was holding it himself; pointing it at the two villains now trading punches.

Without hesitation, and feeling myself falling away from the scene, Mertinon stepped towards them. He fired six, seven, or more times. I watched on—half in shock; half in *terror*—as he plugged both of the combatants in assorted limbs.

Soon enough, the two of them had forgotten the fight, and were rolling about in pain—blood seeping out of their wounds as they did so. Although Mertinon was clearly unfinished, still rapping away on the blaster trigger, there was nothing coming out. The blaster had run itself down in all the excitement. Its payload was spent. I took my chance, before it had a chance to charge itself back up, to slip the blaster back out of Mertinon's vicelike grip.

I tossed the blaster off across the bridge.

Heard it skitter beneath some panel or other.

The two men—Norbortwitz and Big Jo—groaned out in pain from their wounds.

I held very still, wondering just what was going to happen next . . . well, that much seemed fairly obvious . . . they were going to *die* if they didn't get any rapid medical attention. As if he was hooked directly into my thoughts, Brian appeared at my side.

He slipped me a sidelong glance.

Save them?

Or not.

I looked to Brian, and then to Mertinon.

Terry lingered about in the background.

"Do what the hell you want," I said, sounding more bitter

than I would've thought. "I'm going to go catch up with Clive—see just what he's onto . . . and to get some clue as to what he even *needs* me here for."

And, with that, I left my beleaguered crew behind to see to the victims.

———

Using an earpiece I picked up off the bridge and plugged into my eardrum, I located Clive just coming down from the Command Centre—the area which, among other things, would take control of the fleet's cannons.

I suppose he had just got back from posting Foy there in some strategic spot.

He met my eye.

A smile briefly clung to his lips.

Then it faded.

"You heard the news?" he said.

"What news?"

"Big Jo," he said. "He's *dead . . .*"

I had often wondered how I might feel to hear that the boogieman from my childhood was no longer of this mortal coil. I'd always thought that the announcement would be accompanied by fireworks—by rampant celebrations.

But it wasn't like that at all.

Maybe it had something to do with the circumstances, the way that I knew it wouldn't be the end . . . that, at least now, Big Jo had been nothing but a puppet.

"Makes the protocols easier, at least," Clive said. "I mean, I can reprogram things so that you're the official admiral of the fleet . . ."

I must've drifted away then because the next thing I recall hearing was Clive calling out to me.

"Captain? Captain?"

Finally, I turned to look back at him.

"Should I do it? Should I implement the change—make you admiral of the fleet?"

Despite everything—despite the blood which'd been spilled that day—I couldn't help but feel a smile creep onto my lips. "Sounds good, don't it?"

"What?"

"Admiral Wright."

Clive met my eye.

And he gave a weary smile in return.

"Come on," I said, "let's get back to the bridge—there's work to be done."

———

When I got back to the bridge, Brian had already taken care of Big Jo's corpse, while he was currently nursing Captain Norbortwitz in the medbay. Terry had gone to lend him a helping hand. That left Mertinon holding the fort on the bridge when me and Clive arrived.

I wasted no time in getting myself all slumped up in the captain's chair.

Clive took up his place at the navigational screens.

For a couple of seconds, I couldn't help but note just how

thorough the display seemed compared to the systems I had back on the *Nava* . . . and then I gave myself the mental reminder that the *Nava* was a smuggler's craft; beautiful in her way, but by no means cut out to ever become a flagship.

Unsuitable for an admiral such as myself.

I just had to make sure I didn't say so much out loud.

In the *Nava's* earshot.

As Clive made adjustments to our course for Karsedguron-17, I couldn't help noticing how Mertinon had gone some shade of pale. I wanted to ask him if he was okay; if it was the knowledge that he'd killed a man which'd got his knickers in a twist. But I held myself back. Knowing when it was time to give a man space to think things out.

God knows I've had more than my fair share of those solitary, silent moments.

To be honest, before I'd actually had a taste of the job for myself, I always imagined that being an admiral was all fun and games; that it must've felt several shades of awesome to command upwards of a hundred ships, all at the same time. I'd never really thought about the practicalities of the thing; about how it was more akin to steering one great honking mother ship along. Perhaps sensing my flagging enthusiasm, Clive suggested that I send out some scout ships to keep track of our route directly ahead. So I did that.

The scout ships flew out across the vidscreens like a whole host of missiles.

There was, apparently, nothing to report.

I glanced to Clive.

He looked to me.

And then he gave me a firm nod.

It was time for us to make the jump to Karsedguron-17.

There could be no backing away now.

We were going to war.

With Ricky D.

28 KARSEDGURON-17

"SO," I said to Clive, as *Ghost Wave's* proximity alarms alerted us to the groundside defence systems locking onto us, "what now?"

Clive remained calm.

Almost *too* calm.

Even with mine and Mertinon's eyes fixed on him.

"We sit back and watch," Clive replied.

And that was what we did.

Down below, I took in the swirling planet of Karsedguron-17, and—more immediately—the missiles and lasers firing up at the fleet. I watched on with no small amount of interest as the invisible fleet shields absorbed each one of the blows; apparently effortlessly.

Clive leaned into me. "We're absorbing all of that energy, taking it into our tanks, there'll be a nice surprise for Ricky D when he decides to hold fire." He jerked his thumb back over his shoulder to indicate the Command Centre. "Foy's prepping —ready to get them hook, line and sinker."

I said nothing in reply—perhaps it was my new-found, regal, admiral's air.

And, besides, Clive already had everything in the bag.

We'd been witnessing the planetside barrage for what must've been about ten minutes before I turned to Clive. "Just what *is* your plan here? You want to blow everybody off the face of that planet? You want to take care of civilians, too?"

All of a sudden, Clive got all quiet.

An uneasy tension settled over the bridge of *Ghost Wave*.

My heart batted against my ribs a couple of times.

"Well," Clive said, turning to me, "the way I'd envisioned it, I thought this would be the only way. We have to be practical, Captain. Think of all the misery which Ricky D and his kind inflicts on the universe—how many *innocents* he makes suffer. What we have now is a great opportunity; perhaps a *once in a lifetime* opportunity. We can wipe Ricky D out for good. It'll be a mighty blow against a large array of mobsters—of those who do nothing but turn the universe into a great big pile of sludge."

I considered Clive's words for several seconds—again, it seemed like my admiral's role was getting to me. "And what would you say if this was your home planet? What would you say if this was Hortenine-6?"

Clive didn't reply.

He averted my gaze.

"That's what I thought," I replied, glancing to the vidscreens, and the continued onslaught from planetside.

I could see, in a pop-out window, how the energy tanks were

charging themselves up, just as Clive had said. I estimated that in about ten minutes the whole fleet would be ready to fire on the planet; to blow it from the face of the universe.

And it would be *me* who was responsible.

Although it wasn't like I hadn't destroyed planets—or *stars*—before, they had always been, as far as I knew, free from habitation. This was different, though. I knew that if we went through with the plan, if we fired without mercy, that I would wake up in cold sweats every night until the day I died with thousands of screams rattling about inside my skull.

And I didn't want to hear screams.

Never again, if I could help it.

Decided, I shifted myself up from the captain's chair, stalked across the bridge. Before either Clive or Mertinon could say anything, I said, "Bro, you're in charge—stop Clive from doing anything *reckless* . . ."

It wasn't till I'd reached the exit of the bridge that either of them thought to speak up. In the end, it was Mertinon. "Arkle? Where're you going?"

I turned back to him.

Gave a wry smile.

Said, "Planetside."

———

For my trip planetside, I took Milky and Terry.

Just because they didn't seem to have anything better to do.

To be honest, even though they were basically adolescents, they were a far better shot than I was with a blaster pistol. And, it seemed, from the looks of things, that we *would* be needing some blaster pistols . . . and someone who could shoot straight.

With us all suited and booted, we headed down planetside in a shuttle. We landed with a thud just outside the main city, took some speeder scooters through to Ricky D's building.

As we trudged through the deserted streets—the populace apparently somewhat wary of the hundred or so ships which'd cropped up in their skies—I observed the firing lasers on the horizon; and the odd missile which twirled up through the atmosphere; apparently headed for the *Ghost Wave* fleet. Hoping to deal it some damage.

Perhaps I expected Ricky D's building to be on some kind of lockdown, but, just like it had been before, there was no trouble in getting up to his office. I suppose that, since he had his own zombie-staffed fleet of ships, Ricky D had allowed himself a scrap of misplaced confidence; that nobody would be coming knocking on his front door.

Well, we didn't even *need* to knock.

The door was already *goddamn* open.

With Milky and Terry on my heels, we burst into the office.

I cast a quick glance upwards to the skylight, and to the lasers which constantly zapped about the horizon, flashing and fuming.

I don't know if I expected to find Ricky D either huddling behind his desk, a blaster grasped in his hand, ready to go down fighting; or if I thought that he would be on his knees, pleading with us not to wipe him off the face of the universe.

In the end, he was neither.

Just as he had been before, Ricky D was at his desk; his hair nicely gelled, and his eyes firmly fixed on the vidscreen spread out before him. Perhaps his typing motions were marginally quicker than they had been the previous times I'd visited, but that, if it was a change at all, was the only vaguely notable difference.

He glanced up casually to us as we trod in through the doorway. "Captain Wright," he said, a slight smile on his lips. "You'll forgive me for not getting up to shake your hand, but I'm rather tied up at the minute." He jabbed a finger upwards, to the planetside bombardment taking place.

He returned to his busy typing.

Then, as if he'd forgotten something, he looked at us again.

Eyed Terry.

"Hello there," he said. "How've you been getting on? Seems a while since we checked in last, don't you think?"

I turned to inspect Terry.

Read the conflicted emotions passing over his face.

I knew that an astute type such as Ricky D had surely learned how to effectively—*efficiently*—indoctrinate those he needed to; so he might force their arm when he wished it. Would he force Terry's arm now?

I took a step towards Ricky D's desk. "The deal was no good," I said. "You said that you'd get me back my crew; that you'd help me defeat Big Jo's fleet."

Ricky D remained more interested in the goings-on of his vidscreen than the living, breathing human beings standing before his desk.

I decided to continue, unperturbed, as—at least in my mind—I believed was fitting for an admiral. "But the fleet was never under Big Jo's control, after all . . . not since you stuck that chip, that implant, that *whatever*, in his brain . . . since you turned all of his crew into zombies."

No reaction on Ricky D's face.

He just kept about his vidscreen, as if he was dealing with some unpleasantly mundane, day-to-day admin.

I allowed myself a slight smile now, though.

For the first time in this whole experience, I felt as if I was clued into the full picture. And, not only that, I held all the cards. "So," I said, "you wanna negotiate terms of surrender, or what?"

At this, Ricky D did glance up from his vidscreen.

He didn't smile, though.

And, when he spoke, it was as if he was trying to get his lips around a word in a foreign language. " 'Surrender' ?" he said.

But I just nodded to Terry and Milky.

For the two of them to raise their blasters.

———

For the longest while, the only sound I could hear in the office was the distant *sizzle* of lasers scorching the air. I could smell the bitter, sulphuric scent of missile entrails, as they spurted upwards, into the atmosphere. And I could feel the complete stillness of the ground beneath my feet; as if the whole planet was holding its breath.

Waiting for the knockout punch.

For the first time in our exchange, we had Ricky D's full attention.

Perhaps it was the effect of having a pair of blasters trained on him.

If there's something which doesn't often fail to get attention it's a *firearm*.

Still sitting at his desk, Ricky D shook his head as he met my eye. "I don't understand what you mean by 'surrender'. There can *be* no surrender. This is just business. This is the way the world works, for good or for ill . . . what must come to pass shall do so."

"Okay, okay," I said, holding up my palm. "Let's cut all this philosophical, nice-guy gangster bullshit and get down to brass tacks, shall we?"

Ricky D remained still.

His face betrayed no emotion.

Not so much as a raised eyebrow.

Not so much as a quiver of the lips.

"What would the *terms* of a 'surrender' be?" Ricky D said.

I felt puzzled for several moments, not really able to reconcile what he was on about. I wondered if he was stalling for time; that way arch villains have a habit of doing . . . but something about the situation told me that it wasn't the case.

I glanced to Terry, and then to Milky. "Uh," I said, starting out unconvincingly as I shifted my attention back to Ricky D. "That you'll *stop* what you're doing?"

Ricky D merely shook his head at this.

He still retained the hint of a smile on his lips.

"I don't think you quite understand, Captain Wright—I don't think you quite *appreciate* how far and how *deeply* rooted the whole of this organisation really is." He held up his hands, apparently to indicate the building which surrounded us. "The entire economy of this planet depends on my business continuing and"—here he pouted—"I acknowledged that there are *elements* of the business which, from the outside, might seem somewhat unpleasant; *however*, that's not to say that they're not necessary."

This was all beginning to sound a lot like somebody telling me to 'shut up' and not 'worry' . . . something along those lines.

I couldn't quite work out how I should respond to that.

And, as it happened, Ricky D didn't seem keen to give me the opportunity to respond.

"So," Ricky D continued, "if you feel that you must *kill* me, or that you really need to crush the entirety of the planet beneath the force of your fleet, then, please, feel free to do so. But know that, at the same time, you shall be plunging a great number into poverty . . . removing the jobs which *legitimate* society is unable—or *unwilling*—to provide." He hunched his shoulders now. "And what will come out of that but more *evil?* . . . Only this time disorganised, no longer kept in its place beneath a single roof as it is here, on this planet. On Karsedguron-17."

I caught up with everything Ricky D had said.

Then shifted a glance back at Terry and Milky, who looked just as confused as I did.

This was a situation which required *true* leadership.

Which needed a firm and steady hand to take care of business.

I decided to put ourselves back on the offensive.

To take another step forwards.

"That's all well and good," I said, "but what about that whole . . . *thing* you just described which necessitates an entire fleet of ships?"

"Transportation," Ricky D replied, firmly, evenly.

I held my counsel another few seconds, and then managed to get my train of thought back. "And how about all of those zombies you've got up there? How about how you've been controlling them all using neural implants? How come—"

But Ricky D squeezed his eyes shut, an almost pained expression at hearing my words. "Listen, Captain Wright, all of us tend to make *bad* decisions occasionally, and I'm quite willing to admit that I might've put a toe just over the line on that. Along with taking on one of your crewmembers as an apprentice as if he was some slab of meat to be interchanged at will. However"—he shifted another quick glance back to his vidscreen—"I promise you that I have seen the error of my ways; that I've grown to see that these *aspects* of my business may not quite hold to the highly ethical stance which I strive for."

"And?" I put in, thinking that it was somehow my role, as an admiral, to keep the focus of attention on me.

"*And*," Ricky D continued, "with your help, I would like to make some concrete changes."

"Like what?"

"Well," Ricky D said, rolling his eyeballs. "How about we have a rethink on all of those neural-implanted zombies up on the *Ghost Wave* fleet?"

"Okay," I replied, somewhat stunned.

"Now, if you're suggesting that we should set those people

free, then it goes without saying that I'll need some kind of replacements."

"Yeah, well, you ain't getting none of my crew."

"No," Ricky D replied, his voice firm, "that much is apparent."

"Captain?"

I turned around.

Eyed Milky; the one who'd spoken.

"I think I might have an idea."

I turned away from Milky, and then back to Ricky D, who was now pressing his fingertips together and peering over his arched knuckles. His poise and expression was something like a cat considering just how it was going to capture and *skin* a mouse.

But I tried to put that out of mind for the time being.

29   LEAVING KARSEDGURON-17

W ITH EVERYTHING SAID AND DONE, Ricky D graciously accepted Milky's proposal.

This involved, as far as I could gather, harnessing the ghost forms which Big Jo had extracted from the brains of the implanted zombies. And using those same ghost forms to run the whole of the fleet. There would be no need for humans at all.

Not their bodies, in any case.

This struck Ricky D as a terrific idea, and one which would actually *save* him money. No longer would he need to pay for food and other supplies which humans so selfishly demanded almost every day without exception.

It seemed that everybody had come off as a winner.

And without bloodshed.

Once the business deal was through with, Ricky D invited my entire crew out to a nearby noodle-eating establishment on

Karsedguron-17. As a smuggler, I've always had something of a
mean appetite, and one which is hardly mitigated by the
bagatelle that the provider might just so happen to be a
gangster.

And just when the hell did smuggling become such a noble
occupation anyway?

To be honest, I'm sure that I'm far further entwined within
the gangsters' constellations than I would ever like to speculate.
There's very little about my work which is legal.

Otherwise I don't reckon it'd be called *smuggling*.

It felt weird—very weird indeed—to be back up on the
bridge of the *Nava* and to be leaving the *Ghost Wave* fleet
behind us . . . in our wake.

I looked about me, to Mertinon slumped up in the co-pilot's
chair, and then to Foy manning the cannons—the Ship's
Gunner.

Terry was sort of drifting about the fringes, every so often
glancing at the navigational screens over Milky's shoulder,
taking readings of some kind . . . readings that would, surely,
only ever matter to him because, to be honest, I was confident
Milky had everything covered.

Clive was off down with the engines, tuning stuff up, or else
switching it back down.

And Brian was in the medbay, seeing to *who-the-
hell-knew* what.

To return to this vague sort of normality was more than a
touch surreal.

I could still remember how we'd all stood by and witnessed
—accordingly with Ricky D's demands—the processing of the

crew of the *Ghost Wave* fleet. All those humans who had trod off the ships—parked planetside—in an orderly single file.

As if they'd done nothing more dramatic than wake up from a tormented night's sleep.

Once that part of the bargain had been got through with, Milky held up our end of the bargain. He set his program off up and running, for those ghost profiles stored throughout the fleet to work at their various tasks.

I have to admit—even though I've never really needed to be all that convinced about Milky's abilities with computers, droids, and whoever knows what else—that I was impressed to see the entire fleet rise up off the ground and take to the sky. Not so much as hovering for a second before plunging into the murky depths of space above.

Off to carry out the orders which Ricky D had issued.

As I sat in the captain's seat on the bridge of the *Nava*, I could still recall the image of Ricky D standing there, at the terminal, waving us off . . . like he was some kindly seldom-seen relative.

It was enough to weigh down a fella's heart.

But not mine.

Because mine's a smuggler's heart.

Always has been . . . and always will be.

30 NO DESTINATION - NAVAPLASTAS

We'd got ourselves maybe a day or so out of Karsedguron-17 when I started to hear the banging. It began up above our heads, in the ventilation hatches. Everybody on the bridge noticed it, of course. In the end, though, it was Mertinon who summoned the courage to go and check on what the matter was. As I listened to Mertinon's steady footfalls disappearing off along the corridor, a sharp swearword escaped my lips . . . we'd only just got ourselves way out into some clean space.

As peaceful as that might be, it also meant we were a long way from being able to get ourselves patched up if so required.

The whole bridge drifted into silence while we awaited Mertinon's return.

Waiting to hear what the bad news was going to be precisely.

But Mertinon didn't return.

Ten minutes passed.

Then fifteen.

And then half an hour.

Finally, I got up, taking it upon myself to sort this out.

As I left the bridge behind, I couldn't help noticing Terry taking his opportunity and dumping himself into the captain's chair . . . I can still recall how I made a mental note to myself that we'd have words later about *just who* was in charge of the ship; and the certain privileges and reverence which went with it.

I plodded through the corridors of the *Nava*, occasionally using a pipe or a cable to guide my way along. I knew that I should really have got around to getting better lighting put in throughout the corridors; especially with this burgeoning crew of mine.

I passed by a room where Milky was crouched within.

Stooping over various bits and pieces.

Cables and wires.

He smiled as he glanced up at me.

And I shifted a nervous grin back at him.

It was difficult to feel positive at all when the *Nava* was most probably hurting.

When she needed her daddy more than ever.

I stumbled on along the corridor, keeping my mind sharp, and my eyes sharper still.

I picked out the shadows, sure that I could see plumes of smoke.

One of those mirages which would occasionally strike me.

But I reminded myself that I couldn't smell *anything*.

Only the usual blunted scent of grease and oil.

Everything as it should be.

When I turned the corner, into the room which contained the ventilation systems, I expected to see Mertinon perusing the blue, red and green dials within. No doubt scratching his scalp as he considered the sight presented to him. There was one thing for certain. If it *did* turn out to be the case that he was stumped by whatever problem the *Nava* was having then I would be just about the last person to be able to help him.

But Mertinon wasn't pursuing the ventilation systems at all.

In actual fact, he was standing.

But that wasn't what drew my eye.

Not by a long shot.

It was the person standing behind him, holding the laser blade to the tender underside of his throat. His eyes fixed onto mine.

Captain Henry 'Ernest Harry' Norbortwitz.

Ernest Harry.

"Let him go," I said, without thinking.

Norbortwitz made no reaction.

Why *would* he?

He held all of the cards now.

Just as I had believed I had done down planetside . . . with Ricky D.

Norbortwitz slowly shook his head. "No, Arkle, I won't do that."

It chilled me to hear him refer to me by my first name.

I was brought in mind of a time, back when I'd been in my childhood home—the apartment back on Arkle-4. I thought about when the doorbell had gone, and my ma had gone to answer. I remembered it well because my pa was trying to keep me quiet, to keep me occupied watching the vidscreen. But I was strong, even though I couldn't have been much older than nine or ten.

I broke free of him.

Lagged at my ma's side.

Peered out through the doorway.

Eyed the man on the other side.

Ernest Harry.

Norbortwitz.

I can still remember the way he cocked his head to one side as if he'd just been blindsided by some sort of a bolt from the blue . . . some bright idea which'd never before occurred to him. I'm sure my ma saw that expression, too, because she called out to my pa, told him to drag me back inside. I wonder if it was from that moment that Norbortwitz earmarked me as being a terrific potential goon for Big Jo . . . if that was what brought me to join up with the FSA . . . if that was what brought us to this precise split second now; with him having the laser blade held to my brother's throat.

I stared back into Norbortwitz's eyes. "What're you trying to do?" I said. "How'd you think you can win?"

Norbortwitz cracked a smile. He was still wearing the black overalls of the *Ghost Wave* fleet. "Oh, Arkle," he said, "I know I can't *win* . . . not anymore . . . Big Jo's gone; the fleet's gone but that doesn't mean I can't pick up the pieces. That I can't return to Arkle-4. That I can't take advantage of the effective rule Big Jo has held over the place all these years . . . it would be *such* a shame to waste all that hard work, would it not?"

My mind spun back to Arkle-4.

Although I had nothing left there—what with the only surviving member of my family standing right before me at the mercy of this assailant—I couldn't help but feel a knot form in my gut. Just what the hell *is it* with words? Why do they have such power? What is it about them that can drag out those unpleasant memories from the Deepest Darkest Pit of Despair?

"But first," Norbortwitz continued, "I'll need a ship to get back there."

The laser blade brought a bead of blood seeping out from the surface of Mertinon's skin.

Mertinon held still.

He made no reaction.

He stared back into my eyes.

What was he saying?

What was he trying to *communicate* to me?

I thought about the times when the twins—Terry and Brian —would seem to have an almost telekinetic connection. Perhaps that was what me and Mertinon needed right then.

In the end, he had to form the words with his lips. And although his voice was too quiet for me to hear, I could make them out clearly:

. . . Thank you, Arkle.

I hardly had a chance to shift off the spot before Norbortwitz stuck the laser blade directly into Mertinon's throat.

And stole his life away.

I saw red.

———

As Mertinon fell to the ground, Norbortwitz moved towards me.

He bared his teeth.

He swiped the laser blade through the air.

I caught his forearm.

Forced him back.

With a strength I never knew I possessed, I threw him against the wall.

He hit his head.

Then dropped to the ground, beside my brother who was quietly bleeding out.

I ripped my fury away from Norbortwitz, seeing that he was stunned by the blow to his head, and that the laser blade had skittered off across the floor, away from him. I would potentially have *hundreds* more near-death encounters with low-level scumbags, but I might only have one conversation remaining with my brother.

I sank to my knees.

Mertinon lay on his back.

Incapacitated.

I reached out for his head.

Propped it up on my lap.

I felt the warmth of his blood oozing its way onto the leg of my jeans.

It sent a tingle right through my body.

My heart leaped up to my throat.

But I managed to get out the words.

"Mert," I said, apparently unable to quite get my tongue around the longer form of his name right then. "Just hold on a minute, *Mert.*"

It was then that sense struck me.

I leaned back and bellowed out.

Hoping someone would hear me.

"*HELP!*"

My words rattled about the ship, echoing off the metallic bodywork.

The tone came back to me tinny.

Almost like a knife to the gut.

I looked down on Mertinon. Saw his eyes swilling in their sockets. His breath coming rapidly now. That gash on his neck letting loose his life source.

The same blood as my own.

And then, as easily as a snap of the fingers, he was gone.

Just *gone.*

———

I heard a hollowed-out, maniacal chuckle.

Still with my dead brother's head in my lap, I turned to look.

Saw Norbortwitz there.

He was back on his feet—a little unsteady, but holding the laser blade before him with nothing but intent to harm.

I breathed in the air.

Felt my lungs shudder.

And a chill enter my blood.

I remained where I was, down at my brother's side, cradling his head in my lap.

Did I ever believe it would come to this?

How could it ever have *not*?

I stared long and hard into Norbortwitz's eyes.

Those evil, never-ending eyes.

The eyes which'd claimed both my parents.

And now my brother.

Why not let him complete the set?

Why should I resist him?

What *possible* reason did I have to live?

Norbortwitz took another staggering step towards me, his hand shaking but the laser blade which he held remaining impossibly tight in his grip. He only had to plunge it into my heart . . . and that would be the end.

No more light.

No more *life*.

Game Over.

He was only perhaps a trio of steps away from me—from taking that fatal swipe—when I heard a sound come from the corridor. But it wasn't the sound of a person. No hurried foot-steps, or cries of concern. Nope. It was the grinding, pulsing —*humming*—of a machine.

On impulse, both me and Norbortwitz turned our attention to the doorway.

And there stood the droid.

The one which Milky had created, back on *Ghost Wave*.

The Mechadragon.

It stood on its hind paws.

Its claws outstretched.

Mouth ripped-open wide

Its fierce, mechanical teeth glistening in the sharp, even light.

And its scales brilliantly shiny.

Even if I'd wanted to rise up from Mertinon's side, to make some attempt to escape, there would've been no time. The Mechadragon was just too fast.

Its claws retreated into its knuckles.

Before bursting out.

They darted through the air.

Caught Norbortwitz in his mid-riff.

Sent him tumbling backwards.

He dropped the laser blade again.

But, this time, it seemed there would be no chance for him to recover it.

As Norbortwitz slid down the wall, he left a bloody stain. And I couldn't truly believe he was dead—that he had been *dealt* with—until his head hung limp over his chest. Until all signs of respiration vacated him.

Dead.

Both him, and my brother.

Dead.

———

When the Mechadragon backed up from the doorway, I expected to see Milky—proud, and pouting—appear in the gap there; pleased with his day's work, or however long it had truly taken him to create that mechanical monster of his.

But it wasn't Milky who replaced the Mechadragon in the doorway.

It was someone else.

Someone familiar.

Someone who I had seen before . . . *twice?*

I took in her appearance.

The curtly cut black hair.

Thick lips.

But, above all, those sparkling green eyes.

My heart stopped for a moment.

Almost like I was seeing an angel.

Some kind of premonition.

Then I caught myself.

Brought myself back to reality with a *bump*.

The biter . . . the surgeon—who had *cured* Milky and Foy . . . and now, my *saviour*.

She brought her finger down from her earpiece. Giving the Mechadragon whatever order it required to stand by—to go off and reset, and charge, or whatever the hell else it was that Mechadragons *do* in their downtime.

We regarded one another.

The girl and me.

Then, finally, with the lifeless body of my brother sprawled across my lap, I said, "And what might your name be then, honey?"

31 THE NAVA - HEADED NO PLACE FAST

THE GIRL—the biter; the surgeon; the *saviour*—turned out to be called Carole.

Since I'd spent such a long time not knowing the full names of a pair of my crewmembers—of Milky and Foy—I decided to overcome the hurdle right away, and asked her flat out what her second name was. It turned out to be Spax.

Carole Yuv Spax; for richer, or for poorer.

She revealed to us how she had managed to sneak aboard the *Nava* while the other humans who'd been freed from their neural implants had all been filing off *Ghost Wave*. She told me that it'd been a hunch, that she'd noticed Norbortwitz clamber aboard the *Nava* and decided he was up to No Good. Well, I guess I just about have her to thank for getting out of that sticky situation with my life. For not getting my throat slit by some no-good hood.

And now, without having any place to go—or, at least, no place to go that *wasn't* Arkle-4—it seemed that I'd gone and got myself burdened with yet another crewmember.

I have to admit that Brian seemed just a touch put out to have his monopoly on the medbay brought under threat, but, judging from the fact that she was a surgeon, I thought that he should be happy for the educational opportunities it obviously opened up for him.

We . . . I *say* 'we' but really mean *someone* . . . flushed Norbortwitz's body out of the refuse hatch, while we had a decidedly more *reflective* event for my brother. For Mertinon.

I thought I might get all damp-eyed about the whole thing, as I stood by while my brother was loaded into what would prove to be his final resting place; a tube which'd once contained some heavily grease and oil-stained parts. But if Mertinon had gone to the trouble of preparing a will with his last wishes then he hadn't had the wits about him to tell me about it. Or perhaps he had believed his older brother would take just a little more care of him.

That I wouldn't have condemned him to death.

Brought him all this way just so that he might get himself shanked by some Arkle-4 crook. I thought that he was better than that . . . but, then again, I suppose I always thought my parents were better than that. I suppose that everybody bleeds, in the end. Everybody's mortal. We've all got that day quickly rising on the horizon when our number will be up.

When mine'll come, who's to say . . .

As I watched my brother's body spiral off into space—

encapsulated in that box which'd once contained spare parts—I felt my stomach sinking; an almost weightless sensation despite the *Nava's* gravity drives appearing to be in fully working order.

I guess us humans'll never quite feel one-hundred-per-cent normal out in space.

Away from Old Blue.

But, then again, most of us don't even have an option.

The ceremony was all through with in less than ten minutes. There wasn't much for us to say. But, as I watched through a porthole as my brother's body drifted from view for the final time, I couldn't help but reflect on Mertinon's final words.

Thank you, Arkle.

Just as Norbortwitz had slit his throat.

Thank you, Arkle.

Of course, in the coming days, I ran those words through all the appropriate sarcasm detectors, and whatever else. But they all came back clean. For whatever it was truly worth, he had sincerely meant the words he had spoken to me.

Thanking me for this impromptu space adventure?

For taking him away from Arkle-4?

. . . But, with the hours, with the days, I realised what he'd truly been getting at.

What he'd truly been thanking me for.

He'd been thanking me for returning.

For coming back to Arkle-4.

Because he'd thought that I never would . . .

———

It was a few days out following Mertinon's 'funeral', and the melee with Norbortwitz when it struck me out of the blue . . . or out of the black, I suppose, given the endless expanse which confronted me on the vidscreen.

I'd been off in a world of my own; thoughts of the past, present and future all drifting through my brain. I hardly spoke to anyone, and, when I did, it was only so I could put up some kind of façade—give the *impression* that I was still there in mind as well as body.

If I'd been the religious type, I might've thought some kind of spirit or angel, or *god*, had materialised a finger out of mid-air and prodded me in the arm.

Whatever it was, I acted.

On impulse, I turned to examine the co-pilot's chair—left reverentially empty since Mertinon's death. Now, I'd never believed in ghosts, at least when there wasn't any sort of human intervention involved—like back on *Ghost Wave* . . . nonetheless, an idea struck me.

With Foy—her of the peachy eyes—and Clive—him of the monumental *nose*—manning the bridge, I knew I was leaving the running of the ship in good hands. I slunk off into the depths of the *Nava*, first coming across Milky—playing about on the floor of his room with bits and pieces of droids, bots, drones, and who knew what else.

He flipped his plait over his shoulder, glanced up at me and smiled.

With a quick nod and a wink I moved on.

Next up, I came across Brian and Carole.

They were working on some sort of an anatomically correct dummy. They had it all spread out across one of the examination tables. Each of them were fully scrubbed up; Brian's afro tamed beneath his skull cap, while Carole's black hair was kept in place by her own. I noted how Carole's baggy scrubs hid her curves.

And that was probably for the best.

An older gentleman like myself is much better off not spending too long thinking of such things.

Bad for the heart, don't you know . . .

Both of them had some kind of crap-ass electronic scalpel thing they were using to practise.

Good luck to them, I say. And they'd better get studying so they can patch me up the next time I inevitably end up needing some stitching and stuffing.

I did my best not to disturb them as I walked on by.

Deeper into the ship.

Eventually, it was the ventilation systems where I found him. He was crouched over an opened panel with a screwdriver in his hand.

Terry.

I took in the nuts and bolts all scattered about him on the floor.

"Milky too busy with his dolls to pay this any attention?"

Terry flinched at my question.

He spun around.

His eyes locked onto mine.

"Sir?" he said, almost without thinking.

"What you up to here?" I said, squinting.

"Oh," Terry replied, "it's just that I found that a few of the gas canister valves needed tightening, and, you know, one thing led to another."

"And now you're taking the whole goddamn ship apart, huh?"

Terry rose up to his feet. He pressed his lips tightly together.

And then he gave a stoic nod.

"I . . . I'll put it all back, Captain, I promise; it's just—"

But I held up my hand for him to shut his trap.

"Listen to me, okay?"

Terry held still.

His eyes met mine.

I took a deep breath, right to the pits of my lungs, preparing myself. "You're never gonna make much of a mechanic, that's the truth—no shame in it; you just don't have the capacity; the *aptitude* as they used to call it back at school."

"I know, Captain, but—"

Again, I held up my hand for him not to interrupt. "Now," I said, "the question which comes, and the one which you asked me about earlier, well, it's got to do with your place on the ship —just what you *are* good at." I reached up and scratched at the back of my neck; a sort of nervous tick of mine. "Ain't that the question?"

"Yes, sir, I suppose it is. And I—"

Another upturned palm stopped his jabbering once more. "And, from the looks of things here"—I glanced over the complete mess which Terry had made—"it's certainly not got anything to do with tinkering and toying with vital life-preservation systems."

I turned my attention back onto Terry.

And he had better sense than to interrupt me *this* time.

"It just struck me, you know," I said, "that I should put a proposition to you; just float the notion out there, see how you feel about it." I locked eyes with him all the tighter. "Don't want you getting cold feet or nothing, right? I want you on this ship for life."

Here Terry's nervous disposition gave way. " 'For life' ?" he said, his eyes near enough bulging free of their sockets.

"Uh-huh," I replied, feeling like I was almost dealing with some street dog which'd followed me all the way home, and which I had decided, after a whole bunch of hand-wringing and heart-wrenching, to take into my care.

Terry stood very still.

And I decided that I should cut to the point.

"Listen," I said, "I was a lot like you when I was your age— pretty much aimless; nothing much going on. No *skills*. Why, I never thought I'd ever end up so much as setting foot on a spaceship let alone *captaining* one. What I realised was that, for me, it was all about the adventure; the rest could just well and truly go screw itself, you see what I'm saying?"

No response from Terry.

I guess he was still reeling from that comment about me wanting him on the ship for life; still lost in the bomb I'd dropped about *not* wanting to offload him at the earliest opportunity.

"Space travel," I continued, "it's all about experimentation

—all about finding how you get on in different situations; practising different skills." I took in another deep inhalation, and then—call it Mertinon reaching out and poking me from the Beyond; call it what you *like*—I decided to lay all my cards out. "Look," I said, "how'd you feel about being Co-pilot?"

Terry's lips latched open.

If he made any sound at all, then I missed it.

The colour began to fade from his cheeks.

"Kid?" I said, reaching out, clasping hold of his shoulder. "You okay?"

He just continued to stand stock-still.

Stunned.

I glanced about me, as if there might be some kind of medical help on hand, but, of course, it was just me and Terry. I turned back to him, smiled, gripped his shoulder tighter, then said, "Come on, kid, I'll show you to the chair. How about it?"

———

I sank back into the captain's chair, feeling the springs all coiling beneath my substantial weight. It was a strange feeling; for my brother to be gone forever; to know that I no longer had any more blood relatives—that I *knew* of—out there in the Big Bad World. And yet, it was a stranger feeling still to gaze about me and see my crew surrounding me on the bridge, and to realise that, more than anything else, they were all the family I could ever ask for.

I shifted a sidelong glance to Terry, saw him sitting there, in the co-pilot's chair, busily working away at the intricacies of the available jobs.

In the end—since I'd taken the plunge and made the offer for him to be Co-pilot—he'd jumped in with both feet. He had even gone to the trouble of combing his straw hair into a kind of side parting. I suppose he thought it'd grant him a little more respect whenever he got introduced as Co-pilot; that others wouldn't underestimate him on account of his age.

And I was steadily learning the subtle delights of delegation.

I'd never realised just how much day-to-day admin dirge could be offloaded with the simple addition of a Co-pilot to the ship.

I looked about me, to Foy, at the cannons, studying the weapons systems, checking over all the levels, and whatever the hell else. Her quick, peachy eyes taking in all the fine details that, to be quite frank, I had no interest in learning about.

All I knew was that I had the best Ship's Gunner in the galaxy—if not the universe—and that was, after all, the only thing that really mattered.

Clive and his nose were slumped at the vital systems; making sure that the *Nava* kept on flying more or less straight. So that we didn't all end up suffocating in what is—when you get down to it—little more than a big, old tin can.

Milky twirled away with his plait, in a kind of half-awake daze as he perused the navigational screens. But, since we had nowhere to go for the time being, he hadn't much to be keeping his mind on . . . and I couldn't help thinking that he was most likely concentrating the larger portion of his brain's bandwidth on yet more bot, droid and drone designs.

Just as long as he made it crystal clear in their programming that I was very much a *friendly* then it would be fine. The more the merrier, that's what I say . . . or what I feel *compelled* to say . . .

Off in the depths of the ship, I knew that Brian would be stifling his afro once again, working away with the green-eyed Carole; the two of them no doubt coming up with procedures and protocols which would ensure the survival and general well-being of the crew. Now, if only I could get my hands on a Ship's Cook, then we'd be all set . . .

"Captain?"

I turned in my chair.

Took in Terry sitting beside me; grinning from ear to ear.

"What is it?" I said, hoiking my feet down off the control panel.

"Think we've got a job."

"Oh yeah?"

"Look," Terry said, indicating the vidscreen, and the job which he'd chosen out of a whole hatful.

As always, my eyes hardly penetrated the surface of the paragraph of description which accompanied the job offer. On impulse, my eyes meandered down to the number at the end.

And all those *glorious* zeroes.

My heart ticked a little harder.

I reached out and gave Terry a well-done pat on the head. "You're really picking this up sharp, boy, I'll give you that."

"Captain?" Clive said, from behind me.

I turned in my chair.

Eyed Clive.

"What's up?" I said, already feeling jubilant about the prospect of collecting the fee.

"It's just . . . those *jobs*," he said, "I don't know; there's always a catch when there's so much money on the table. And I—"

Although I was on the brink of interrupting Clive, Terry ended up doing the job for me.

"No pain; no gain," Terry said.

I cracked a smile at Clive. "Couldn't have said it better myself." I nodded to Clive, seeing that he looked a touch put out. "Don't worry, you can stay behind this time. No pressure. Nobody expects you to play the hero *every* time . . . gotta give your captain some glory once in a while, huh?"

Clive remained stone-faced for a long few moments, and then he finally gave me a wry grin by way of response.

I cast a glance over at Foy, who was wearing a wicked smile.

There was no need to ask her if she was in.

And Milky was still away with the fairies.

Brian and Carole would do what they were told.

Or they would if they wanted to eat in the none-to-distant future.

"Okey doke," I said, turning back around in my chair, eyeing Terry. "Set course for the job." I rubbed my hands together as if it might've been kicking up a chill on the bridge. "Got a good feeling about this job. A *real* good feeling about it."

And, if anyone didn't feel good about the job then they didn't take the chance to air their concerns. Their loss. And, to be quite honest, they've gotta take on some of the responsibility for siding with a space smuggler.

It's not like our psychology is too complex.

Money. Nothing else.

But, family, well, that runs it a close second.

And it's growing closer every day.

THE END

AUTHOR'S NOTE

Thank you for taking the time to read one of my books. If you would like to hear about my latest releases you can sign up for my newsletter here: www.raymondsflex.com

Thanks for reading!

Raymond S Flex

Homeward-Bound Haul
The Second Arkle Wright Novel

Copyright © Raymond S Flex, 2017.
Published by DIB Books
All rights reserved.

Cover design and layout copyright © DIB Books, 2017.
Cover art copyright © Angela Harburn / Shutterstock, 2017.